OPERATION BA

By

Robert Cubitt

Carter's Commandos Book 9

Books by the same author:

Carter's Commandos Series

Operation Absalom (Carter's Commandos Book 1)
Operation Tightrope (Carter's Commandos Book 2)
Operation Dagger (Carter's Commandos Book 3)
Operation Carthage (Carter's Commandos Book 4)
Operation Leonardo (Carter's Commandos (Book 5)
Operation Terminus (Carter's Commandos Book 6)
Operation Pegasus (Carter's Commandos Book 7)
Operation Banyan (Carter's Commandos Book 8)

Non-Fiction

A Commando's Story
I Want That Job
The A to Z of (Amateur) Golf
I'm So Glad You Asked Me That: A Book Of Answers
I'm So Glad You Asked Me That Again
I'm So Glad You Asked Me That The Third
I'm So Glad You Asked Me That Goes Fourth

CONTENTS

1 – Lunch

Glasgow 1973

It wasn't a restaurant with which Carter was familiar. He had passed it often enough, but on a Civil Servant's salary he could never hope to cross its threshold. But he wouldn't be picking up the bill for this lunch, fortunately.

The Maître D' was waiting at his station just inside the inner doors. Behind him silverware sparkled and crystal glass twinkled, accompanying the buzz of muted conversations from the well-spaced tables.

"I'm lunching with Mr Green." Carter announced in response to the man's greeting.

"Of course, Sir. The gentleman has already arrived." The man's accent was Scottish, but not the broad dialect of Glasgow. The suburbs, perhaps, or maybe even Edinburgh, Carter thought.

The man snapped his fingers and a waiter scurried across. "Rory will escort you to your table." He announced. "Table Six, Rory. We hope you have an enjoyable meal, Sir."

Carter was sure he would be forgotten in an instant, as the Maître D' readied himself for the next arrivals.

So, Prof is here already, Carter thought. Typical of a former Warrant Officer, Carter mused. He knew Carter would be punctual, so he had made sure he was at least five minutes early. It was an unusual courtesy for the high and mighty, who usually like to keep people waiting so they could recognise their differences in status.

But Archibald Green wasn't that sort. He may have climbed the greasy pole of politics, but underneath it all Carter knew he was the same old Prof Green.

And there he was, smiling at him across the room. He had aged, of course, just as Carter himself had aged. His hairline was receding, and furrows sat at the corners of his eyes and mouth. Long political lunches and expensive dinners had added inches to his waistline but Carter would still have recognised him across a smoking battlefield.

"Prof!" Carter extended his hand, which Green took in a strong handshake. "Or perhaps I should address you as 'Minister' now?"

"If you do that I'll make you pay for lunch, and I doubt you could afford it." Green replied with a broad grin. He sat back down as the waiter withdrew Carter's chair to allow him to sit with the minimum amount of effort. No sooner were Carter's knees bent than the waiter picked up a crisp linen napkin, shook it out of its folds and draped it across Carter's lap.

"May I get you a drink, Sir?" Rory asked, glancing at each of them in turn.

"A bottle of the house claret." Green replied. "You do still drink red wine, don't you?"

"Like it was going out of fashion." Carter replied. At Green's nod, the man scurried away to fulfil the order.

"You must have won the football pools to be inviting me here." Carter observed.

"With my newfound status goes a generous tax payer funded expense allowance." Green replied. "You've been following my career, then, if you've noticed my elevation."

"I spotted your name in the newspaper reports of the re-shuffle." Carter replied. "Northern Ireland. How on earth did you end up there?"

"I know too many secrets to be sacked, so they did the only thing they could to get me out of the way. Northern Ireland is the political equivalent of the Land of Nod[1]."

"Why would they want to sack you anyway?"

"I intervened in an incident when a young researcher was being harassed by a senior Minister. Said Minister didn't like it and tried to get the PM to sack me. I was a junior Minister at Health at the time and destined for promotion if the Whip's office was to be believed. Anyway, I know a lot of things about a lot of people, so it was assumed that I would reveal all to the gutter press if they sacked me, so Northern Ireland it is, in the hope that I'll keep quiet."

"You're not like that though. You don't go telling tales out of school."

Green gave a wry smile. "You know that, Lucky, and I know that, but most politicians think that everyone behaves with the same lack of integrity as they do, so they don't know that. Which is why I'm now Minister of State for Northern Ireland."

"But still, I've been most impressed by your meteoric rise up the greasy pole."

Green chuckled. "I got a bit lucky. Not long after we got back from Malaya[2] there was a by-election in a safe Tory seat. They needed a bit of cannon fodder to put up against the Tory candidate, and I happened along at the right time. I wasn't expected to do anything other than put up a good fight and lose graciously, but someone got hold of a photo of the Tory in the arms of a woman who wasn't his wife and sent it to the News Of The World[3] and the Tory voters stayed at home on polling day, which meant I pretty much walked into the seat. For some reason the good people of my constituency, despite being Tory in terms of the demographics, keep voting for me."

"Any idea who leaked the photo? It wasn't you was it?"

"Certainly not. The consensus is that it was his wife. He was a serial offender, apparently, and I think she'd just had enough of it and stopping him from being elected MP was her revenge. She probably hired a private detective to get the photo. They divorced soon afterwards."

"Is there a lot of that sort of thing in politics?

"You have no idea. If I ever wanted to get rich, I could do so just by blackmailing members of my own party. If I started on the Tories as well, I'd give Onassis[4] a run for his money."

"I'm surprised that more of it doesn't get out." Carter observed.

"Mutually assured destruction.[5] as our American cousins would put it." Green replied. "If you tell what you know about me, I tell what I know about you and nobody wins. As you well know, I'd never have been elected if my own little secret had got out. I might even have gone to prison. And that goes without mentioning our little escapade in Thailand, which was totally illegal. Even now I'm legally allowed to be who I am, it would lose me enough votes for it to end my career if it got out."

The waiter arrived and poured their wine and was replaced by another who handed them menus.

After he had gone, Carter spoke again. "Things are changing though, aren't they?"

"Too slowly for my liking, but it's not in my interests to speak out. That was the reason I was sent to Northern Ireland. The researcher who was being harassed was of the same persuasion as me. The minister involved is a real homophobe and makes no secret of it. There aren't many in our party, but he is one of them. Anyway, the researcher is now working for me, though he's probably worse off in Belfast if his secret ever got out. I can't imagine the Wee Frees[6] taking kindly to him."

The waiter took their order, both of them opting for the fresh Scottish salmon. "Well, I have to wonder why you've invited me to such a fine restaurant," Carter said. "I'm pretty sure it wasn't just for a catch up, because you'd be happier doing that in a pub. I remember Paddy O'Driscoll always saying that when the Army starts being nice to you, it's time to start worrying. So, I'm quite curious as to what you hope to persuade me to do while we consume fine wine and salmon."

"Ah yes, Paddy. Funny you should mention his name." He was interrupted by the arrival of the waiter bearing their food. Green remained silent until after he had gone.

"So, what about Paddy?" Carter re-started the conversation, his curiosity piqued.

"Perhaps I'd better start at the beginning." Having taken only one small forkful of his salmon, Green laid his cutlery down on his plate and assumed a thoughtful gaze. "I won't swear you to secrecy; that would be an insult. But obviously what I'm about to tell you is highly sensitive. If it ever got out that I was discussing this with you, I'd be out of office so fast my head would spin and nothing I know could save me, even if I wanted to use it."

"Well, I have to say, that's one way to get my attention." Carter chuckled.

"It's no laughing matter. Lives are at stake here. Lots of lives including Paddy's. Amongst my many portfolios is oversight of the intelligence operations in Northern Ireland. I get daily briefings on what is happening and discuss the security strategy with the senior police, military and intelligence people. While I don't get involved in day to day operational matters, they all have their political implications and I'm there to make sure that they don't go against Westminster policy. That's how I got to hear about what I'm going to tell you.

As you've probably heard, the Provisional IRA have been pretty inept in mounting their terrorist campaign. They've scored more 'own goals'[7] with their bombs than they've had successes and so far their use of firearms hasn't been that effective. They've fired a lot of rounds but not hit many targets.

But in recent weeks we've noticed a change. Their fieldcraft has improved, as has their shooting and their success rate with bombs has increased and the number of their own side killed by their own bombs has fallen. Special Branch suspected that they had improved their training, and someone was tasked with looking into it. They soon discovered that they did indeed have a new training regime, masterminded by a former British soldier. They did more digging and discovered his nickname in the Provos was 'the Commando'. Eventually it was discovered that he had served with the commandos during World War 2 and then with the Australian army's commandos. Does that sound familiar?"

"You mean…" Green gave a warning glance as the waiter returned to see if they needed anything. They waved him away.

"No names, no pack drill[8] as we used to say. But yes, I do mean him."

"OK, but I can't see what that has to do with me. You aren't trying to recruit me to go after him, are you. Because if you are …"

"No, at least not in that way. But I am hoping you can pass on a word to the wise, so to speak. I can't do anything because of my position, otherwise I'd gladly talk to him. But he respects you and I'm hoping he'll listen to you. The intelligence services are getting close to identifying him and if they do, catching him will become their number one priority. They'll ask for the assistance of the Irish Special Branch if he's on their side of the border and there's every possibility they'll co-operate. I'm hoping that a word in his ear will persuade him to take early retirement and go and live quietly back home in Mayo before it's too late."

"Will I be in any danger? You know I promised Fiona I wouldn't …"

"Hopefully not. It would just be a quick trip to Donegal and back. She'd hardly know you were gone."

"Donegal … but that's in the Republic, isn't it?"

"It is. But word is that's where he's based himself. There's a small town there, about twenty miles west of Londonderry, called Letterkenny. The Provos use it as a sort of rest and recreation centre; somewhere they can relax. If the Irish government knows about it, they're turning a blind eye. But a lot of the Provos from Derry, Strabane and Armagh have relatives in the border counties of the Republic, so they always have somewhere to stay, and their faces are familiar enough so that they don't stand out."

"How would I find him? I can hardly go through the streets asking for him by name."

"The Irish gossip the same way as they breathe. I think that if you go into the right pub someone will probably engage you in conversation. The purpose of your visit is bound to be raised and if you mention looking for an old army comrade, word will get back to him. It's a small town; everyone knows everyone and as a stranger you'll stick out like a sore thumb. But the natives aren't hostile. There are a few British living in the area. It has wonderful scenery and great golf courses, and an Englishman's money is as good as anyone else's, so the locals live and let live and the Provos don't want to attract attention to the area, so they let sleeping dogs lie."

"So that's it. I just go to this Letterkenny place, sit around in pubs talking to people and he'll find me. Is that the plan?"

"Pretty much. I'll make a few arrangements and let you know what they are, and you can take it from there."

"You sound pretty sure I'll do it."

"You're Paddy's oldest mate. You knew him even before Danny Glass or me. If I know you as well as I think I do, you don't want to see him end up in prison if it can be avoided. I don't want to sound cocky, but I'm pretty sure you won't turn me down."

Carter gave his old friend a hard glare. "You're taking too much for granted."

"I know, and I apologise. But will you do it? Not for me, but for Paddy."

Giving a big sigh, Carter's shoulders slumped in unaccustomed defeat. "If it's for Paddy, I don't suppose I have much choice. The number of times I nearly got him killed, including the last time in Thailand, means I at least owe him a chance to decide his own fate."

Green's face split in a broad smile. "Thank you, Lucky. I knew I could count on you. Now, eat that magnificent salmon before it goes cold."

2 – Letterkenny

It was a small, rather nondescript town, as far as Carter could see. He knew of a dozen like it scattered across the lowlands of Scotland and he guessed that the Scottish influence had come from Northern Ireland

It was a warm, sunny day, so he decided to leave his car at the Mount Errigal Hotel, the place at which Prof Green had booked for him to stay. The hotel itself was modern and comfortable, but rather out of place, as though someone had dropped a late 20th century building into an Edwardian town.

Carter was advised to fly into Northern Ireland's Aldergrove Airport, where he was met by a rather earnest young man who handed him the keys to a hire car and briefed him on everything he needed to know. The man wasn't local and Carter wondered if it was the harassed researcher of whom Green had spoken. The briefing was followed by a lengthy drive along the A6 road past Lough Neagh, over the Glenshane Pass, through the small town of Dungiven and into Derry, or Londonderry as the road signs announced it. He was stopped at checkpoints at both ends of the double decker bridge across the River Foyle before skirting the notorious Bogside housing estate. There was another Army checkpoint before he was waved through the Customs checkpoints on both sides of the border and into the Republic.

The most noticeable difference that Carter could see was the condition of the roads. They were in need of repair and hardly a hundred yards went past without him having to swerve to avoid another pothole.

Here the road was designate the N13 and took him across the isthmus at the southern end of the Inishowen Peninsula to Letterkenny. It was a pleasant enough drive, with some nice views across Lough Swilly. Or it would have been without the potholes, with traffic quite light. He passed the occasional tractor but there was very little other traffic in either direction.

From the hotel he walked back to the N13 and turned right towards the town. The view was dominated by the spire of a large church, which he would later find out was actually a cathedral. The road was lined with the sort of commercial premises that litter the approach to many towns, until he got closer to the centre, where he passed the Fiesta, which advertised itself as Letterkenny's premier entertainment venue and then, on the other side of the road, the Golden Grill, which made the same claim. What had once been the town's railway station was now the bus terminal, with a Swilly Bus Company single decker vehicle parked outside the only remaining building, though there was an old railway aggregate truck to remind passer's by of the building's original purpose.

From there the road sloped upwards past small shops and the town's cinema. At the top of that road others converged to form a junction which none of the cars seemed to be able to negotiate without attracting the tooting of horns. To the left a grand building identified itself as the Court House and to the right was a scruffy building describing itself as Gallagher's Hotel. Behind him, forming one corner of the junction, was a boarded up building that threatened to crumble into dust if anyone so much as looked at it. Posters for a forthcoming international folk festival were plastered across the peeling paintwork.

Carter had to smile at the pretentious use of the word 'international' in the festival's name. It was out of place for a such a small town. But he guessed it was accurate if acts from the nearby North travelled the short distance to appear.

A sign on the wall above a pharmacy told him he was entering Main Street, which was both a name and a description.

Here the road became a little busier, with vehicles parked along both sides forcing others to navigate with care along the narrow street. Anywhere else the street would be one-way, Carter mused, but such ideas had yet to reach the town.

Shoppers, mainly women, busted to and fro, wicker baskets in hand as they did their daily rounds. Some stopped to exchange pleasantries or, if Prof Green was to be believed, gossip. As a stranger he attracted some curious glances, but not hostile ones and he was given nods of greeting and the occasional "grand afternoon".

Small shops dominated Main Street, interspersed with the odd pub or betting shop. He came to the market square, where he was able to get a closer view of the church with its soaring spire. He considered walking up the side of the square to take a closer look at the magnificent building but was deterred by the steepness of the slope.

It must be a sign of his aging, Carter thought, that he considered such a short journey too challenging to undertake. Only ten years earlier he would have sprinted up that hill and wouldn't have felt out of breath when he reached the top..

He continued down the gentle slope, passing a building on the far side of the street bearing the sign of the *Garda Síochána.* The small saloon car that stood outside, with the dome of a blue light on its roof, provided an easy explanation of the building's purpose without having to translate from the Gaelic..

Reaching what appeared to be a major junction, diagonally across from him he saw a new red brick building announcing itself to be Dunne's Store. He'd heard of them, one of Ireland's biggest chains of department stores which had obviously only recently arrived in this backwater. Ahead the road curved into the distance while to his left it rose gently to the hills on the far side of the River Swilly. where some houses stood.

He crossed the street, turned and retraced his steps back up the hill, heading towards the end where he had started. He had spotted the place he was interested in as he had passed it and would now give it closer attention. He navigated around a group of women clustered around the entrance to Dillons' Supermarket, which stood across from the market square and continued until he was almost opposite a pub that announced itself to the world as the grandly named Central Bar.

The earnest young man had told him to avoid two pubs in the town, Jacksons, which was on the other side of the river from Dunne's Store, and The Cottage, which was further up the street from where he was standing. They weren't known IRA haunts, but they did attract a younger crowd where he might encounter hotheads keen to make a name for themselves. The Central Bar was more the sort of place, where older men gathered to gossip over a pint of "the black stuff".

The outside of the pub looked unprepossessing. A pair of windows were either side of the front door, frosted up to half their height so that wives couldn't see their husbands inside.

Just as in Scotland, women didn't go into a pub unaccompanied by a man and if they were accompanied, they would only go into the lounge bar if there was one.. The more usual place to see a woman drinking would be in a hotel and, even then, only if accompanied by a man.

It didn't look like the Central Bar had a lounge.

Taking a deep breath, Carter crossed the road and entered the pub.

A couple of dim bulbs lit a scruffy interior. A bar stretched along one side and wooden chairs lined the wall, with rickety looking tables arranged in front of them. Most of the space was empty. Just as in Scotland, men drank standing up until they were too old, or too drunk, to do so.

In the far corner a couple of older men sat, half-drunk pints of Guinness on the tables in front of them. Like the women in the street, they gave him a curious glance followed by a nod by way of greeting, before returning to their conversation. They wore corduroy trousers, tweed jackets, shirts and ties, cloth caps perched on the backs of their heads. The barman was middle aged, wearing a white shirt with sleeves rolled to the elbow and also wearing a plain coloured tie. Jeans and tee-shirts didn't seem to have reached Ireland yet, at least not in the Central Bar.

"Grand day. Can I get you something?" The barman asked.

Carter scanned the beer pumps. It didn't take long because there were only three of them. One was for Guinness, one for Harp lager and middle one displayed a small plastic sign declaring the brand name Smithwick's. Carter assumed it was local brand of bitter and ordered a pint.

Reaching for a glass the barman spoke again. "By the sound of it you're not from around here."

He hadn't posed a question, but it invited an answer. Carter guessed it was the way things were done around here. Not intrusive but engaging anyway. His accent was distinctly northern, but not the broad vowels of Belfast. It was more rounded, easier on the ear.

"No," Carter replied. "I'm from Scotland."

"You're not Scottish though." The barman replied, setting Carter's pint down in front of him. "We used to get plenty of Scotchies over on holiday before The Troubles started."

"Ah, yes, Glasgow Fairs week, the big holiday period. No, I'm English by birth but married a Scottish woman. I live there now, on the coast south of Glasgow."

"Ah, I've got relatives that way me'sel', Saltcoats."

"Just along the coast from us. I've been there a few times."

"Have you ever met the Gallaghers?"

"I can't say I have." Carter took an experimental sip at his beer and decided it was better than the gassy keg brews that seemed to have taken over the pubs in Scotland in recent years.

"Ah well. It's a common enough name I suppose. We've plenty of them around here. That will be twenty five pence please."

"Do you take Ulster Bank notes?[1]" Carter had been given a wad of them when he arrived at the airport. "They'll draw less attention than Bank of England notes." The young man had told him. "They'll fit with your cover story of working in the North for a while."

"Aye, but I'll have to give you your change in Irish coins."

"That's fine." Carter replied. "I'm sure you'll be getting some of them back."

As the barman counted out Carter's change, the door opened to admit a new arrival. He was similar in age to the existing customers, excluding Carter, and must have gone to the same shop for his clothes. Tweed ties were definitely a local fashion.[2]

"Afternoon, Tommy. Your usual?"

"Aye, thanks Jimmy." The new arrival replied. "I see we have a visitor." He turned his attention to Carter.

"Just passing through, doing a bit of sightseeing." Carter responded to the unspoken question.

"We don't get many visitors these days, thanks to what's happening across the border. Even the Irish don't come here much now, because they have to travel across the North to get to us."

Carter knew that he was expected to comment. "Are you that cut off from the rest of Ireland?"

"We are. It's either cross the North through Omagh and Strabane. or take a very long route around by Leitram. There's a very narrow neck of land between Fermanagh and the sea that keeps us connected to the other twenty five counties of the Republic. We call ourselves 'the forgotten county', because the politicians in Dublin forget all about us until they need our votes at election time. Hopefully Neil Blainey[3] will stick a firework up their arses down there, the gobshites."

"Put not your trust in Princes, as someone once said." Carter replied.

The man laughed. "Aye, politicians are the same everywhere, I suppose. What brings you to our wee neck of the woods?"

"I'm doing some work for Harland and Wolff in Belfast and they don't need me for a few days, so I thought I'd take a look around. I've heard that Ireland is very beautiful.

"Most people in the North stick to the Giant's Causeway or the Mountains of Mourne." Again, a statement rather than a question, but inviting an answer.

"Well, I'd heard that an old friend of mine was here in Letterkenny, so I thought I'd see if I could track him down."

"And you thought you might find him in the Central Bar did you." The man laughed.

"Hey, that's my pub you're talking about!" Jimmy retaliated.

"No offence Jimmy, but it's not the smartest establishment in the town."

"Well, you don't seem to mind." The barman responded. "You're in here every day."

22

"Well, a pub is as good a place as anywhere if you're looking for my friend. He's seen the inside of a fair few in his time." Carter filled the silence.

"Does this friend have a name?"

"Patrick O'Driscoll" Carter replied. "He normally answers to Paddy though. He's originally from Mayo but spent a lot of the time out of the country."

"How did you meet a Mayo man in England?" Tommy sounded genuinely surprised at the notion.

"We … er, we worked together for a few years."

"Ah, worked together so you did. Look, you're amongst friends, so if you mean you served in the Army together, just say it. There's no shame and judging by your age, I'd say you fought the Nazis. We cheered you on from this side of the water and fair few of our boys died fighting alongside you. So long as you're not still a soldier we've no issue with you."

"You certainly won't have." Jimmy replied. "I heard you made a fortune smuggling poteen[4] across the border and selling it to the Yanks during the war. That and butter and the odd side of bacon."

Tommy chuckled but didn't deny the accusation.

"I don't suppose you've come across my friend.?" Carter asked.

"Can't say I have, but it's a small town. Go into enough of the pubs and someone is bound to know him. Do you know where he works?"

"Can't say I do. I only heard he was here through another friend and he didn't have any details."

"What's his trade?"

"I'm not sure he has one, other than being a soldier. I know he studied Irish history at Galway University. Oh, and he was from a farming family I believe, so he probably knows one end of a cow from the other."

"Well, he might be lecturing, either the Tech or at St Eunan's College. That's the big boys' school up the road a bit from the cathedral."

"Is that the place with the very high spire."

23

"That it is. It's higher than the one on Salisbury Cathedral, so they say[5]."

"Maybe I'll ask at both colleges then." Carter noticed that the man had finished his drink. "Can I get you another?" Carter nodded towards the empty glass.

"That's very Christian of you. I'll have a Paddy's"

"You'll have a Guinness and leave the man with money in his pocket." The barman leapt to Carter's defence. "You've to keep an eye on this one, mister. He'd skin you alive if you let him."

"What is a Paddy's, anyway?" Carter asked.

"It's Irish whiskey." The barman replied.

"In that case, I'll have one of those and get one for Tommy here."

Tommy beamed: the barman just shrugged and lifted a glass to the optic. "Suit yourself. It's your money."

* * *

By the time Carter got back to his hotel he was feeling decidedly lightheaded. It had been a while since he had drunk whisky, or whiskey[6], in any quantity and he wasn't used to it. But he'd enjoyed the afternoon, though he didn't seem to be any closer to finding Paddy O'Driscoll.

After a short nap to clear his head, Carter ate a passable dinner in the hotel's dining room and settled into a comfortable chair in the lounge to read a copy of the Irish Times which someone had left lying on the bar. He planned to try one of the other pubs, or perhaps the bar of Gallagher's Hotel, for news of O'Driscoll but he would leave that until a bit later.

The dominant story in the newspaper was the continuing trouble in the North, with a catalogue of recent bombings and shootings. Two soldiers had been killed in Belfast the previous day and a suspected terrorist had died in Derry, in an exchange of fire with the Royal Ulster Constabulary.

Footsteps alerted him to the arrival of another guest and he looked up. He almost didn't recognise O'Driscoll, who was standing looking at him.

If Carter considered the aging process to have been unkind to him, O'Driscoll had been treated far worse. His once fit physique had run to fat and his belly hung so far over the waistband of his trousers that Carter couldn't tell if he was wearing a belt. Like the men he had seen earlier, Paddy wore a tweed jacket and trousers with matching tweed tie providing an ornament for his white shirt. Rolls of fat bulged above the shirt's collar and led upwards to a florid face, the dominant feature of which was a bulbous and veined 'boozer's nose', as Carter's late father would have described it. The one remaining feature that Carter recognised was the thatch of thick, almost untamed red hair, but even that was now predominantly grey, with only a little of the original colour showing through.

Biting down on his gasp of shock, Carter rose and offered his hand to be shaken, fixing a smile on his face to hide his emotions at the sight of his old friend. "It didn't take long for news of my presence to reach you, Paddy."

O'Driscoll returned the smile. "Well, it's a small town. Those that aren't related by birth or marriage know everyone else by name. I was back home when a neighbour called round to say there'd been a man in the Central Bar asking after me. A telephone call to Jimmy, the owner, was all it took to lead me to the Mount Errigal."

"The same would probably happen if you turned up in Troon, looking for me." Carter had to admit. "Can I buy you a drink?"

"I'll just take a glass of orange juice, if you don't mind."

"Of course. make yourself comfortable. I'll be back in a minute."

Well, thought Carter, there was a first. Paddy O'Driscoll drinking orange juice! There was a story there for the telling, Carter felt sure.

After ordering the drinks Carter returned to the lounge and re-took his seat. When the drinks arrived, O'Driscoll raised his glass in salute. "What was the old toast? Here's to us."

"There's none like us" Carter responded.

"There's some like us."

"But they're all dead." Carter concluded, raising his pint glass to his lips and taking a pull at his beer. "How's Rosie these days?" Carter asked.

"If you can track her down, you can ask her yourself." O'Driscoll replied morosely. "For I've not seen her since 1966."

Carter didn't know what to say. Should he console Paddy, or was it through the man's own choice? Well, there was only one way to find out.

"I'm sorry to hear that. Can I ask what happened?"

"You can and I'll tell yez. I've nothing to hide. After the Yanks went into Vietnam I was there and back all the time, working with the Americans alongside their Green Berets. As you probably know, Australia was providing military support up there and I was part of the effort[7]. I was at Long Tan[8] in '66, where we lost 18 men but left 240 Vietcong dead and held control over the province."

Carter couldn't help but hear the pride in O'Driscoll's voice; the pride of a soldier who knew he had done his job well. But that had been only seven years earlier. How had he gone from being a fighting commando to the physical wreck that Carter now saw before him?

"I was doing six months in-country and six months out. I guess Rosie got lonely during my six months away. Anyway, after Long Tan I was granted some leave and I got back to our house to find a note on the table saying she'd met someone else, and she'd be in touch to tell me where she was. The note was dated three months earlier and the table was thick with dust. Well, she never did get in touch, or if she tried she didn't reach me.

I didn't take it too well, I have to say. I loved Rosie so much. I climbed into a bottle and didn't get out for a long time. On my next trip back to Vietnam I led a patrol into an ambush and almost got us all killed. I had three wounded men out of twelve and one of those died later. One of the men must have reported me, because my CO said I was drunk when I took the patrol out. I couldn't deny it because it was true. I was hardly ever sober, only a little bit less drunk some of the time. So, my career was ended there and then. I should probably have been court martialled, but they kept it quiet and I was allowed to resign my commission.

Well, it turned out that no one in Australia wanted to hire a drunken ex-commando, so after a couple of years drinking myself into oblivion I spent the last of my savings on an aeroplane ticket back to the Auld Country. I kept myself going with farm labouring, mainly for relatives or old friends who knew me before the war and took pity on me. Then one day I just caught a glimpse of myself reflected in a shop window and saw what you see before you now. That would have been a little less than two years ago.

I went to my parish priest and asked him where I'd find my local branch of alcoholics anonymous, and he told me there was a meeting that night in the church hall. And when I plucked up the courage and walked in, there was the auld sot there himself." O'Driscoll let out a chuckle, which turned into a cough, smothering it with his hand.

"So, I've been sober now for one year, nine months and twenty three days and I still take it one day at a time." O'Driscoll continued after he had caught his breath. "But I'm no fool, Lucky. You didn't come all the way to Letterkenny to hear my tale of woe. So, what brings you to this backwater."

"A mutual friend is worried about you. So, he asked me to see if I could find you."

"And why didn't this mutual friend come himself?"

"He's not at liberty to do so." Carter answered.

A wry smile played around O'Driscoll's mouth. "So, Prof Green is pulling strings up in Stormont, is he?"

"I didn't …" Carter started to reply.

"Don't kid a kidder, Lucky. You don't have to say his name." O'Driscoll cut across him. "I know that my presence has been noted by the security services and I know who they report to in Belfast. How much do they actually know?"

"They know that there is an Irishman who has served in both the British and Australian commandos. They know his nickname is "The Commando" and they suspect him of being involved in the training of Nationalist paramilitaries in the North. But they don't know your real name. Prof deduced it was you, but he hasn't told anyone … Yet."

O'Driscoll nodded his head in understanding and took a sip of his orange juice. "What I wouldn't give for a drop of the Irish right now." He said morosely. "Yes, that would be Prof. He wants to give me a chance to get out before it's too late and they come after me. So, he asked you to come and try to persuade me to see sense, as he and you would both see it."

"That's pretty much it." Carter responded. "Can I ask, what you're doing mixed up with this bunch of terrorists. It's hardly your style, especially not after what you saw in Malaya. And what you saw in Vietnam too most probably."

"You're right. It wasn't my style, and I was keeping well clear of it down in Mayo. Right up until January 30th in Derry last year. What those paratroops did was unforgivable. I couldn't stand by and watch innocent Irish men and women getting shot in the street. Could you?"

Privately Carter had to admit he would find it hard to ignore something like that, but he wasn't there to encourage O'Driscoll, he was there to dissuade him.

"They say they were armed."

"They can say what they like. I have it from eyewitnesses that they weren't. Good men and women, not involved in violence themselves and with no reason to lie. If I believed that even one of them was carrying a gun that day, I'd walk away now. But I don't. "

He stood up and drained his glass. "It's been good seeing you, Lucky. But tell Prof I'm doing what I believe to be right, and I'll take the consequences."

Carter stood as well. "Paddy don't go. Stay and have another … orange juice. We can at least chat over old times."

"Thanks Lucky, but I don't think I can. And I think it's best if you climb into your car and get back across the border tonight. I don't know if anyone knows I came here, but as I said earlier, it's a small town and the staff in this hotel all live in it. Tongues will wag. The IRA hates informers and I don't want anyone thinking I might be that. And you don't want anyone thinking I might have told you something important. Get yourself back home to Fiona and the twins and forget you were ever here." He turned his back and waddled towards the door, his ungainly bulk once again making him appear to be a stranger in Carter's eyes.

"Goodbye, old friend" Carter muttered towards his retreating back. "I hope we meet again one day, in happier times."

* * *

The harsh wind scythed across the Inishowen peninsula, cutting into exposed flesh and making the three young men huddle down inside their inadequate clothing. The summer was over for them and this was just a precursor of the autumn gales that would follow. Little stood between them and the Polar ice caps.

The fourth man was better dressed for the climate, in thick tweed and waxed canvass, his feet shod in heavy boots that were so well worn that they had the softness of chamois leather. He had to shout to make himself heard above the noisy rush of the wind.

It was hard to believe it was only the first week of September, but they were at the most northerly part of the island of Ireland and the normal rules of meteorology didn't seem to apply up here. Tomorrow it might be sunny enough to cause heatstroke, or they might get a blizzard. Neither would surprise the local people. They'd just give their normal greeting of "a fine soft day", which seemed to cover every eventuality from a little light drizzle to a category five hurricane.

"Perhaps in future you'll listen when I tell youz to wrap up warm." Paddy O'Driscoll shouted above the whine of the wind in nearby power lines..

"Can we not gae hame and do this tomorra?" one of the young men asked.

"And when you're stuck out on a freezing moor being hunted by the British Army, will youz be asking them if yez can 'gae hame and do it tomorra' instead." O'Driscoll mocked the young man in a similar accent.

"But …"

"But nothin'." O'Driscoll cut him off. "You are here to learn how to fight the British. If youz want to gae hame you are free to go." He waved his hand towards the car parked on the narrow lane that passed by them on the lower ground. "But if you do that, you will never be given another chance to fight the British. Is that what you want?"

They shook their heads and muttered that it wasn't what they wanted.

"OK, why do you think I brought you out here, into the middle of nowhere?"

They looked at him expectantly, as though he had made a statement rather than asked a question.

"Well, have none of youz any idea?" He tried again.

"Because there's no one around to see what we're doing." One of the young men ventured.

"Aye, that's one reason, but not the only one. Who else would like a go?"

More silence.

"OK, I'll tell you. If you can learn what I have to teach you out here, in this wilderness, then when you get back to Derry, or Strabane, or Omagh or wherever you've come from, you'll be able to do it there. Not only that, but doing it out here will give you confidence. If you can beat the wilds of Inishowen, you can beat any Brit squaddie. Got it?"

They nodded their understanding.

"When will we get guns?" One of them asked.

"Not while you're with me." O'Driscoll replied. "I'm not here to tach you to shoot. I'm here to teach you how to look after yourselves so you don't get shot.

Any eejit can shoot a gun. That's the easy part. But keeping yourself hidden, for hours at a time, so that you can shoot the gun at just the right moment, that's hard. It's very hard. Then being able get away afterwards, while half the Brits in Northern Ireland are trying to track you down, that's harder still. That's what I've brought you out here to teach you. By the end of this week you'll be able to hide yourself behind a pimple and not be seen by a Brit patrol.

If you learn what I have to teach you, you may live to draw your old age pensions. If you don't, you'll be dead before Christmas.

Oh, they'll write songs about you, to be sure. They'll sing about how the heartless, Godless Brits killed you, just a young man cut down before you've had a chance to live, like Kevin Barry[9]. But it'll make no difference to you because you'll be six feet under, so you won't hear the songs being sung and you'll certainly never sing them yourselves."

He paused, letting that sink in. He had given the same speech a dozen times before, standing on the very same spot, but it never seemed to break through the cockiness of the boys they sent him.

Oh well, all he could do was try.

He searched in his pocket and brought out a one Punt[10] note. "Now, you remember passing a wee shop about five miles back along the road?" O'Driscoll asked. They nodded their heads. "I want the three of youz to get back in the car and go there and buy me a pork pie for me lunch. Got it?"

They gave him a puzzled look, not answering.

"In the name o' the wee man." O'Driscoll snapped in frustration. "Do yez not understand simple instructions."

"Aye, we do. It's just that we didn't come up here to go shopping."

"No, you came up here to learn." O'Driscoll barked back. "Everything I say or do up here has a reason to it. In this case, while you are going and buying me my lunch, I'll be hiding somewhere here, but you won't be able to see where. Then, when you get back, you'll try to find me. I've a five Punt note in me pocket that says you won't find me within twenty minutes. How does that sound?"

"Aye, that sounds alright." One of them replied.

"Right, but there needs to be a few rules about where you go lookin' or you'll wander off and get lost. So, first of all, I'll be on this side of the road. Second, you see those rocks up there." he pointed up the slope of the hill to a rocky outcrop about four hundred

31

yards away from their present position. "I'll not be anywhere past those rocks. Now, you see the poles carrying the electric wires?"

He indicated the thick timber poles that marched in a straight line across the hillside, the nearest being about a hundred yards from them. "The third one to the right has a white stripe painted on it, as does the third one to the left. I won't be past either one of those. That gives a large rectangle for you to search, but you can see all of it from here."

Inside the area he had indicated there was nothing but a few stunted gorse bushes, worn down by the winds.

"We'll find yez easy." The one who had so far stayed silent finally spoke.

"Well, if you do you get that fiver."

"And what if we don't?"

"Yez get to walk all the way back to that shop, because at the end of twenty minutes I'll be in the car and on me way. I'll wait for yez there.

Now, get off and don't you dare think of stopping short and coming back to try to get a look at where I'm hiding. If you don't produce that pork pie when I ask for it, I'll know you've cheated."

"What if they haven't got any pork pies?" One of them asked with a smile.

"They have, because I phoned them this morning to ask. And I asked them to keep me one back and told them there'd be three gormless eejits coming in to collect it. Now, get off with yez."

He watched them as they returned to the lane and climbed into the car he had borrowed. He couldn't afford one of his own, but he knew plenty of people well enough to ask for a loan, providing he left it with a full tank of petrol when he'd finished with it. The one that had elected himself to drive turned the car in the road and sped away with a shriek of tortured rubber. O'Driscoll shook his head. He had a shrewd idea that the youngster had learnt to drive in other people's cars and they hadn't always given their consent for the lesson.

Of course, they could stop and drop one, or even two, of them off to spy on him but it would make no difference. By the time they'd got into a position to see without being seen, he'd be well hidden.

Once the car was safely around the side of the hill, O'Driscoll dipped into the holdall that sat by his feet. From it he pulled a ghillie suit[11]. It was made up of a pair of dun coloured overalls of the sort that a farmer might wear when tending cows, with bits of green, brown, black and grey hessian stitched to it and then shredded to leave it looking like a very large, bad hairdo.

He slid it on over his other clothes, feeling it tight around him. A couple of years earlier he would have described it as 'snug'. A couple of years before that it would have been a good fit. But even he had to admit that it was now tight. He had gone on size alone when he had bought coveralls and the size he had chosen was the one he had been when he had been a much slimmer man.

Crouching, he used his fingernails to pull away some of the grass and dug out some of the soil beneath. He spat into his hand and then smeared the soil into a paste which he applied to his forehead, cheeks and jawline. Those flat planes were the ones that reflected light the most and the soil would prevent that, as well as breaking up the outline of his face, making it a less recognisable shape.

The final touch was a green balaclava with more hessian stitched on, and a pair of woollen gloves, also adorned with hessian. Standing where he was he would still be visible to the searchers when they returned, but he wouldn't be standing there. He would be lying in the place where he always lay and where no one had taken less than twenty minutes to find him.

He picked up his holdall and made his way up the hillside. To the untrained eye it looked relatively smooth, just the gorse bushes breaking up the eye line, but any soldier would have been able to pick up the hollows that they would call 'dead ground'. Ground that the eye couldn't see into from any more than a few yards away and which soldiers used to conceal themselves.

He had once seen a demonstration down on Salisbury Plain, while still a new recruit, of an entire platoon hidden away in plain sight.

They had been dressed in their ordinary khaki, not the sort of camouflage he had just adopted, but he and the other recruits hadn't been able to pick out even one of the twenty four men, their Sergeant and their officer.

It had stuck in his mind over the years, which was why he had included the demonstration for his own groups of recruits, because actions spoke louder than words.

There was plenty of time for O'Driscoll to conceal himself before the three volunteers returned. It was a round trip of at least twenty minutes on the narrow lane and, once in his ghillie suit, he needed a lot less than that.

One of the many differences between soldiers and civilians, O'Driscoll mused, was the way they perceived land. For a civilian a piece of land was something to walk over, build on, cultivate or keep animals on. For a soldier it was something to be fought over and part of the success or failure of the fighting was how well it could be used for concealment.

Land was never flat. It undulated like the waves of the sea which had been frozen in place. You stood on the crests of the waves to give you the best view and you hid in the troughs because they provided concealment.

The civilian walked across land, his feet sometimes climbing the sides of the waves and sometimes descending into the troughs, but they never realised what that meant for the soldier. The whole purpose of the challenge he had set the volunteers was to demonstrate that viewed in the right way, any piece of land became a hiding place.

He headed diagonally up the hill for about fifty yards, knowing exactly where he was going. Most of the "dead ground", the troughs between the frozen waves, ran side to side across the hill, but there was one which ran down towards the lane and that was the one he was looking for. It had probably been created by water running down the hill, but there was no sign of water in it now. Not only would it conceal him, but it would allow him to crawl back down the hill unseen to reach the lane and get to the car.

Opening the front of the ghillie suit, O'Driscoll pushed the canvass holdall inside, to lie flat against his body. It left his hands free, but made the overalls tighter still, straining the seams across his back and under his arms, threatening to burst them. He lowered himself into the shallow trench, his head towards the road. Controlling his breathing, he settled down to wait.

* * *

The howling wind blew the sound of the car's engine away from him, so he saw it come around the shoulder of the hill long before he heard it. It slowed, coming to a stop and one of the occupants got out of the rear seats before the car moved forward once more.

Good, O'Driscoll thought. They had used their time to devise a plan to search for him. That was rare. Most of them just came back and wandered around aimlessly. It would make no difference, of course.

The car passed the spot where it had been parked that morning and dropped the second youth off roughly opposite the third pole on the left, supporting the power cables, before being turned around to return to a parking place roughly in the centre of the search area.

The third youth emerged and raised his hand in a signal.

With his camouflaged head low to the ground, O'Driscoll still had the advantage of height; not much, but enough so that he was looking down towards them, while they were looking upwards, with the bulk of the hill behind O'Driscoll's head. They walked forward about twenty yards and the youth in the middle stopped, while the other two turned inwards and walked towards him.

It made sense, of a sort. If O'Driscoll wanted to get to the car, it would make sense for him to conceal himself close to the road. Which was why O'Driscoll hadn't done that. It was a lesson Lucky Carter had taught him. Work out what your enemy most wants you to do, then do something completely different. Preferably do what your enemy least wants you to do.

They met in the middle and started some sort of discussion. That was as far as their planning had taken them, apparently.

35

They spread out, but not very far. Poking listlessly around the gorse bushes, they headed up the hill, the undulations in the ground meaning nothing to them, least of all suggesting a means by which someone could stay concealed.

Taking the occasional peek above the level of the trough, tilting his head so that only the side of his face and one eye broke the horizon, O'Driscoll watched until they were past him and then started to crawl along the shallow depression. He used his elbows and knees, raising his body until his belly skimmed the grass, pushing with his knees and toes to move him forward, lowering himself and then repeating the movement. A 'leopard crawl', they called it in the Army, as it mimicked the way a leopard supposedly crept up on its prey. It was slow going, but from solid experience he knew there was every chance he wouldn't be seen.

He checked again, craning his neck to see behind him, but they were on the opposite diagonal from him and still heading up the hill. He could break cover and dash for the car and would make it before they had time to reach him, but that wouldn't serve his purpose. The exercise was about effective concealment, not about getting to the car before them. That was just their punishment for not being sufficiently observant.

He crawled forward once again, the depression getting shallower as he neared the road. His back would be visible now, if they knew what they were looking for. But that was the purpose of the ghillie suit. It broke up his outline, blending it with the natural features and their colours, confusing the eye.

He could smell the tarmac of the lane now. It was probably no more than a dozen feet from him. Which meant the car was about forty yards away to his left. He changed direction, seeking out a similar furrow that would run parallel to the road, as most of them did. His eyes picked it out, downhill to his right. He eased his way towards it. It was no more than six inches deeper than the ground on either side of it, but that was enough.

Turning his head slightly he looked for the three searchers. If he had still been in the army his faced would have been smeared with ochre, black and green stripes to break up its outline, but he didn't have access to that sort of warpaint anymore. It didn't matter. It would take exceptional eyesight to pick out the round shape of his face from the camouflaged balaclava that covered the rest of his head, and the mud he had smeared across his face.

The three were ambling across towards the rocks that marked the furthest point of the search area he had defined. Perhaps they thought there might be a cave, or at least a significant crack within which he might hide, but O'Driscoll knew there wasn't.

This was the riskiest part of the game. It only needed them to look to their left and then recognise his shape. It wasn't a high risk, but it was a risk, nonetheless. Paddy played by the rules. If they called out and pointed at him, he would give himself up. But there was no sound to be heard over the howl of the wind through the power cables above the hillside.

Reaching a point level with the car, O'Driscoll turned towards it and slithered around behind it. Thoughtful of them to have left it with the driver's door furthest from him, preventing them from seeing him climb into the vehicle. They could have locked it, O'Driscoll thought. It would have made no difference, as he had the spare key in his pocket, but they didn't know that.

He shook his head at their stupidity as he saw the ignition key in its slot, the fob swinging as his movement rocked the car a little. They knew that he was trying to reach the car and he had told them of the consequences if he succeeded, yet they had made it easier for him.

He didn't rate their chances against the British, but perhaps the hour long walk to the shop might give them pause for thought.

He slid behind the steering wheel, keeping his body low. He turned the ignition key but didn't start the engine. Instead, he let the handbrake off and allowed the car to roll along the lane, powered by gravity. Once it was doing about ten miles an hour he depressed the clutch, put the car into second gear and let the clutch out. The car jerked almost to a standstill, then the engine fired and the car leapt forward once again. Wriggling his body he managed to get himself upright in the driver's seat.

Looking over his shoulder he saw the three volunteers running full pelt down the hill, waving their arms. No doubt they were shouting too, but they were far too late. He steered the car around the shoulder of the hill and they were lost to sight.

*   *   *

Sipping at the mug of tea he had persuaded the shop's owner to make him, O'Driscoll bit into his pork pie, which had been left in the glove compartment for him.

He was no longer wearing the ghillie suit and he had wiped most of the mud off his face using his handkerchief, so as not to invite too many questions from the shopkeeper. On the passenger seat beside him lay a copy of the Irish Times, which he had bought to give him something to read while he waited.

But it wasn't the previous day's events, as reported in the newspaper, that occupied his mind. It was the recent visit from Lucky Carter.

It had unnerved O'Driscoll.

He wasn't worried about being caught. So long as he was on this side of the border it was unlikely that the Irish authorities would take any interest in him, let alone arrest him. There was no evidence to link him to the IRA except rumours and the Irish wouldn't risk a prosecution which might be embarrassing in the eyes of the Irish public if it failed to convict him.

No, his worries ran deeper. Carter had asked him what he was doing mixed up with this bunch of terrorists and he hadn't really thought about it that much until he was asked the direct question.

He was as loyal an Irishman as any on the island and he believed wholeheartedly in a United Ireland, but did he believe that the way the Provos were going about it was the right way?

That something had to be done on the other side of the border was self-evident. Half a million men women and children were being denied the same rights as the other half million and he knew of no other country where that was the case.

Well, there was South Africa, of course, but everyone condemned them for Apartheid. Which was ironic considering that the government that condemned South Africa was the same government that was supporting a political system in Northern Ireland that was, in many ways, similar. But it wasn't the colour of the people's skin that was being discriminated against, it was their religion.

He knew of one other country where it had happened, and he had fought in a war to put a stop to it. But were the two things similar?. There were no concentration camps for Catholics. Their property wasn't confiscated, so no similarities there. But they were denied jobs because of their religion, he knew that, just as the Jews had been in Germany.

Oh, they weren't asked if they were Catholics directly, but they didn't have to be. They were asked their address and that said everything. All the major towns and cities of the North were divided up by religion. You didn't have to ask what way a man worshipped his God, you just had to ask his address to get the answer.

And then there were voting rights. You had to own property to vote for councillors or members of the Stormont parliament and very few Catholics owned much more than the clothes on their backs. And in the country areas where some Catholics owned farms, the constituency and ward boundaries had been so gerrymandered[12] that they looked like a plate of spaghetti, to make sure that the few Catholic landowners could never elect one of their own to a position of power.

But was violence the way to change that?

They had tried peaceful means, protest marches and the like, but that had led to the marchers being attacked. It was why the Army had been sent in, supposedly to protect them. But the Army were now part of the problem, not part of the solution.

But blowing up women and children? That couldn't be right. That made the Provos as bad as the Protestants, if not worse.

The end justifies the means, he had been told. But that was the argument used by tyrants since the dawn of time.

He took another morose bite of his pork pie. But it wasn't him doing the bombing and the shooting. He was just trying to keep young men alive, he argued with himself.

Yes, but young men who would bomb and shoot if they were told to do so.

It was hard to make a moral argument for what he was doing, he realised. And, if nothing else, Paddy had always regarded himself as being a very moral man.

*   *   *

The wind had died down a bit as he addressed the three volunteers once more. They had trudged into the small parking area in front of the shop in a foul mood, looking daggers at O'Driscoll sitting reading his paper. Paddy didn't care. He had been through this a dozen times before and he knew that learning a lesson the hard way made it stick better. At Achnacarry it hadn't been unusual for lessons such as that to be hammered home with the handle of a trenching tool across the buttocks, just to make sure it was properly understood.

"You cheated." The biggest of them challenged him.

"Tell me how I cheated?"

"You were hiding across the road."

"Did you see me there?"

"No! But …"

"If you didn't see me, then how did you know I was there?"

"Because we couldn't find you?"

"That just means you didn't know what you were looking for. Now, you three go into the shop and get yourself something to eat and drink and then I'll drive you back up the hill and you can see how I did it."

"Now, how do you recognise things?" Paddy asked them, once they were standing back on the hillside.

40

They looked at him blankly, clearly not understanding the question.

Paddy gave his head an exasperated shake. "That power pole there." he pointed at the nearest pole. "How do you know it's a power pole?"

"Because it looks like a power pole." One of the three replied.

"OK, tell me what it looks like."

"Well, it's tall and thin, made of wood, with arms across the tops and those glass things that hold the wires ..."

"Exactly." Paddy interrupted him. "You recognise its shape, its colour,. If it had been sunny today you would have recognised its shadow, the fact that it has cables running over it and a whole lot of other things.

That's why you didn't see me. Because you couldn't see the shape of me. I was there right under your noses, but I didn't look like me."

He pulled the ghillie suit out of his holdall and held it up. "I was wearing this."

"Youz are having a laugh." The big one said. "That wouldn't hide you?"

"Would yez like to bet another hour's walk back down the hill on that?" O'Driscoll said, a smug smile on his lips.

"Prove it." One of the others interjected.

"I was just about to. But this time you can watch me."

O'Driscoll climbed back into the ghillie suit, put on the balaclava and gloves and headed up the hill to his hiding place. Without warning he dropped down to the ground and started to crawl forward. After about thirty yards he stopped and stood up again.

"Now, did you see me?" he shouted, before walking back towards them.

"I thought I saw you." One of them ventured. "But then you stood up and I realised that it wasn't you."

"Precisely. And that, gentlemen, is today's lesson in a nutshell. You can hide yourself in plain sight if you know how to do it. And that allows you to wait until your enemy is in the best place for you to get at him. You could lie in wait for hours and they would never know you're there until it's too late.

Then, when you make your escape, you can hide yourself again, right under their noses, and they'll think you've got away.

Let me introduce you to what we call the seven S's of concealment: Shine, Shape, Shadow, Silhouette, Spacing, Sound and Sudden Movement. For the rest of this week I'm going to teach you how to avoid those seven things, which will allow you to avoid discovery. If you learn the lessons, you have a reasonable chance of drawing your old age pension. If you don't you'll either end up in prison, or dead.

It's up to you.

Now, let's start with disguising your shapes.

*   *   *

A half-eaten burger sat in front of O'Driscoll, alongside a cold cup of coffee. There was nothing wrong with the burger or the coffee; he just wasn't in the mood for them. It was Thursday evening and on Thursday evenings he went to the Four Lanterns burger bar. He did it because if his contact wanted to tell him anything, he knew that it was the place to find him.

After two days of practicing concealment in a variety of locations, O'Driscoll has started to the teach the volunteers about surveillance and counter-surveillance. He had learnt the skills himself from the Australian SAS, undergoing a course of training on how to be a close protection officer, otherwise known as a bodyguard. The job for which he was trained never materialised and he had gone to Vietnam instead, but he hadn't forgotten the basics.

It is hard to follow someone, either on foot or in a vehicle, if they know you are going to be there, so O'Driscoll had taken them into Letterkenny, Buncrana and Donegal town and set them to trailing unwitting subjects as they went about their innocent business. O'Driscoll observed the volunteers and if he thought they did anything that was likely to alert a more surveillance aware person, such as an undercover police officer, then he brought to their attention later.

For counter surveillance he followed each volunteer in turn and they had to try to shake him off. None of them succeeded, but he had to commend them on some of the tricks they used, because he had taught them those tricks.

At the end of the week, he dropped them back at their B&B and never expected to see them again.

Now he waited for his contact so he could be paid. Sometimes he turned up and sometimes he didn't. He only made contact if he needed O'Driscoll to take on a new group of volunteers.

A steaming cup was placed on the table, and he heard the sound of a body lowering itself into the seat on the other side of the table. O'Driscoll interrupted his contemplation of his half-eaten burger and greeted his contact without looking at him. "Evenin' Ger."

Ger could be short for Gerald, Gerard or Jerome. O'Driscoll didn't know which and cared less.

"Evenin' Paddy." Ger replied. A brown envelope was slid across the table towards O'Driscoll. It was slimmer than usual and O'Driscoll hoped it was because it contained Twenties and not tens, but he felt that he was probably being optimistic. Technically he was a volunteer and as such he didn't get paid. But he was recompensed for out of pocket expenses and typically they just gave him a wad of cash. The Provos weren't the sort of people who expected to be handed receipts to account for the money.

O'Driscoll picked up the envelope and slid it into his jacket pocket.

"So, how did they do?" Ger asked. He always asked after O'Driscoll had trained a new batch of volunteers.

"The young one, Ruari, I wouldn't use on anything more complicated than carrying messages. He's keen, but he just doesn't seem to have a knack for the work. Maybe it's his age, but I think he's a danger to himself. The other two, Colm and Ryan, are OK. They stand a fighting chance of not getting themselves arrested or killed if they remember what they were taught."

"What about their attitude?"

"Typical teenagers, I'd say. Thought they knew it all and got a bit arsey when they found they didn't, but not the worst I've had. What about the ones that have been out and about for a bit longer?"

Once O'Drsicoll had trained the volunteers and they went back to the North, the only way he could find out how they were doing was if Ger told him. Like most teachers, he always took an interest in his former pupils.

"Seamus got arrested a couple of weeks ago, but it wasn't his fault at all. He went to visit his auntie and the Police raided her house while he was there. The armchair he was sitting on had a gun stashed inside it. Turns out that his cousin, who's twelve or thirteen, had found the gun and took it home and hid it. What he was going to do with it we have no idea. It was probably ditched by one of the boys after doing a job. Probably being chased by the police or the Army and planned to go back later to collect it, but the cousin got there first. Anyway, it turned up in the house when they searched it."

"Were they after Seamus?"

"Apparently not. We suspect that the cousin had been shouting his mouth off about the gun at school and word got back to the RUC that way. Just bad luck that Seamus chose that time to visit.

Martin and Hugh are off to Libya next week, to one of the training camps there."

"They're doing well enough to have been chosen for that?" O'Driscoll knew that the two young men were better than the average, but they had to be the pick of the litter to get themselves sent to Libya for more intensive training.

"Aye, they've been good enough to get themselves noticed. Anyway, I've got to get going. I'll let you know when we want you again." Ger started to rise from his seat, leaving his drink untouched.

"About that. I've been thinking …."

"Not getting cold feet on us, are you Paddy?" Ger sat back down, leaning towards Paddy in what he probably imagined was a threatening manner. But Paddy wasn't to be intimidated by this man. He knew that Ger was just a go-between. He was trusted enough to carry messages and talk to Paddy on behalf of the more important figures, but no more.

"You don't need me anymore, not really. You've got plenty of trained people now who can teach the stuff I teach. And they're younger and fitter than me. I'm getting too old for running around the hills in all weathers."

"It hasn't anything to do with that Englishman you met up with a couple of weeks back, has it?

"You know about that?" Paddy asked, surprised it hadn't been mentioned before.

"We know everything that goes on in this wee town, Paddy. And you better not forget it. Now, what did he want?"

"He was an old pal from my Army days. He'd come over to see me because he'd heard I was back from Australia."

"Heard from who?" Ger persisted.

"I don't know. The ex-commandos keep in touch with each other. If someone gets sick, or needs help, word goes out and if anyone is able to help, they go and see them. It's just something we do for each other. I'm guessing that someone had heard I'd been a bit fond of the bottle and word got back to him. He was my CO back during the War. We went through a lot together."

"Is that all it was? You know what we think about touts[13], don't yez?"

"I do, and I'm no tout. We met up, I told him I had my problem under control, we chatted for a bit and that was that. I promised I'd go to the next reunion at Honfleur, but I doubt if I will, because if the Brits found out what I was involved in, it would be too risky. I have no intention of seeing out my days in a prison cell." It was close enough to the truth and, unless someone had overhead the actual conversation, it would be enough to convince Ger that there was nothing for him to worry about.

"So, why the sudden desire to pack it in."

"Everyone retires some time. I just think this is my time. I'm a risk to you, you know that. I'm only ever one offer of a free shot of Tullamore[14] away from losing control again and if that happens, who knows what I might let slip. While every other grown man in Ireland meets up in a pub, we're here in a burger bar. Why do you think that is?"

"OK, Paddy, calm down. I get it, you want to retire. But now isn't a good time for us. It will take time to find someone to replace you. We may have to wait till ... till some things have been done, shall we say. Could you hang on till next year?"

"I guess so. But no later than March, please. I'd like to get back to Mayo for the spring."

"What will you do?" Ger asked, seeming to actually care about Paddy's future.

"I haven't thought that far ahead yet. I might see if I can get some work lecturing at Galway University. I might even go looking for a wife. Maybe get down to Lisdoonvarna for the festival.[15]"

"Well, good luck with that." Ger said, with a grin, getting up from his seat. "I'll be in touch" he threw over his shoulder as he left the burger bar.

That conversation had gone about as well as Paddy could have hoped, and a little better than he had expected. He had anticipated some sort of pushback from Ger on his decision to quit his involvement with the Provos. They tended to view their supporters as making a lifetime commitment, much as religions did. And, just like religions, any attempt to distance oneself from them was seen as heresy.

Of course, the decision didn't lie in Ger's hands, but if the go-between was happy to pass on the message without making a fight of it, the chances are the people in the North that did make the decisions wouldn't be too fussed. They probably had bigger fish to fry these days anyway, than worrying about one middle aged man wanting to go back home.

It was a load off his mind, Paddy had to admit to himself. Since his visit from Carter, he had agonised about his involvement in terrorism. It didn't fit in with his values and beliefs.

Oh, sure, the political aim of a United Ireland was close to his heart, but the methods by which the Provos were trying to achieve it weren't to his tastes. He had been raised to fight for the right of people to make their own choices and that wasn't what the IRA were fighting for. They would force half a million Protestants to relinquish their nationality and he, Paddy, had fought a war for the right of people to choose their political leaders and not have them imposed on them.

It wouldn't end with a United Ireland, Paddy knew. It would end with a United Ireland run by Sinn Fein, whether people wanted them or not. People who use guns to get what they want don't put them away when they got it. They clung on to their guns to prevent others taking what they had fought for.

That Mao Tse Tung fella knew what he was about when he said that political power comes from the barrel of a gun[16], Paddy mused. The only thing in question was who holds the gun and Paddy was pretty sure that the Provos intended that it should be them.

3 – Glasgow

On an RAF aircraft heading from Singapore to North Borneo, 1955.[1]

"So, Ewan, what's this proposition you want to talk about?" Carter undid his seat belt and half turned in his seat to face his companion. "I can tell you now, if it involves guns I'll be turning you down flat. I've had enough of those now."

Former Commander Ewan Flamming RN laughed. "Nothing like that. But, as you have probably worked out, I spend some of my time, when not writing spy novels that no one seems to want to read, doing odd jobs for … shall we say a certain organisation in London. It's part of government, but not a part that seeks the limelight."

"And what has that got to do with me?"

"One of the services I provide is what you might call talent spotting. You have some undoubted talents which I have observed over the years. They mainly involve killing the enemies of Her Majesty's government, but I think they run much deeper than that. I think my employers might consider you to be something of an asset."

"What me, a spy?" Carter blurted out.

Flamming raised a warning finger to his lips."Shhh. Keep your voice down. There's only so much noise four Rolls Royce engines can drown out, you know."

"Sorry, but I don't think I've heard anything so ridiculous. I couldn't be … I couldn't work for them. I don't even speak any foreign languages. A smattering of German perhaps, picked up during the war, even less Italian, but that's all. Besides, Fiona would never stand for it. And before you say she wouldn't have to know, I'm afraid she would wheedle it out of me somehow. She's a very persuasive woman and she can read me like an open book."

"I would love to see how you explain this little jaunt to your wife then." Flamming chuckled. "But that's by-the-by. It isn't what I have in mind, and you need have no fear of Fiona knowing about it. It's an office job mainly, with maybe the odd trip to an embassy or two abroad. You'd be based in London. I'm sure we could work out some sort of deal to cover the cost of your accommodation. And if Fiona doesn't want to move to London, we can probably work out something to allow you to get home at the weekends. My employers can be very flexible for the right man. How do you think I can afford to live in the Caribbean for half the year?

But really, I'm sure Fiona would welcome you taking this job if it is offered. I think it's the sort of thing you would enjoy, but which Fiona could accept you doing without having to worry about you coming home in a coffin."

"So, what would the job be?" Carter had to admit that his interest had been piqued.

"My employers get a lot of information across their desks of a military nature. We need someone to make sense of it for us."

"There are thousands of former soldiers who could do that for you. In fact, you only have to walk into one of a dozen London clubs and throw a pebble to find someone suitable. I know you employ quite a few in that role already, you didn't have to come all the way to Singapore to find me."

"I happened to be coming here anyway," Flamming sounded unusually tetchy. "When I heard your name mentioned, I got hold of the report on your operation from Warriner and that was what put the idea into my mind, Steven. Your talent isn't just in fighting, or your knowledge of military matters. You have a habit of doing what the enemy least expects and that is where I think you can be of use."

"I must admit, I do seem to be able to put myself into the other chap's boots and see things from his point of view. If I can work out what he would least like me to do, then that seems to be the best thing for me to do to beat him."

"Precisely. Now, let's say if Nikita Kruschev[2] were to send a few divisions into Hungary to quell a rebellion against communism[3], what do you think he would least like us to do in reply?"

50

"Off the top of my head, I think he wouldn't like it too much if we were to position a few divisions on his flanks, say on the Baltic and Black Sea coasts. It would mean him having to look in three directions at once."

"There you have it. Straight away you saw the opportunity to distract him and give the Hungarians some breathing space. Not that the scenario is ever likely to happen, you understand."

Carter gave Flamming a shrewd look but decided to say nothing.

"So, that's all I would have to do. Just sit in an office analysing military intelligence and coming up with possible scenarios about the best way to counter the threats that are posed. The ones that the enemy would least like us to employ."

"Pretty much. Of course, your role would only be advisory. What the politicians and military bigwigs actually do would be down to them, but your thinking would be in the list of options for consideration.

"I have to say, it sounds more interesting than going back to the shipyards and I'm not really cut out to be a farmer. I don't mind helping out from time to time, but the smell of manure isn't my favourite perfume.

"Good man. So, can I put your name forward?"

"I don't see why not. They may not even want me, so there's no harm in testing the waters."

"Oh, I can assure you that if my name is on the recommendation, they'll want you."

*　*　*

Glasgow, January 1974

Carter stuck his head around the door of his boss's office. "You wanted to see me, Hamish?"

"Yes, Steven. What have you got on at the moment?

"The usual. Monitoring the two factions in Glasgow and the lowlands, to make sure they never escalate their disagreements beyond the current football rivalries. We're keeping our eyes on a couple of individuals from both sides who might be trying raise the stakes, but there's nothing significant on the horizon right now. You've seen the weekly summary, haven't you?"

"Yes, but I really wanted to make sure you haven't anything significant on your plate right now. Nothing that your deputy can't look after for you."

"Alex has a handle on things. I'm sure he could cope. Why? Do they want me down in London?"

Carter's time with MI6, Britain's foreign intelligence service[4], had been relatively brief. After commuting back and forth to Troon each weekend for almost a year, he had dozed off during Sunday lunch and Fiona had decided that things couldn't continue as they were. He was no use to man nor beast if he was perpetually tired, she said, so she gave him an ultimatum: get a job closer to home or come and work on the farm.

Fortunately, Carter's bosses had been understanding. His main role didn't really occupy him for a full week and most of what he did could still be done from somewhere other than London, so if he could find something to occupy the rest of his working week he could work from one of the many government offices in Glasgow or Edinburgh.

By that time, Carter had established relationships with people in the other intelligence service, the one that took care of domestic matters, known by the public as MI5 even though it wasn't its proper name. A few calls and a couple of lunches later and he was being interviewed in an unobtrusive office in Glasgow, with a view to helping to keep an eye on security threats in Scotland.

Although the people of Scotland were no more of a security risk than their neighbours south of the border, the presence of several Top Secret military establishments, including those of their friend and ally the USA, meant that there was always interest from agents of the Soviet Bloc, who had an unusually high number of consulates in Scotland considering so few people from Warsaw Pact countries were allowed to travel. Since 1968 the role had expanded to keep a closer eye on the Catholic and Protestant groups that had sympathies with their counterparts in Norther Ireland, to make sure that what was happening over there didn't spill over onto Scottish streets.

"What about our other friends. The ones with snow on their boots[5]?"

"The usual. Occasional trips to have picnics along the side of our picturesque west coast sea lochs. We have a team keeping tabs on them to see if they meet up with anyone or take an unusual interest in loose bricks, but with diplomatic passports and number plates, there's not a lot more we can do.

Hamish chuckled at the reference to the sort of place that made a good 'dead letter drop', where an agent could leave a message to be picked up later by their handler, with the two never having to meet face to face.

"Any new faces?"

"No, not since the last staff rotation. I shall miss old Sergei. He was so clumsy a blind man could have followed him."

"As you speculated at the time, perhaps he was being clumsy on purpose, so we didn't notice someone else being a little more subtle."

"Well, if that were the case, he failed, because we spotted Nicolai quickly enough." Both were codenames but they fooled no one. The game of cat and mouse between the resident KGB agents, the ones protected by diplomatic immunity, and the security services was the tip of an iceberg as they all knew. The real problem were the agents who lived quiet, apparently respectable lives and so stayed under the radar of the ever watchful British.

People like Gordon Lonsdale, Harry Houghton and Ethel Gee, collectively known as the Portland Spy Ring, who had been uncovered in 1960.[6] Fortunately, Carter hadn't been involved in that investigation, which had only been exposed thanks to a Polish defector.

"So, why do you want me to clear my desk all of a sudden?" Carter asked, returning to topic as he often had to with his aging and easily distracted superior.

53

"Oh yes. Well, some damn fool of a senior analyst in the Belfast team has been stupid enough to seriously injure himself while on a skiing holiday. He will be back at work in due course, but Belfast needs a steady hand to take over his desk for a few weeks. Normally such an absence would be covered by other members of his team taking up the slack but, as you may imagine, things are pretty hectic over there these days, so there is no slack. I've been asked if I can spare someone and, as your team doesn't seem overly stretched at the minute, I thought you might go over and steady the ship for them.

"Will it involve …"

Hamish gave a wry smile. He had met Fiona and knew her views on Carter taking risks. "He did enough of that during the war." She scolded. "I'm not having him do it again, not now he's got grandchildren on the way."

"Don't worry. It's strictly deskbound. You'll be put up in a hotel in what is considered to be a safe part of the city. It's used quite a lot by visiting politicians and civil servants, so security is pretty tight."

"Well, it seems to be a done deal. But, for form's sake, do you mind if I talk to Fiona about it this evening. You know how she likes to be consulted about these things."

Hamish waved a dismissive hand. "So long as she agrees in the end, then no problem."

"And if she doesn't?" Carter asked with a cheeky grin.

"I'll pass it to the Edinburgh office. But you know I don't like them getting credit for anything."

It was true that the rivalries between offices sometimes got a bit tense and Glasgow had no greater rivalry than the one with Edinburgh.

4 – Strabane

If he was being honest with himself, Carter was rather bored. Having been led to believe that he would be heading up a team of intelligence analysts in Belfast, he found that one of the resident staff had already been given temporary promotion to cover the accident prone skiing enthusiast and he, Carter, now found himself at the desk of the promoted man.

It wasn't the loss of status that bothered Carter, and Civil Service rules meant he couldn't lose any of his salary for doing the job of a lower grade official. It was just that the new incumbent was an officious jobsworth and a poor leader. The team was suffering because the acting senior analyst kept changing the priorities, demanding that reports that could wait be ready in hours and intelligence information that might be vital for the soldiers and police on the ground was being sidetracked and delayed in favour of the trivia.

It was something with which Carter was familiar after his years in both the Army and the Civil Service. Getting simple and often unimportant tasks done made it look like the team was productive, but in doing that it was failing in its purpose.

Bullshit baffles brains, as the old Army saying went. Make a room smell of fresh paint and an inspecting officer would think that everything had been painted in preparation for his visit. His ego received a boost because of the perceived effort that had been put in for him, while real problems escaped attention because the officer felt that everything was in tip-top condition. Stories were abundant in the Army of poor quality, or badly led, soldiers being sent out on "manoeuvres" for the day so that they didn't catch the eye of inspecting officers; and it seemed to work.

Carter felt like letting Prof Green know what was happening, in the hope that he might intervene, but realised it would probably be counterproductive. It was clear that the man, McAnally, had the ear of the head of the department. They were old friends from years back, having joined the service together. Such loyalties were hard to overcome, however inefficient it made the department.

Recognising that rocking the boat served no real purpose, because he was only going to be there for a short time, Carter sighed inwardly and got on with the job he had been asked to do, which was to analyse financial data to try to identify money laundering routes used by the terrorists. Cut off the money supply, it was argued, and you cut off the means to buy arms and explosives.

The fact that Carter was bored wasn't because there was insufficient to do. It was because McAnally's own desk dealt with most of the department's trivia as well. The absent skier, no doubt, knew of McAnally's shortcomings and gave the important work to people who would do a better job. He gave it to the other people in the room with Carter.

It was another old trick that Carter had come across in the Army. If an officer turned out to be useless, or a bit windy, he was sent off to a stores depot to count paperclips, or somewhere else where he could do little damage. No doubt there was probably a manager in London happy to have shuffled McAnally off to Belfast to become someone else's problem, at least for a while. The London based Civil Servants only did twelve month attachments to the department before being replaced by fresh faces. Only the local staff were permanent.

Carter's ears perked up as he heard a voice being raised in his temporary boss's office.

"Why haven't you got the latest updates on Strabane?" The voice asked. The reply was too quiet for Carter to hear. He had heard the name 'Strabane' a few times that morning as well as seeing it on the evening news on his hotel room TV set the previous night.. Apparently there was some sort of ruckus going on in the area and the whole world was wondering what it might mean. Well, the whole world that was the security community in Belfast.

And it seemed that McAnally, whose job it was to tell them that, was unable to do so.

The raised voice was lowered, which suggested that McAnally had managed to mollify his visitor, but it didn't mean that he had given a satisfactory answer. A few minutes later a door slammed, signifying someone's departure. Carter caught a glimpse of camouflaged material through the corridor window, but it wasn't possible to identify the soldier wearing it. But Carter had a suspicion that it was someone senior enough to get away with using a raised voice in McAnally's office, which meant at least a full Colonel and Carter knew only one of those in Belfast who was also part of the intelligence community.

The door to the office opened and the head of McAnally's secretary appeared. It was an office shared with three other analysts, but she had no trouble identifying the one she was looking for.

"Mr Carter, I wonder if you would mind popping into Mr McAnally's office." Her broad accent went right to the heart of the city they were in. She was a young looking fifty years old, and Carter guessed she had worked for the department since leaving school, if she was trusted enough to be privy to the goings on in this office.

"Certainly." Carter stood and lifted his jacket from the back of his chair. McAnally wasn't one for the informalities that were normal for Carter in his own office.

Taking the few steps along the corridor, Carter stopped to gather his thoughts, before raising his hand to knock. He was pre-empted by the secretary, who stepped around him, knocked once and entered without waiting for a response.

"Mr Carter for you, Sir." She announced, before withdrawing. The smile she had been wearing as she entered, slipped from her face as soon as her back was towards McAnally and Carter doubted that there was any love lost between the two.

Carter stepped through the door to replace her on the threshold. "You wanted to see me, Robert." He said.

It was clear that McAnally was about to reprove him for the use of his first name, but he stopped. Firstly, he and Carter were the same grade, but McAnally's was only temporary while Carter, despite filling a more junior post, was substantive. If he started that game, Carter could tie him up in all sorts of knots in terms of Civil Service etiquette.. Secondly, it was likely that McAnally wanted Carter to do something to get him out of the trouble he was in, and it would be unwise to get the meeting off on the wrong foot.

Instead, he said "Take a seat please, Steven." A fake smile made its way to his mouth but failed to reach his eyes.

Carter didn't trust the man as far as he could throw him. Which was surprisingly far, Carter thought, as they were on the top floor of the building and it was a long way down to the ground. He dismissed the thought before it could take root and instead did as he was bid, pulling a chair from the side of the office to place it in front of the desk at an angle so that he didn't have the low winter sun in his eyes.

"Thank you Steven." Carter was unsure for what he was being thanked but nodded an acknowledgement anyway. "We have a bit of a situation and I'm wondering if you might be the person to get us out of it."

Get you out of it, Carter thought. There is no 'us' in this. Instead, he said. "I'll do what I can."

"We were expecting a report on the trouble that's blown up in Strabane over the last few days, but it has failed to arrive. Our man on the ground there seems to have dropped off the radar." He paused, unsure of what to say next and probably hoping for Carter to fill the gap.

For his part, Carter could see where the conversation was leading. If the mountain wouldn't come to them they, or rather he, would have to go to the mountain. Well, he had promised Fiona that he would keep well clear of any danger, and he had no intention of breaking his word.

"Erm, yes. I was rather thinking that someone needs to go to Strabane and make contact with our agent there. Either get his written report or get a verbal one instead."

Again, Carter stayed silent. Even to enter into the conversation could be construed as him volunteering.

He remembered an old Army joke, where a Sergeant appears in front of a squad of men and announces that he's looking for two volunteers. An inexperienced soldier pipes up and asks what they would have to do and the Sergeant replies "Good man, now who's going to be the second volunteer?"

"I was thinking that … er … with your background, you might be the man to do the job."

There it was, out in the open.

"Why me? I'm not a field agent. I've never been trained in field work." Carter replied. He knew it wouldn't make any difference. McAnally had already made his decision. If Carter refused to go, no doubt pressure would be brought to bear from above.

"I know that, Steven, but you're a former commando. Your reputation precedes you. You've operated behind enemy lines. You know how to look after yourself."

"But you must surely have field operatives that could do the job. Someone who already knows how to blend in. I only have to open my mouth for anyone to know I'm not from around these parts. I'd give myself away in a moment."

"It would take too long to make contact and brief one of them on what is needed. This is too urgent to permit such a delay. Besides, it would mean revealing their identity to the man in Strabane and we can't risk that. You know the importance of anonymity in this game Carter.

You don't have to talk to anyone other than the agent. We'll tell you where to find him, all you have to do is say the codeword we give you and he'll let you in. Then you either get his written report or memorise what he tells you and then you leave. It's a two hour drive there and another two hours back. Say you spend a maximum of two hours with him if you have to take a verbal report. You'll be back here by …" he made a great show of consulting his watch, "… Seven this evening. Call it eight if you have your lunch first. We'll provide a car and driver, of course, and the driver will be armed."

Carter looked for any angle that could get him out of doing the job. He could refuse point blank. He had the right as it wasn't his job to go scurrying across Northern Ireland and if it was necessary to provide him with an armed escort it definitely fell outside of his job description. His was an office job, which was the only reason he had accepted the temporary appointment. He cursed his reputation as a war hero. Not for the first time it was putting him in danger when he could be enjoying a quiet life.

But if he did refuse it might put him in a bad odour with his superiors, not just here but also in Glasgow and even London.. Having good intelligence saved lives and if his inaction meant that the intelligence picture was incomplete and someone died as a result, it would be seen as his fault.

He cursed his sense of duty, which was the cause of even more trouble than his reputation. If he didn't go, someone else would be sent. And that someone would be less experienced than Carter. He considered the two men and a woman with which he shared an office.

There was young Michael, barely out of University and hardly shaving. He had a local accent, which would help but he'd be a quivering jelly, which would give him away in a moment if he ran into trouble. Then there was Eric. More mature, a twenty year man if Carter recalled correctly. But he was an academic type. He was a wizard at chess, as Carter had cause to know, but jumped at his own shadow. He had been sent over from London to do a tour here to earn his stripes but was hating every minute of it.

Finally, there was Aisling. She was another youngster, but a feisty type. She wasn't experienced enough for field work anymore than the other two. She might make the grade if she was given the right training, but she was also as green as grass when it came to operating outside of the office.. She would see it as an adventure and would probably go if she was asked.

And if anything happened to her, Carter would have that on his conscience. She was about the same age as his daughter. Could he really let her go on this job?

The answer was a resounding 'no'.

There was a new phrase going the rounds in the press these days: male chauvinism[1]. Was he guilty of that? No, he decided. It was all about suitability to do the job. Of the four people in the office, he was the only one who was experienced enough to do it whilst being at the minimum of risk.

"Will I be armed?" Carter asked, admitting defeat.

"If you want to be. I won't insult you by asking if you have any firearms experience." McAnally's wry grin was genuine this time, happy now that he had what he wanted. "Any preference for type of gun?"

"Browning nine millimetre." Carter answered without even thinking. It was a weapon he had become familiar with during the war and again in Malaya and carried a bigger punch than the Webley he had been issued with as a newly commissioned officer. He doubted that there would be a Webley to be found anywhere anyway. They had gone out of service a few years before.

"That's settled then." McAnally was cheerful now, having passed his problem on to someone else. "Get yourself along to the canteen for some lunch and I'll sort out the details and set up a briefing for you and your driver."

*　*　*

The driver's name was Jerry and he had been born and bred in Belfast. He drove like a professional, putting the minimum of effort into each manoeuvre, keeping pace with the traffic and easing past it when the opportunities arose. The Austin Maxi didn't have a standard engine under its bonnet, Carter felt sure. The way it accelerated spoke for that. He wondered what else might not be standard.

But the important thing about the car was that it was nondescript. Even its colour was a bland shade of beige.

Jerry didn't speak much, other than to comment on the skills of the other drivers they encountered, usually in four letter words. Carter put him at around fifty and guessed that this hadn't always been his job. He'd have guessed at police, but Jerry could also have been ex-military.

Once past the turning for Aldergrove Airport they took the same route as Carter had used on his visit the previous year, as far as Dungiven, then they took a turning onto the B74, the direct road to Strabane.

"We could go via Derry and along the Foyle valley." Jerry remarked, "It's a better road but it'll increase the distance."

"Whatever route you think is best." Carter replied from the front passenger seat.

He shifted the weight of the shoulder holster under his armpit. No matter which way he moved it, it felt uncomfortable. He thought he'd be given a belt mounted holster, but the armourer explained to him that it would be more visible when he got out of the car. "Seeing a gun will make people think you're either a terrorist or undercover police and you don't want either. If you need a gun, then the sorts of places you'll be going won't welcome a cop and if they think you're a terrorist, they'll assume you're from the opposition, because they'll know their own boys."

So, the uncomfortable shoulder holster it was. Carter felt tempted to take it off and put the weapon in the glove compartment, but that would make it too difficult to reach if he needed to get at it. He hoped he wouldn't need it at all.

Along with the gun went a spare magazine of bullets, giving him twenty rounds in all. "If you need any more than that …" the armourer had grinned, "…then you're as good as dead anyway unless the cavalry arrives."

On that cheerful note Carter had left the sanctuary of the central Belfast office block and joined Jerry in the car.

The houses started to become closer together and small factory units and other commercial premises replaced open fields.

"Almost there." Jerry commented.

The flags on the lampposts told him they were passing through a 'Loyalist' area. Carter also noticed that kerbstones were painted red, white and blue.

"Is that normal?" Carter asked.

"Aye, in some areas. It's like a dog marking its territory. Flags can be ripped down, but it's harder to uproot a kerbstone. You'll see green, white and orange painted ones in the Nationalist areas."

They reached an army checkpoint made up of concrete blast walls painted olive green, with skeins of barbed wire along both sides to keep people from approaching along any route other than through the approved one, which brought them into the firing line of the soldiers manning the sangars[2]. Jerry and Carter both produced their driving licences when a soldier ordered them to. There was no pretence of politeness and Carter suspected the soldiers came in for a fair amount of abuse from drivers and passengers.

Both of them could have produced official ID that would have seen them waved through in an instant, but that might be noted by watching eyes and that was a risk Carter couldn't take. His visit was supposed to remain a secret and anything that attracted attention would go against that principle. The soldier took their licenses into a sandbag protected hut, while another kept them under observation from a sangar. His rifle wasn't pointed directly at the car, but the amount of adjustment needed to bring the vehicle into the soldier's sights was tiny.

The soldier returned, passed the licences through the driver's side window then waved them on without another word.

"Cheery sort." Carter observed.

"You're lucky. We caught them in a good mood. He could have had us out of the car and searching the whole thing and us stripped to our underwear too." Jerry reminded him.

"What did he do when he took our licences inside?" Carter asked.

"Probably nothing. There's a rumour going around that they're connected by some sort of computer to a central record that holds all the identities of the people of Northern Ireland, their driving licence details, passport information and all that sort of thing. but that's bullshit. But the Army doesn't contradict the rumour and taking the licenses away like that helps to keep it going. They will have a paper list of suspect names, so he may have checked against that."

They were easing through the town centre now, with traffic stopping and starting at this busy time of day,

Carter eyed the crowd uneasily, aware that it was quite feasible for someone with a gun to get up close to the car and take a shot.

He was feeling paranoid, of course. No one knew he was coming, so there was no reason they should come under attack. But he was a lot happier when they were out of the narrow streets and moving back through the suburbs once more.

*　*　*

The house had seen better days, Carter could see that. It was a large place, standing in its own grounds on a lane just off the Omagh road. Ivy crawled across all available surfaces and what could be seen of the painted render on the walls was peeling and cracked, with chunks missing in places. It looked like it might have been a country doctor's pride and joy, perhaps thirty years earlier, but now it would take more money than Carter could ever afford to restore it to its former glory.

"Wait here." Carter ordered Jerry. His orders had been clear, the driver mustn't see the person Carter was expecting to meet. Just to be sure, Carter made him park at the side of the house, where the front door wouldn't be visible from the driver's seat.

The door knocker was old and tarnished, but still loose enough on its hinge for Carter to lift it and make three loud raps. They were greeted with silence. Carter had noted before that when a house is empty, it takes on an air of silence that was beyond the mere lack of noise from inside. He was always able to tell when a door would be answered and when it wouldn't. On this occasion he was sure nobody would respond to his knock.

However, he waited patiently, before trying a second time, getting the same result. He stepped across a weed infested flower bed and peered through the window into what was probably a sitting room. It was empty.

He returned to the door and tried for a third time but he knew already that there was no one at home.

He walked around the side, the one furthest from where Jerry waited in the car, and found himself in a large, overgrown garden. Approaching a pair of French windows, he peered in again. It was a dining room but was as empty as the sitting room. Continuing his circuit, Carter reached a rear door. The window alongside revealed it to be the kitchen.

On impulse Carter grabbed the doorknob and twisted it. The door fell open under his hand.

"Anyone at home?" He called. But he didn't even get an echo in reply. The January dusk was fast approaching, and the interior of the house was gloomy. He stepped over the threshold and found the light switch on the wall beside the door.

The kitchen was clean and tidy, and it was apparent that the interior of the house was better looked after than the exterior. A plate, cup and cutlery sat in a drainer next to the large empty sink, where the tap dripped sporadically. A green limescale stain on the bottom of the sink said it had been leaking for many years. Whoever lived in this house might be houseproud, but they weren't much good at maintenance.

Opening the fridge beneath a work surface, Carter peered inside. There was an open bottle of milk in a recess in the door, a butter dish, the butter having been scraped. A fish lay in a newspaper wrapping on one of the shelves. A crisper drawer at the bottom of the fridge was empty. Not much of a salad eater, Carter concluded. On the top shelf lay a block of cheese, wrapped in plane white butcher's paper. Reaching for the milk, he lifted the foil cap and took a tentative sniff. Fresh enough to have been bought recently, Carter thought. Or maybe it had been delivered. Probably no more than a day old.

He closed the fridge and began opening cupboards at random. He had no idea why. Perhaps he was looking for some clue as to whether the occupant intended returning to the house. A tall cupboard revealed a well-stocked larder, while a bread bin contained half a sliced loaf wrapped in greaseproof paper that bore the logo of, Carter assumed, a local bakery. As with the milk, he tested it for freshness. The top slice was dry, fit for nothing more than toast, but there was no sign of mould.

He moved into the hall, glancing into the dining room. The far wall was dominated by a sideboard. It was the sort of place where someone might store papers in a drawer, so he investigated. He was right. The drawer on the left hand end held some official looking letters and when Carter lifted them, he found a passport underneath.

"I think he's beyond our help." Carter heard a voice behind him, unmistakably that of Jerry. He turned his head to confirm what his ears told him.

"What do you mean?"

"He's not here, quite clearly, and you found the back door unlocked. Once upon a time no one locked their doors, or they left a key in the lock, so visitors didn't have to knock, they just walked in. But that all stopped when The Troubles started. But you found the back door open."

"His passport's here."

"That doesn't mean anything. There's lots of people have an Irish passport as well as a British one. It's all legal and above board, part of the peace treaty of 1922. But even if he didn't have an Irish passport, he doesn't need one to move around. If you were to cross the border, no one would ask to see a passport. It's part of the same agreement."

Carter recalled his visit to Letterkenny the previous year. Jerry was right, no one had asked to see his passport when he crossed the border in either direction. The only people who were interested in his identity were the soldiers and they accepted his driving licence.

"You said you think he's beyond our help. That assumes the worst."

"Car keys on the worktop by the back door." Jerry nodded his head back towards the kitchen. "I'm guessing if we open the garage we'll find the car that goes with them."

"He might have taken a taxi."

"But he wouldn't have forgotten to lock up before he left. This guy is an informant. He can't afford to take risks with his security.

Locking doors would be second nature to him, especially as he's Catholic. The IRA don't take kindly to informants. Well, neither do the Loyalists, but to be a tout, as they call them, is the worst thing you can be if you're a Catholic. It goes back to the Easter Rising and the troubles afterwards."

"How do you know he's a Catholic?"

Jerry smiled and pointed at a rather garish picture hanging on the wall above the sideboard. It was a depiction of Jesus, holding his robe open to display a crimson coloured heart. "No Protestant would ever have one of those on the wall. I've not looked but I'm guessing there'll be a Holy Water font by the front door, too, so he can bless himself when he leaves the house."

"You're very observant." Carter complimented him.

"I wasn't always a driver. I was a copper in London for twenty years before I decided to come home. There's some habits you never lose and one of them is taking in small details. They tell you a lot about a person. This house tells me the occupant lived alone."

"Even I spotted there was only one plate in the drying rack."

"Yes, but also no family photos on the sideboard. It's the most obvious place to display them."

"Maybe they're in the sitting room." Carter replied.

"Let's take a look see, shall we?"

He led the way along the corridor and into the lounge. Carter flicked the light switch and the details of the room sprang into sharp relief. The furnishings were dark and heavy; a leather Chesterfield style sofa with two armchairs. There was a dark wooden coffee table with a few magazines on a shelf below. The cover of the only one Carter could see showed a man holding a fish, a big smile on his face. There were half a dozen pictures on the wall, but all were sporting prints, mainly of men standing up to their waists in water, wielding fishing rods, with fish leaping at the end of the line.

"Bit of a fisherman by the looks of it." Carter observed.

"Aye, we've got some good rivers and the coastal fishing is grand. I do a bit m'sel when I have the time."

The final bit of furniture in the room was a TV cabinet, the doors lying open to allow the screen to be seen. On top of it was a crucifix mounted on a stand.

"He seems to be religious."

"A man living in fear is always ready to meet his maker." Jerry replied.

"You seem determined he's dead." Carter remarked.

"I can't be one hundred percent sure without seeing a body, but the car keys and unlocked back door are fairly conclusive as far as I'm concerned."

"So, what's the scenario. There's no sign of a struggle. At least, not down here."

"We can check upstairs if you like, but I think it's most likely he heard a noise outside, made to attract his attention, then when he went to look to see what it was he was grabbed. It means whoever took him didn't risk leaving any fingerprints. Very professional."

"But that doesn't mean he's dead."

"No, but if that's what happened, we'd better hope he is dead because if he isn't, it means whoever has him is interrogating him and I wouldn't wish that on my worst enemy."

Carter led the way upstairs and found no more evidence of a disturbance than they had downstairs. The only furnished room was the front bedroom and it was neatly made up. The wardrobe was full of clothes, mainly suits in dark colours, and the chest of drawers was filled with shirts and underwear. A copy of the Bible lay on a bedside table, under a Dick Frances novel with a bookmark showing how far it had been read.

"Of course, he might just have gone for a walk." Carter suggested.

Jerry nodded towards the window, where darkness had fallen, despite it being only four in the afternoon. The dark, lowering clouds had brought an early dusk. "Nobody in Northern Ireland walks outside after dark. If he planned to be away this late he'd have taken his car."

He was being a right Jeremiah[3], Carter thought, but there was no evidence of the man's whereabouts.

They gave the other rooms a cursory glance then headed back down the stairs. Carter went back into the living room where he had spotted a telephone sat on a small circular table next to the chair opposite the TV set. Lifting the handset, he placed it to his ear. The familiar purr of the dial tone was noticeable by its absence. Either the man hadn't paid his phone bill, or someone had cut the line.

"No dial tone." Carter reported.

"That just about settles it then." Jerry replied. "It's a routine thing if the IRA are coming to visit. They don't want anyone getting a three nines call out and spoiling the party."

While all the facts led to Jerry's conclusion, Carter still wasn't convinced. There was something about the scene that suggested it had been carefully stage managed. Maybe the man had wanted to make it appear that he hadn't left the house voluntarily.

But there was no way of proving that, so on the basis of what he knew, Carter had to accept Jerry's version of events. Coppers were supposed to have a 'nose' for such things, Carter knew from the numerous detective series he watched on TV.

"Well, he clearly isn't here, so I need to call Belfast for fresh instructions. Perhaps they can tell me where his dead letter drop is so I can ..."

"Oh no you don't. You're not going near any dead letter drop." Jerry's tone suggested no argument about the matter.

Having assumed that he was in charge of the operation, Carter now realised that he might not be.

"Why not?"

"If he's been interrogated, it's the first bit of information he would have given up, in the hope of appeasing his torturers. And that means they'll have it under observation, to see who approaches it. An informant needs a handler and the handler's identity is useful information. He might even be killed when he goes near it. So, no visits to dead letter drops."

It seemed that Jerry might be more than just a driver-cum-bodyguard "You seem remarkably well informed about fieldcraft." Carter observed.

"I worked with Special Branch in London for a while. I know all about dead letter drops, cut-outs, brush passes and all that sort of stuff. I'm not just a pretty face, y'know."

"So it seems. But if he has a handler, what am I doing here? Surely the handler is closer."

"So as not to give away the handler's identity. He's probably running several informants. Get hold of him and the whole network gets blown."

It was a chilling thought and meant that their presence in the house, and its meaning, might have been noted. "But I still need to contact Belfast for instructions." Carter persisted.

"I'll use the car radio." Jerry told him. "Wait here."

"Won't we be out of range?" Carter called towards Jerry's retreating back."

"Multi-channel radio, Mr Carter." Jerry called over his shoulder. "There are relay stations all across the Six Counties. I speak to A, A speaks to B and so on until the message gets to where it is needed and the reply comes back by the same route. Or A just phones the office for me."

He was back about ten minutes later. "Belfast says to get back there as soon as we can. Wipe down all the places you know that you touched, starting with the light switches and the drawers on the sideboard."

"Why?" It seemed like a strange thing to do.

"Someone is eventually going to realise this man is missing, or his body is going to turn up somewhere, so this will become a crime scene. Having our fingerprints all over the place will muddy the waters and maybe even bring us under suspicion of being involved. I'm sure you'd rather not become a suspect for a murder you didn't commit."

Carter didn't bother replying. He just pulled his unused handkerchief from his pocket and started wiping down the handset of the telephone.

* * *

After locking the back door and dropping the key through the letterbox, Jerry had them back on the road and speeding through the now deserted streets of Strabane. The lights of the town were soon disappearing in the rear view mirror.

After about five miles, in the depths of the countryside, a light appeared in the road, the only one visible. It was bright and moving from side to side. Rain on the car window splintered the beam like a kaleidoscope, causing Carter to raise his hand to shield his eyes.

"Army mobile checkpoint." Jerry said by way of explanation. "Probably UDR[4]."

As they approached the light Jerry slowed the vehicle, bringing it to a final halt several yards short of whoever was holding the torch.

Only when the figure holding the torch approached the car did Carter see that he wasn't wearing the usual camouflage of the British Army. He wore a dark coloured coat and trousers and on his head he was wearing a balaclava helmet. The lower part of his face was covered by some sort of bandana, wild west style.

"Oh shit!" Jerry exclaimed.

Carter needed no further explanation. He reached for the Browning nestled uncomfortably in his armpit.

"No!" Jerry barked. "It's already too late for that. If you draw that gun you're dead." Sure enough, Carter could see that aligned alongside the torch was a handgun and it was pointing straight at him. He looked around behind them to see a man standing in the road, not far behind the car, with a rifle aimed through the rear window."

"How did they know?" Carter whispered.

"Someone watching the lane, I'd say. They saw us arrive in and reported back. Since then, we've probably had people reporting ahead of us as we passed through the town. It wouldn't be hard to

71

guess the road we'd take. They probably have the Derry road covered as well."

"What now?"

"You're guess is as good as mine, Mr Carter. If they wanted us dead we'd already be lying in pools of blood, so think positive. Where there's life there's hope, as they say."

The car door was yanked open and the torch carrier shone the beam inside. "You!" he pointed the gun at Jerry as he backed away from the door to forestall any attempt to grab the gun. "Get out and on your knees. Quick now or I'll kill ye."

Jerry did as he was told.

"Now you. Out on your side and on your knees as well."

Carter obeyed. Rain ran down his face and the wetness of the ground seeped through his trousers, cold against his flesh. A minor discomfort. Carter's mind raced, looking for any way he might overpower the men. Another man approached Carter from the front, Tucking a handgun into the waistband of his trousers as he came.

"There's a marksman with a rifle behind yez." The man reminded him, raising his voice loud enough for his companions to hear him as well. "He'll use it if yez does anything stupid."

He felt himself being patted down expertly, the Browning being removed and tucked into the waistband of his searcher's trousers alongside his own weapon.

"Clear." The man announced, stepping away from Carter and drawing his firearm again.

"Clear." Came an answering shout from the other side of the car, signifying that Jerry had also been searched and disarmed.

"OK, up!" The man in front of Carter commanded.

He heard the sound of an approaching vehicle and for a brief moment Carter's heart lifted as he contemplated rescue, but the hope died almost at once. The vehicle drew to a standstill behind them as its headlights lit up the scene.

"Turnaround and start walking." Carter was ordered. "And don't even think about trying to make a break."

The man must be a mind reader, Carter thought, because it was just what he had been thinking. The man's night vision would have been ruined by the headlights and a few brief steps away darkness beckoned. Once in it, Carter would back himself against any part time terrorist.

So, Carter just walked down the side of the vehicle, which turned out to be a Ford Transit van. The side cargo door was already open and a man waited inside, a gun at the ready.

"Get in!" The man behind Carter barked.

Carter did as he was told and was immediately grabbed by another man, who had been concealed inside, and was thrown to the floor. Rough hands tied him at the wrists and ankles before pulling a foul smelling bag over his head. He was left lying on the floor.

More commands were shouted as Jerry was escorted to the vehicle and Carter felt the vehicle's suspension rock as his former bodyguard climbed in, then he was subjected to the same rough handling.

The suspension rocked again as the terrorists climbed out and the cargo door was slid shut and the lock clicked into place with an air of finality.

The vehicle moved off only moments later.

"Is that you, Jerry?" Carter asked, his voice muffled by the bag over his head. If anyone other than Jerry answered, it meant they weren't alone in the back of the van.

"Yae, I'm here, Mr Carter."

"Call me Lucky, everyone does."

"The name doesn't really match the circumstances, Mr Carter." There was heavy irony to be heard in Jerry's voice.

"You're right, Jerry. Make that Steven. So, what do you think will happen now?"

"Well, as I said in the car, if they wanted us dead we already would be, so there's that. But we'll be questioned about who we are and what we were doing in that house. Once they've established that, they'll want to know what we know about what the man in the house was up to, who his contacts were, his handler, the whole lot."

"That's not much. All I know is his codename and that he was supposed to be giving us … me, information on the local troubles."

"But they don't know that yet." Jerry replied. "If you'll take my advice Steven, you'll answer their questions as best you can. It will be a lot less painful. You don't know enough to make it worth your while being beaten up for the sake of pointless heroics."

"Is that what you'll be doing."

"Pretty much. I know a bit more about the security set up here than you, but not that much more than they already know from their own insiders."

"So why grab us at all?"

"I think it's probably because you're a new face. You're an unknown quantity as far as they're concerned and that makes you of interest."

"But I'm only an analyst. I interpret what's going on and they know that already."

"Yes, but they don't know you're an analyst. Once they find out they'll probably be quite disappointed."

"But they won't let us go, I'm guessing."

"Steven, for the first time on this trip you are absolutely right."

Carter felt a steely resolve building inside him. He remembered all the way back to 1941 and the day after his arrival at the Commando training depot at Achnacarry House[5]. He and the other volunteers were sent by truck to the foot of Ben Nevis and told to run up the mountain. Once at the top they were instructed to run back down again. Thinking they would find their trucks waiting for them at the bottom, they were surprised to find them absent and that they were expected to continue running until they got all the way back to Achnacarry once more.

It was enough to break some of the volunteers and they went back to their original units that day, never to return. But not Carter. He gritted his teeth, ignored the blisters that had formed on his feet inside his boots, put his head down and started running once more. That same determination had got him through the war in one piece and he wasn't going to let this new challenge end his life.

Woe betide whoever had taken them prisoner.

5 – London

Danny Glass climbed down from the cab of his lorry and stretched, trying to unravel the knots that had formed in the muscles of his back. Feeling a little more comfortable, he started to untie the ropes that secured the tarpaulin covering the empty beer kegs that made up the lorry's cargo.

"Danny!" A shouted voice made him turn, to see a familiar figure walking quickly across the transport yard.

"Evenin' Arthur. What can I do you for?" Glass asked the yard's foreman.

"You've got a visitor. Arrived about an hour ago. Wouldn't tell me what he wanted. When I told him you wouldn't be back for a while, he said he'd wait." He gave Danny a curious look before continuing. "Got the air of a copper about him, if you ask me. What you bin up to then?"

"You know me, Arthur." Glass chuckled. "Pure as the driven snow. Want to buy a watch? Second hand. Offer me a fiver and I'll throw in the hour and minute hands too." He laughed at his own joke.

"Seriously, you know the company policy on anything dodgy."

"Honestly, Arthur, I have no idea why he might want to talk to me."

"Well, better not keep the man waiting anyway. Get along. He's in my office cluttering the place up."

"But I've gotta unload …"

"I'll get one of the lads to do it for you. Just this time, mind." He wagged a warning finger at Danny before turning away to search out someone to unload the empty beer kegs.

Glass strolled across the brewery yard towards the corner where the transport foreman had his small office. He was as curious about what the visitor might want as the foreman himself.

Despite his joking, he was an honest man and had no reason to fear the police. He hadn't witnessed a crime, so far as he knew, so it couldn't be that. A sudden thought crossed his mind and he wondered if his wife, Edith, was OK. But he dismissed the idea. Arthur had said he had the air of a copper, not that he was one. If anything had happened to Edith they'd send a uniformed officer, not a detective. And a detective would produce his warrant card, just like they did on Dixon of Dock Green[1].

No, this was something else, but he couldn't think what. He was naturally suspicious of authority, feeling that they were always out to do the working man down in some way.

Despite the cold weather, the door to the office was open and the man was seated on the far side of the foreman's desk; the side normally used by visitors.

"You were looking for me." Danny said without preamble.

The man unfolded himself from the rickety office chair. He was tall and thin, Dany could see, despite the thick winter coat he wore. Glass guessed the coat probably cost more than he earned in a week..

"Mr Glass. My name is Allan Drinkwater. How do you do."

He extended his hand for Danny to shake. Drinkwater was a suitable name, Danny thought, taking the man in. He was like a long streak of piss. He had one of those annoying accents that Glass remembered from the war; braying tones that suggested too much 'breeding' and not enough brains. The sort of officer who thought he knew it all just because he'd been to OCTU[2]. But this one seemed harmless enough.

"That's me." Glass said, shaking the hand. "Call me Danny." The man didn't invite him to call him Allan. "What can I do for you?"

"A very good question, Danny, the answer to which we will get to in due course. Firstly, though, I must ask you a couple of questions. Do you mind answering them?"

"So long as they ain't going to get me into any kind of trouble."

The man dismissed his fears with a condescending chuckle. "Don't worry. You aren't in any kind of trouble. Now, can you tell me, do you know a Steven Carter, sometimes referred to as Lucky Carter?"

"After four years of fighting side by side, I probably know him as well as any man. Why, what's he got himself mixed up in this time?"

"All in good time, Danny. Now, do you know Patrick O'Driscoll. You may know him better as Paddy."

"Same again. He was my best mate. I was best man at his wedding."

"And when did you last see Mr O'Driscoll?"

"That would be 1956. Me, Prof and Colonel Carter all went out to Australia for a year to train Australian commandos. Paddy was the training officer in charge of the depot." Danny thought it better not to mention the detour to Malaya that had happened in the middle of their year out there. If the man didn't know about it, it wasn't Danny's place to give away government secrets.

"And when did you last have any contact with him?"

Danny had to think hard about that one. Truth to tell, he had lost track of the last time he had heard from his friend.

"Hmm. Maybe a Christmas card, about three … no, at least four years ago."

"Not since then?"

"No. Definitely not since. I'd remember."

"That doesn't sound like a very close friendship." Drinkwater observed.

Glass's lip curled in a sneer. "What you civvies will never understand is the bond that soldiers have. I might not see Paddy for twenty years but when we meet, not only will we re-start our last conversation from the very point we left off, but we'll even remember whose turn it is to buy the drinks as well."

"A bit like public school then." Drinkwater was unwise enough to say.

"If public school involves a lot of charging Jerry machine guns, then yeah, exactly like that." Danny Glass made no effort to conceal his contempt for such an ignorant reply.

Drinkwater had the decency to blush at his faux pas. Glass said "Wanker" just loud enough for him to hear.

79

"Er, yes, now, how about Colonel Carter. When did you last hear from him." Danny noted the switch to military rank, to mirror his own use of it.

"That one's easier. It was my birthday last month and he sent me a card. He never forgets. birthdays and Christmas, regular as clockwork. The same for Prof Green, though I think he's got an underling sending them now. You haven't mentioned the Prof."

Drinkwater's face took on a sour expression, suggesting that he might be the 'underling'. He also ignored the reference to Prof Green and Danny noticed it. "When did you last see Colonel Carter?"

"I saw Colonel Carter last summer, in August. The commandos have an annual reunion, when we visit Honfleur to commemorate a raid we did there back in '42. That was bad business[3]. We lost over half the commando that day. Prof Green, sorry, Mr Green ..." Danny corrected himself with a grin, "... was due to go too, but there was some sort of government crisis. That almost goes without sayin', doesn't it. This government seems to be in crisis every day."

Drinkwater ignored the remark. "When you say you got a card from O'Driscoll ..." Danny frowned at the lack of use of any sort of title, unlike the way he had referred to Carter and Green. "... Can you remember where the card was posted? For example, can you remember what nationality the stamp was?"

"Not a clue. My wife usually opens the post 'cos I'm out at work by the time the postman delivers. She gets home before me. You could try askin' her, but I'd doubt she'd remember. But what's this all about? I've answered a whole lot of questions and I'm pretty sure you already knew the answers to some of them, because I'm guessing you work for the Prof."

"I was just coming to that, Danny. And I thank you for your patience. I did indeed know the answers to some of those questions, but not to all of them. But there was a reason for asking them, especially the ones relating to O'Driscoll."

Again, Danny noted the lack of a title for Paddy. Was it because he was Irish? It wasn't long ago it was possible to see signs in the front windows of boarding houses saying 'No blacks. No dogs. No

Irish.' He'd even seen it on the doors of some of the pubs where he delivered beer. Those times were changing, thankfully, but it showed how intolerant some people were. Just because the signs weren't there anymore, it didn't mean the landlords and landladies weren't thinking it still.

Danny decided to take a stab in the dark. "This is about Paddy, isn't it. What's he done? Or, more likely, what are you trying to fit him up for having done?"

"What makes you think that?" Drinkwater seemed genuinely surprised at the allegation.

"Well, the Irish are hardly flavour of the month right now and it's been *Mister* Carter or *Colonel* Carter since you arrived, but it's only been plain 'O'Driscoll' for Paddy."

"A keen observation, Danny. You are correct, this is related to '*Mr*' O'Driscoll. But we're not trying to fit him up for anything. Indeed, all we want is for you to talk to him on our behalf."

"What, me? Go all the way to Australia again? You must be out of your tiny mind to think I'd drop everything and go there without a by-your-leave."

"Oh. Mr O'Driscoll is much closer than Australia, Danny. There would still be some travel involved, but not so much you couldn't be back home pretty quickly. But let me explain first."

"Well, time's getting' on." Danny took a theatrical look at his watch. "I'm due to knock off in five minutes and I don't think the foreman's going to pay me overtime just to sit here battin' the breeze with you."

"Please bear with me. I'm sure you're as anxious to help your old CO as we are."

That brought Danny up short. "What has this got to do with Colonel Carter? I thought you said it was about Paddy. And just who is the 'we' in this little chat." Danny paused, a thought clicking into place in his head. "Hang on. This is something to do with the Prof, isn't it. He's behind this."

"I'm afraid I'm not at liberty ...."

81

"It's OK, you don't need to say it out loud if it's going to cause difficulties. He's an important man now, a Minister no less. But when a posh bloke turns up at my place of work, talking about my old friends, but hasn't said who he works for, I don't need to be a genius to work it out. So, someone we won't name has sent you here to ask me for a favour and that favour has to do with two mutual friends. Correct me if I'm wrong."

"You are not wrong, Danny." Drinkwater conceded with a sigh.

"OK, you have my undivided attention." Danny moved to the side of the desk normally occupied by the foreman and lowered himself into his well-polished seat. He pushed a sheet of paper to one side and rested his elbow on the scarred surface of the desk.

"Thank you. Perhaps I had better start at the beginning, though there are a few things I can't tell you. Not because it might cause difficulty for my employer, but because they are covered by the Official Secrets Act. Are we clear on that."

"Yes, don't worry, *we* are clear. I know how to keep my trap shut."

"Very well. Mr O'Driscoll returned to Ireland in 1968 after he was discharged from the Australian army. He went back to his native Mayo, but in recent months we think he has taken a more active role in what is happening in Northern Ireland, though not on the side of law and order."

"Are you sayin' Paddy's a terrorist?"

"Let's just say he is suspected of being one. On behalf of my superior, last summer your friend Colonel Carter went across to Ireland for a very unofficial meeting with Mr O'Driscoll to warn him about the risks he might be taking. It is safe to say the meeting didn't go as well as it might and Colonel Carter came back and reported his lack of success. We thought that was the end of it and Mr O'Driscoll would just have to take his chances.

Now, do you know what Colonel Carter does for a living?"

Drinkwater's sudden change back to questioning threw Danny for a moment. "No … er … Not really. He told me he worked for the government, some sort of Civil Servant, but didn't go into details. In the commandos you learn when to ask questions and when not to. That was clearly a time not to. If he had wanted me to know what he did, he'd have told me."

"Quite right, but I assume you drew a conclusion from his reticence."

"Yeah. I drew a conclusion. I concluded he was some kind of spook, you know, a spy or something. Not the James Bond type, but maybe the George Smiley sort."

"Close, but not actually a spy. He's office bound. Or I should say, he was supposed to be office bound. Two days ago, he went to Strabane, County Tyrone, to meet with someone. He was asked to go by his boss, who had no right to make such a request. But that is something that will be dealt with in due course." Danny suspected that someone's career had just turned into a job but didn't feel sorry for whoever it was. Lucky Carter's maxim had always been to never ask someone to do a job that you wouldn't be willing to do yourself, and it appeared that the unknown functionary had broken that rule.

"The important thing is that Colonel Carter disappeared off the face of the earth, along with his driver. Our belief is that they have been taken by the Provisionals, but for what purpose we can only guess."

"I'm not sure where this is going. Surely you don't want me to go and try to find them?"

"Oh no. We couldn't ask that of you. No, we have the whole of the police and the Army in the North out looking for the pair of them. We have no need to draft in a civilian to help, not even one with your war record. No, we have a different job we would like you to do."

The penny dropped with a thunderous clang. "You want me to go and talk to Paddy and see what he knows. Maybe persuade him to ask his Provo pals to release Lucky and the other bloke."

"That's right, Danny. That's exactly what we want you to do."

Glass leant back in his chair and let out a low whistle. "That's some ask. People are getting killed over there."

"We wouldn't expect you to put yourself in any danger. We'd even have people keeping a watchful eye on you to make sure you were in no danger. Of course, you won't see them … unless they need to act."

"In that case, why send me? Why not get one of them to do it?"

"First of all, it's not their job. They have more important things to do and speaking to O'Driscoll would mean giving away their identities. Secondly, it's the personal nature of the request that is important here. You and Paddy O'Driscoll are old friends. It's a friendship that has stood the test of extreme adversity; you've fought side by side. And Paddy respects Colonel Carter. It's probable that he doesn't know what's happened to him and if you tell him, he might be persuaded to help, even if it's only for old time's sake."

"And our mutual friend can't go himself because his face is all over the TV and newspapers in Northern Ireland. He'd be an even bigger prize for the Provos."

Drinkwater didn't reply. He didn't need to.

"You wouldn't have to go into the North. In fact, we don't want you anywhere nearer the North than a place called Letterkenny. That's where your friend Mr O'Driscoll bases himself."

"How soon do you want me to go?"

"Time is of the essence, Danny. They've already been missing for two days. That's a lifetime in Northern Ireland, quite literally. There's flight to Dublin from Heathrow at nine thirty this evening. We'd like you to be on it.

We'll arrange a hotel in Dublin and a hire car and you can set out for Letterkenny first thing in the morning. It's about a six hour drive using the route we want you to take. It's much longer than the direct route but it avoids travelling through the North. We hope you will be able to make contact with Mr O'Driscoll tomorrow evening or maybe the next day. Hopefully no longer than that. Once you've talked to him, whatever the outcome, you just retrace your steps and fly back. We'll make sure you have an 'open' ticket, so you can use any BEA flight that has an empty seat[4]."

"I can't just walk out of here for two days, maybe more. I'll get the sack."

"Don't worry, we'll square it with your boss. We'll pay your wages while you're away, with a bit extra on top."

"If you think I'm doing this for the money, you can take a hike. I'm doing this for my mates."

"I'm sorry, Mr Glass. I didn't mean to offend you." Drinkwater struggled to backtrack from his faux pas. "I just mean that your employers won't suffer financially because you aren't here and you won't be out of pocket either."

Glass was slightly mollified. "You seem to have it all worked out. But what do I tell my wife? I can hardly waltz in and say 'Hi love, just popping over to Ireland for a couple of days.' She'd have more questions than you asked and I'd have more trouble answering them."

"In cases like this, it might pay to be honest, within reason. Tell her that you have an old friend that needs urgent help. Maybe suggest that it's Scotland you're going to, rather than Ireland."

"But that doesn't tell her what reason I have for going to Scotland."

Drinkwater gave a heavy sigh. "In my experience, there are three reasons that get people into trouble: sex, crime or money. Pick the one your wife will find easiest to believe. Maybe combine money with crime and make up some story about Carter being threatened by loan sharks and he needs some muscle to help him deal with them."

"I doubt Edith will fall for that and any hint of sex being involved will have her on the train up to Scotland armed with a carving knife to separate Lucky from his family jewels. Never mind. I'll think of something."

"OK. I'll have a taxi waiting at your house for seven pm. I'll be in it to go over the details with you."

Danny looked at his watch. "Bloody hell. That's less than two hours."

Drinkwater gave a self-satisfied smile. "In that case I won't detain you any longer."

6 – The Box

In many ways, their prison wasn't that much different from the one Carter had suffered in Thailand. It was an elongated cube shape, made from metal rather than bamboo, but about the same size. There was a double door which only had handles on the outside and, presumably, a padlock to prevent them getting out. The roof contained a single electric light secured behind a heavy wire cage. There were no furnishings, but a plastic bucket sat in one corner, its lid fighting a losing battle with the noxious smells emanating from within.

And that was before either of them had used it.

As soon as they were locked inside, Carter pulled his hood off and threw it in the corner, before exploring the space to see if there were any weaknesses. He was disappointed to find there were none. The metal was thick enough not to flex even when he applied his weight to it. He suspected that it might be a shipping container of some sort. Their use had mushroomed over recent years as ocean going shipping companies switched to using them as their preferred mode of cargo handling. They had invested huge sums of money in building massive new ships to carry them and ports had had to adapt to cater for the switch, sometimes building whole new port facilities on new sites, leaving the traditional seaports bereft of business.

Carter had witnessed the decline of Glasgow docks as a consequence, just one of many British casualties to the new transportation systems.

They had no tools with which to attack the metal, and the seams he might attack would need something stronger than his fingernails to make them yield.

But that didn't stop Carter thinking about escape. He lay prone and started doing press-ups, counting out loud. After he had done fifty, he sat up and asked Jerry to hold his feet while he did sit-ups.

"What's the point of all this?" Jerry asked, as Carter grunted away.

"Got to be ready when the time comes. If we get the chance, we have to make a run for it and if we do, then we need to be able to outrun them. That means being fit. Could you outrun those bastards if you had to?"

"Point taken." Jerry said, letting go of Carter's feet. He laid himself face down and started doing his own press-ups. He got as far as ten before he collapsed onto his belly, gasping for air.

"It's a start." Carter clapped him on the back.

"Fuckin' fags." Jerry responded. "They'll be the death of me."

"Well, they've taken them away from you, so now might be a good time to stop smoking." Carter chuckled.

"Are you going to be as cheery as this all the time. because if you are, you're probably going to get right on my tits before we've been here for long. Never mind the Provos killing you, I might just do the job for them."

"Maintaining morale is as important as keeping fit." Carter replied. "If we start to believe this is the end, we may as well shout for them to come and take us outside and shoot us."

"True. It's the first time I've been on the wrong side of the door, so you'll have to forgive me if it takes a wee bit o' time to adjust."

"It's more than my first time, but these circumstances are a lot different." He looked around the room again. "Looks like we're not the first to be brought here." He pointed to dark patches and smears on the metal surfaces. "Blood, do you think?"

"I hope so. Some of the alternatives don't bear thinking about. You've been locked up like this before?"

"Yes. If we're here for long enough I'll tell you about it."

"I've got a few stories of my own I can tell, so it'll help to pass the time."

They had travelled in the back of the van for what seemed to be a long time, but unable to see their watches they were unable to guess with any accuracy. Carter suspected they had been on the road for around four hours, but he could be as much as thirty minutes out in

88

either direction. Finally, the van had lurched and splashed its way across a rough surface before drawing to a halt.

Carter and Jerry had the bindings at their feet cut so that they could walk, then were hustled across an uneven surface until they were thrown into their prison. The bindings at their hands were cut then the door slammed shut.

"Any idea where we might be?" Carter asked after Jerry had recovered his breath enough to attempt some sit-ups.

"Not a clue. I tried to keep track of the turns, but after about half an hour I lost it. They turned the van around and headed back towards Strabane, then turned left which would take us South towards Omagh. But with the number of turns after that, we could be anywhere. We could even be back where we started."

"So even if we get out, we have no idea in which direction we should be running."

"Well, we're on an island. So long as we reach the sea at some point we'll be able to narrow things down to a choice of two directions: left or right.

Carter chuckled. If he'd been able to choose with whom he could be imprisoned, Jerry wouldn't have been a bad selection. He might have made a commando, had he decided to join the Army. No, he would have been too young, Carter guessed. He was in his mid-forties. He would still have been in school when the war was on.

Without warning, the overhead light went out.

"Looks like it's time for bed." Jerry said. "Nighty night, sleep tight."

*　*　*

The interrogation started the next morning. The door was opened with a bang and a masked figure ordered Carter to put on his hood. The pistol in the man's hand brooked no argument.

A second man entered the box and tied Carter's hands behind his back, before shoving him out of the box, causing him to stumble on the unseen step down to ground level.

A hand gripped his upper arm painfully, squeezing the muscles, then he was half dragged, half escorted, across a rough surface before he stumbled again on another step.

Carter heard something being dragged across a metal floor. "Sit." The unseen voice commanded. Carter bent his knees tentatively and found there was a seat behind him. His hands were untied, then tied again, this time to the chairback. His hood was yanked off and he found himself in another brightly lit metal cube, facing a man seated on the far side of a plain wooden desk that had seen better days. The man wore the familiar black balaclava used by all the terrorist groups, and the lower half of his face was covered with a black bandana. The only visible part of his face was the bridge of his nose and a pair of piercing ice blue eyes.

The man wore an olive drab jacket of the sort that could be purchased at any military surplus store. Again, it was part of the uniform favoured by paramilitary groups on both sides.

Although Carter couldn't see him, he felt the presence of at least one of his guards behind him. Would they start with an interrogation, or would it go straight into torture? Carter wondered. It made no difference to the information he would impart. Whatever he knew would be of little use to the terrorists.

Even as he sat there, Carter knew that the intelligence staff in Belfast would be going through the files with a fine tooth comb to examine the operational recommendations that Carter had made over the previous weeks and then they would change the plans to neutralise the effect of anything Carter might give away. It was standard procedure in these circumstances. He wasn't expected to remain silent, so it was now just a matter of damage limitation.

"Name." barked the man on the far side of the desk. It was intended to intimidate Carter, but anyone who had ever faced a Sergeant Major in the British army wouldn't be cowed by that tone of voice.

"Steven Carter." He replied. They already knew that, having relived Carter of his wallet and the various forms of identification it held. The only reason the man was asking was because it was known to be a tendency amongst prisoners of war to answer questions more freely once they had started. Ask the easy questions to get them talking, then they'll just keep talking.

"Who do you work for?"

"The Security Service. You might know them better as MI5."

The man blinked in surprise, perhaps not expecting Carter to reveal such sensitive information. Carter decided to help him out. "You have my building pass and I'm sure you know which departments are based in that building. I'm pretty sure you don't normally kidnap people who work for the Department of Agriculture and Fisheries." There were several other government departments in the building, but that one served its purpose as an example.

"Very funny, G Man[1]. OK, what sort of spy are you? How many agents do you run?"

"None. I'm an analyst, not a spy. I haven't even been here that long. Just a few weeks to cover someone who is off sick. I look at the intelligence reports that come in and try to work out what's going on in Northern Ireland. I pass my conclusions on to other departments, and they decide what they are going to do to try to stop whatever it is from happening."

"What departments do you pass it on to?"

"The ones you'd expect. Other parts of the Security Service, both here and in London. The police, especially Special Branch, and the Army"

"If you aren't a spy, what were you doing in Strabane? It doesn't sound like an analyst would get out of their office much."

"You're right. One of our informants had failed to report in. It was decided that someone needed to find out what had happened to him, so I was sent, probably because I was available."

"Is it normal to send analysts out into the field?" the man sounded genuinely amazed at the idea.

"No, but I'm not your ordinary analyst. I may look like a middle aged Civil Servant, but I was once something very different. But that was a long time ago."

The man gave him a thoughtful look. Carter felt as though his eyes were boring into his soul.

"So, who were you sent to find?"

"A local informant. I don't know his name. Before you ask, his codename was Mayfly."

The choice of codename had puzzled Carter until he had seen the inside the of the man's house and his interest in fishing. He remembered from somewhere a fisherman saying that his favourite lure for catching trout was a replica of a mayfly.

"Did you find him?"

Carter knew the man already knew the answer to that question. It wouldn't surprise him if Mayfly was locked away in another of the shipping containers somewhere close by.

"There was no sign of him at his house. He may have gone for good or he may have just gone to visit a neighbour. I couldn't risk waiting around to see if he'd come back."

"What about your pal, the one who was in the car with you? What's his name?"

"I only know him as Jerry. He was my driver and I guess he was my bodyguard as well."

The terrorist laughed. "Seems he wasn't too good at being a bodyguard."

Carter didn't bother replying. The evidence spoke for itself. He didn't blame Jerry for their predicament. He had seen what he expected to see: a UDR patrol on a remote country road. They probably set up a dozen check-points of that sort every night. He himself had made a far bigger blunder during the war which had resulted in him spending a brief time as a prisoner of war.[2]

"OK, G Man, so you analyse intelligence and try to make sense out of it. What were you expecting from this tout; this Mayfly?"

"He was supposed to be providing information about the riots in the area over the past few weeks. Were they just a part of the on-going troubles, or were they a cover for something else? Perhaps they were going to try to set the Army up for another Bloody Sunday type incident. We didn't know and when we don't know about something, we worry about it until we find out."

The man subjected him to another long gaze before speaking again.

"But you didn't find Mayfly, so you still don't know. OK, what do you know? What have you been analysing since you arrived in Northern Ireland?

"I've mainly been looking at where you get your money. We know some of it comes from collections around pubs, but that's chicken-feed. We know that some is being raised in the USA, but again it isn't the big bucks. To run a war like this you need a lot of money to buy arms, keep your people fed and watered, that sort of thing. You aren't doing that from collections in pubs and bars."

"And what have you decided?"

"There are a lot of places in Belfast and Derry where it isn't safe for Her Majesty's tax inspectors to go. Nor the customs inspectors either[3]. We suspect that there are businesses operating in those sorts of areas which either generate income for you, or which are used to launder money for you. Either way, they end up buying the guns and explosives which are being used to kill people. I've been analysing the reports from various sources in an attempt to identify some of those businesses so they can be closed down. Slot machine arcades are of particular interest. Not only do they generate quite a lot of money from the people who play the machines, but they handle a lot of cash which can't be traced, which makes them ideal for money laundering."

"Would you like to name one of those businesses?"

"No, I wouldn't. But I know that if I don't you'll find a way of making me tell you, so I may as well tell you anyway. Dessie's Arcade on the Falls Road has attracted our attention. The number of people who go in there could never account for the amount of cash they bank."

"Any others?"

"That's the only one I'm sure about."

"In that case tell me about the ones you aren't sure about." The man's gaze hardened, and his tone had become more menacing. The figure behind Carter shuffled his feet, as though expecting to be told to do something.

"There's a hairdressers on the Antrim Road; Uppercuts it's called. We've had information that suggests we should take a look at it. There are also two bookmakers' shops in the Ardoyne on which I was going to start working, but I haven't had a chance yet."

"It seems like a lot of work to be doing considering that no one will ever collect the tax on that money."

"As I'm sure you know," Carter replied, "This has nothing to do with tax. If we can cut off your money supply, you'll find it harder to operate, The sorts of people who are selling arms to you don't take cheques. But you do need bank accounts for other reasons so we are interested in those accounts to tell us where the money originates. That's how we got on to Dessie's."

The man laughed and his humour even touched his eyes. "OK, Carter. That will do for today."

Abruptly the man stood up and left the room. Carter's hands were untied, re-tied and then he was escorted back to their prison cube.

"How'd it go?" Jerry asked, once he and Carter were alone again.

"Just a softening up, I think. They wanted to see what they could get out of me without working too hard."

"Aye, they'll go away now and cross check what you've said with other sources. If they think you've lied, or held something back, it will likely not go well."

Carter didn't doubt that. The world is never short of hangmen and torturers, he thought. Someone had said that to him after they had discovered Belsen Concentration Camp and he had wondered how a supposedly civilised country could do things like that to their fellow man.

But it was true. No matter how civilised a society thought it had become, someone could always be found who would willingly torture another person, then justify it by saying it was for the good of the people. No doubt whoever tortured him would say the same.

Because Carter had no doubt that the next time he was interrogated, the man with the piercing blue eyes wouldn't be anywhere near as nice.

7 - The Mount Errigal Hotel

Unlike Carter, Danny Glass took a more direct approach to finding O'Driscoll. He drove straight to the Central Bar, parked outside, entered and asked if the barman's name was Jimmy, then asked him to pass a message to Paddy.

Jimmy denied knowing anyone by the name of Paddy O'Driscoll, so Danny suggested the message be passed to Tommy Gillan instead. He didn't hang around after that.

Drinkwater had told him that he would be as safe in Letterkenny as he would be in London, which didn't reassure Glass. As a lifelong resident of the city, he frequented places where Drinkwater had never been and was never likely to go, so they had very different ideas regarding the safety of the city of Danny's birth. Danny was therefore sceptical regarding any reassurances that Drinkwater might give.

After checking into the Mount Errigal Hotel he had an early dinner then settled into the lounge with a pint of Guinness and the previous evening's edition of the Evening Standard, turning straight to the sports pages.

"In the name o' God, who will they send next, the Band of the Coldstream Guards?" Paddy O'Driscoll's voice drew him from his newspaper.

"Paddy! So good to see you." Glass leapt to his feet and pumped his old friend's hand. O'Driscoll went one better and pulled him into a bear hug,

"People will talk." Glass protested after a moment.

"Let the feckers." O'Driscoll laughed back but relented and released Glass. "I've ordered drinks. I see you're sampling the local brew." O'Driscoll nodded towards Glass's almost empty Guinness glass.

"I thought I might. You Irish are always sayin' it never tastes the same outside Ireland, so I thought I'd test the theory."

"And your verdict?"

"Can't tell the difference, to tell you the truth. But then again, I'm more a black and tan drinker usually." He referred to the mix of stout and pale ale that was drunk in some London pubs.

"Good God man, do yez want to get yoursel' killed? Never say those words in Ireland if you know what's good for you."

"Oh, yeah, sorry. I forgot. It means something different over here.¹"

"It certainly does. So, Prof Green got nowhere by sending Lucky Carter over to talk to me, so he's having another go by sending you, is he?"

"That's not why I'm here. Though I am surprised to find you throwing in your lot with the Provos."

"It's not something I'm proud of. To be honest, I don't do that much for them and I'm far more interested in keeping Irish boys alive than I am in killing British boys or even Loyalists."

"What do you mean?"

"I mean that every so often I get a phone call from the North and I go and take half a dozen lads out across the hills of Inishowen for a few days. It's pretty wild up there and you can go for days without seeing another cratur. I try to teach them enough soldiering to stop them getting themselves killed. They're going to do what they're going to do whether I like it or not. So, I do what I can to make sure they don't get themselves killed while they're doing it. I don't teach them how to make bombs and I don't teach them how to fire guns."

Danny grinned, "That's a good job too. You couldn't hit a barn from the inside."

O'Driscoll chuckled. "I have to concede, you were always a better shot than me Danny. But they have other people to do those things."

"That doesn't seem to be what the British think."

"Just clever propaganda. Having a former British commando in the ranks is supposed to scare youz lot. It's also supposed to scare the Prods. But my fame is overrated."

"So, what do you do the rest of the time? How do you earn a living?"

"I suppose you could call me a private tutor. It pays enough for me to keep body and soul together. I teach ten and eleven years olds enough Irish to get them into the Convent or the College. Pretty much everything the two schools teach is taught through the Irish language, even Latin, so they won't keep up if they haven't got a good grasp of it. Then, at the other end, I make sure the seventeen and eighteen year olds are fluent enough to pass their Leaving Cert. You can't get any job that's paid by the government if you can't speak Irish. Officially you don't need it to get into an Irish university, but if you haven't got it, you're not to get a place. And if you don't get a place, all that's left is Queen's in Belfast or going over the water to an English university. And those that leave rarely come back at the end.

"Do a lot of young people do that?"

"Ireland's greatest export has always been its young men and women. It's not just the language though. Eamon de Valera[2] and the church between them have held Ireland back for so long that we're almost in the dark ages compared to the rest of Europe."

"Why was that?"

"Dev was American born. His mother made sure he grew up with very romantic notions about Ireland He saw the entire population making hay and herding sheep in their cloth caps and shawls. So, he's done almost nothing to modernise the country. As for the clergy, the gobshites. They'd have us illiterate and on our knees prayin' all day if they could. I tell yez, if some of the things I've heard are true, there's going to be an almighty scandal about the clergy and the nuns one day."

Glass decided not to open what was obviously a wound and changed the subject. "Maybe this new Common Market thing we're all in will help."

"Aye, well, we hope so. Something needs to change. You just have to take a look at towns like Letterkenny to see how we're hanging on by the skin of our teeth. It's not just in the North that people are getting restless."

"I didn't realise you were so anti religion."

"I'm not anti-religion at all. What I am is anti-priests and anti-nuns. The gobshites. The Christian brothers are even worse, and they run a lot of the church schools. Evil bastards, they are, who live by the motto 'spare the rod and spoil the child'."

Glass realised this line of conversation was threatening to overshadow the reason for his visit so he thought it might be time to change the subject.

"Well, good as it is to catch up, it's not why I'm here …"

"I know why you're here and I'll give you the same answer as I gave Lucky …"

"No, I'm not hear for the same reason as him. Though if I could persuade you to cut your ties with the Provos I would. No, I'm here because Lucky has gone missing in the North and we were hoping you could help track him down and maybe intervene with whoever has him to …"

"Lucky's missing in the North. In the name o' the wee man, how the feck did that happen?"

"I don't know the full story. All they told me was that Lucky had to go to Strabane to meet someone and he hasn't been seen since."

"But what … why … For feck's sake, what was he even doing in the North?"

"That I do know. You know he works for the government now?"

"Aye. He mentioned it in one of his letters when I was in Australia, but he didn't say what he was working at. What was he doing?"

"He was working for the security people, you know, the cloak and dagger mob. Not as a field agent though. They described him as an intelligence analyst. Why that should take him to Strabane I have no idea, but it did and now he can't be found. They've got a whole load of people out trying to track him down, but nothing so far."

"So, you've been sent to find out what I know."

"Not in any official capacity. I'm still just a lorry driver for the Griffin Brewery[3]. Someone thought that you'd be more likely to listen to me than to a stranger."

"By 'someone' I take it you mean Prof."

"His name hasn't been said out loud, but I think that's a reasonable guess. I haven't actually spoken to him. It's all been arranged through one of his minions."

"Look, if I knew anything, I'd gladly tell you. I don't forget old friends and Lucky was probably the best officer I ever served under. But I just don't know anything. Like I said, I take lads out onto the hills to try to stop them getting their heads blown off when they do whatever they were going to do anyway."

"But you know people who might know. Could you talk to them and mebbe put in a good word. Mebbe a deal could be arranged, you know, like they swap spies at Checkpoint Charlie[4]."

O'Driscoll's face took on a pensive expression, and he studied his glass of orange juice. "OK, for Lucky I'll see what I can do, because I know he'd do as much for me if our positions were reversed. I'll meet you here tomorrow evening."

"Not until then?" Glass was dismayed. "I was hoping to be on the road back to Dublin by breakfast time."

O'Driscoll gave a rueful smile. "I'm sorry Danny, but the people I need to talk to aren't sat by the phone waiting for me to call. I don't even have any phone numbers that will let me talk to them. It will take me most of the day to get a message to them asking them to ring me. I'll let you know if I hear something before then."

"What am I supposed to do in the meantime?"

"You've got a car, so take a trip out to Glenveagh[5]. It's beautiful out there and there's nice old house you can take a look around, if you like that sort of thing."

"Isn't it dangerous for me to be wandering around. You know, 'cos I'm British."

O'Driscoll laughed. "I'll put the word out with the local hot heads. You'll be left alone. Enjoy a bit of free time. I'd recommend a trip to the beach at Bundoran, but it's a bit cold in January." He turned his back and left the lounge before Glass could distract him anymore.

* * *

As Danny Glass entered the hotel foyer a receptionist caught his eye.

"Good afternoon, Mr Glass. Mr O'Driscoll phoned and made a dinner reservation for you both for seven pm."

"Thank you …" Glass peered at the young man's badge "… James. Can you ask the dining room if they would find us a quiet corner. We have confidential business to discuss."

"Of course, Mr Glass. We aren't busy at this time of year, so there'll be plenty of room."

Danny headed up to his room, impatient to find out what 'O'Driscoll might have discovered.

"Are you paying for this dinner?" Glass asked as O'Driscoll sat down at the table, thirty minutes late.

"No. Whoever sent you is paying for it." O'Driscoll said, in an equally bad mood.

"You sound like you've had a bad day." Whatever was getting to O'Driscoll, it was bound to be worse than having to delay his dinner for half an hour.

"Frustrating, rather than bad. I've been running from pillar to post and back again." He glanced around the room to make sure no nearby diners could eavesdrop, but the closest was several yards away across the large dining room. "Everyone has denied knowing anything about Lucky, but everyone admits something is going on. The amount of police and Army activity speaks for itself. I think that my asking has made them more worried, not less. But I'll tell you this, I don't think my … associates have him. At least, not the ones in County Derry or County Tyrone. I can't answer for any of the other commands. I don't have any contacts there."

"How do you mean?"

O'Driscoll glanced around again before saying anything. "The organisation in the North is in cells. No more than four or five people working together. No one knows the identity of anyone in another cell and they don't know the identity of anyone in the command structure. They get recruited by third parties and communication is done through cut-outs. That way if someone gets picked up by your lot, they can only give away a small number of others. The only people who have the full picture in their area is the senior commanders. That's the Brigade commander, his deputy, the intelligence officer and the quartermaster. There'll be bodyguards and runners too, but they won't know anything worth knowing unless the senior ranks need them to. Above that, there's only the Army High Command. That's a very small number of people and they co-ordinate the activity between the different brigades[6].

After a lot of to-ing and fro-ing I finally managed to get to talk to the intelligence officers in the Derry and Tyrone brigades. They're not normally people I speak to and even now they're just a voice on the end of a phone line. I don't know their names. I usually deal with the quartermasters. Anyway, they say they have no knowledge of anything like a kidnapping in their commands. If they do know anything, they're either very good liars or they don't trust me enough to tell me anything. But I genuinely believe them.

I mentioned the man in Strabane that also seems to have gone missing and that got them a bit more excited. They have lost track of someone. They wouldn't give me a name but he dropped off the radar several days ago. I didn't suggest he was an informer, but it won't take them long to work that out for themselves. It's the only reason one of yours would go visiting."

"So, if the Provos don't have Lucky, who the hell has?"

"Now, I didn't say the Provos don't have him. All I said was the people I talked to deny having him. From the outside it looks like the IRA is a single unified organisation, but it isn't. Within it there are extremists that don't think the Army Command is going far enough. They want to hit more sensitive targets and to be bolder in our attacks. Some of them want to take the fight across the water into England and even further to the British Army's overseas bases. The High Command knows those people exist within the ranks, but they can only do so much to keep them in check. It could be that there's a … oh, I don't know what you might call them … shall we say 'radical' group and they've grabbed Lucky, though we don't know what for."

"What's your gut feeling on that?"

"I don't know. If they have, it would be the first major operation they've mounted without authority. But that doesn't account for the man in Strabane going missing. I can see them taking Lucky, but if no one knew the other mane was an informer, why did he disappear?"

"Coincidence? Maybe he just got cold feet. You've said how much the Irish hate informers. Maybe the strain was getting to him, and he just decided to get out."

"Possible, I suppose. But there is a third possibility. Maybe it wasn't my side that took him."

"But who else … you mean the Loyalists?"

"Why not? They may have done it for reasons of their own and the fact that Lucky was visiting an informant from the Nationalist side would make yous lot think it was the Provos who snatched him. You'd be looking in the wrong places."

"But why would they do it?"

"For the same reason the Provos would do it. Either they want information they think Lucky might have, they want to send a message of some sort to the government, or they want to bargain with him. It was you that suggested some sort of prisoner swap. Maybe they've thought the same thing."

They fell silent as the waiter approached with their food, but they were both so deep in thought that they didn't resume their conversation after he had left.

"Where does leave us then?" Danny asked after a while. He had only toyed with his food, his appetite having deserted him.

"Up shite creek without an oar." O'Driscoll replied.

"Well, there's not much to keep me here now, I suppose. I'll head back to Dublin after dinner so I can get the first flight out in the morning."

"Are you giving up so easily?"

"I'm not giving up. But if you can't do anything to help Lucky, then neither can I. If I cross the border I'll stick out like a sore thumb. If I so much as open my mouth I'll give myself away. I haven't got a clue where to start looking. I don't even know where the bloke's house is, the one who went missing and started all this off. So, I'm more of a liability than an asset. I'll report back to Prof's minion and tell him what I've learnt, which is precious little. He can take it from there." His face fell. "I suppose I'll have to go to Scotland and tell Fiona."

"Why you?"

"There's been nothing on the news about Lucky. The people in Belfast seem to be trying to keep it quiet. So, I doubt anyone has said anything to Fiona in case she starts making a fuss. And we both know that Fiona would be quick to do that. So, if they won't say anything, I guess I'll have to. At least I can tell her we tried to do something."

"We could actually try to do something." O'Driscoll said, without taking his eyes off of what was left on his plate. Unlike Danny, his appetite was undiminished.

"How do you mean?"

"Well, you may not know where to start in the North, but I know people who do. I also have the right accent. Well, close enough to get by. At least it's identifiable as Irish and not English. Someone knows something and if we can find that someone, we can start to follow the trail that will lead us to Lucky."

"Are you mad? Sorry, of course you're mad. You've always been mad, from the day I first met you. But are you now clinically insane? What did they put in that orange juice of yours, LSD?"

"No, I'm not clinically insane. I just think I stand more of a chance of tracking down Lucky than the security forces in the North. I can open doors that would be slammed shut in their faces. But I also need someone to cover my back and there's no one I would trust more to do that than you. My friends in the North might help me find Lucky, but they wouldn't necessarily let him go if we found him. So, it has to be you."

"You're fuckin' serious, aren't you?"

"Never more so in my whole life." O'Driscoll's tone was sombre.

"I'm going to the toilet." Glass stood up abruptly and stalked from the room. His head was spinning. He was fifty three years old.

Paddy was about the same. Years spent driving a lorry had left him unfit and Paddy was in far worse shape than him. It was madness for them to go chasing wild geese around Northern Ireland.

But then an image of Fiona flashed across his mind's eye. He hadn't seen much of her since the end of the war, so the image was of a young woman, cradling a pair of toddlers in her arms. One of the toddlers was a boy by the name of Patrick, named after O'Driscoll, and the other was a girl, named Danielle, named after him.

But the worst part of the image was the tears rolling down Fiona's face as he told her that her husband was dead, and he had done nothing to save him.

And he would have to be the one to tell her, he knew that. He couldn't leave that to some nameless official. And he definitely couldn't leave to the lanky streak of piss, Drinkwater.

Prof might do it, but Danny would have to be there to tell her what he had tried to do in Ireland. Only O'Driscoll wouldn't be there, because he would risk being arrested.

Danny washed his hands and picked up one of the fluffy hand towels that the hotel provided. He stared at his face in the mirror above the sink.

Paddy! Of course, that gave him leverage he could use.

But then there was his own wife. She had been suspicious of his sudden departure anyway and if he stayed he would have to find some excuse for the delay. That he might not make it home himself never crossed his mind. If he allowed that thought to dwell, he might as well just walk straight out of the hotel and get into his car.

He straightened his back, as though preparing himself for an inspection by a senior officer.

Returning to the dining table he sat down heavily, leant towards O'Driscoll, placed his elbows either side of his barely touched dinner plate, clasped his hands together and spoke over the top of them.

"If I do this, you have to promise me something."

"What's that?" O'Driscoll asked.

"If I go with you, you have to agree to cut your ties with the Provos when we're done."

"Why do you want me to do that?"

"It's simple enough. I can't bear the idea of reading the news of your death in the newspapers. I don't know how long this … whatever it is over there …is going to go on for, but I know that the Provos aren't the type of people to let your talents go to waste. They won't be happy just letting you run around the hills teaching a bunch of lads how to camouflage themselves.

No, they'll want more from you and they'll want you on the other side of the border when you do whatever they want. And I think you'll end up either dead at the hand of some paratrooper or in prison. I don't want either to happen.

So, when this is over, whether we find Lucky or not, I want you to go back to Mayo and put your life to good use there. It's what Lucky would want as well."

"Now don't you go telling me what Lucky wants …"

"He wanted it enough to risk himself coming and talking to you last year. He wouldn't have done that if he hadn't believed it was the right thing to do. He doesn't care about what's going on across the border …. No, that's not true, he probably does care about that … but he cares about you more. And you care enough about him to risk your life to save his.

I think, when this is over, we should all hang up our green berets and go into permanent retirement. You in Mayo, me in London and Lucky in Scotland."

"You missed out Prof." O'Driscoll grinned.

"Well, he's chosen his own road, but I suspect he won't stay in politics much longer, at least not as an MP. According to the newspapers, Northern Ireland is a political graveyard. I reckon he'll announce his retirement at the next election, whenever that is, then he'll be offered a seat in the House of Lords, where he can spend his days drinking the best quality Port and serving on committees.

"I can't see Prof liking that, but I think you may be right. I can't see him settling for being a backbencher in the Commons."

"So, do you agree? Will you cut your ties with the Provos?"

"If it's the only way to get you to help me, then yes. I'll promise to do that."

"Good!" Glass offered his hand and O'Driscoll shook it solemnly. The bargain had been sealed more securely than any written contract could make it.

8 – Claudy

The village of Claudy sat halfway between Dungiven and Derry. It's main claim to fame, as far as Glass could see, was that it was alongside one of the two roads that could be taken to get to Strabane. The other turned off in Dungiven itself and then merged with this one a few miles further south.

They had chosen it as their start point for no better reason than every search has to start somewhere. They could have started in Strabane and tried to pick up the trail there, but O'Driscoll thought there was the possibility that the informant's house might still be under observation and even that depended on them being able to identify the house itself.

"No, that's not really why we're here." O'Driscoll confided as they sat in Glass's hire car. "There were three bombs set off here two years ago. Thirteen people were killed including a nine year old child. The attack was laid at the door of the Provos, so the people here have no love of the nationalist cause. If the Loyalist paramilitaries are anywhere in this area, then people here will know about it."

"You think it was the Loyalists who took Lucky?"

"I'm keeping an open mind. I'm still in contact with one of the lads I trained in Inishowen. I'm giving him lessons in Irish whenever he comes across the border. He's bright lad. I've asked him to keep his eyes and ears open to see if he picks anything up from the Republican hangouts in Strabane."

"Did you tell him why we want to know."

"No, and he didn't ask. Like I said, he's a bright lad. I think he'd be better off working for *Sinn Fein* than for the Provos, but that's his choice."

The village was dominated by two buildings. One was the church and the other was the Orange Hall[1]. But there was also a GAA[2] pitch, so there must have been some resident Catholics. O'Driscoll drove them along the main street until he spotted what he was looking for. "This place will do." He said.

"How do you know it will welcome you, if the village is strongly Protestant?" Glass asked him as he looked at the sign advertising the premises as being available for bed and breakfast.

"Well, you see that wee statue outside the front door." O'Driscoll appointed along the garden path towards the closed in porch at the front of the house."

"Yes, what of it?"

"Well, that's the 'Wee boy of Prague' as he's known, after a statue that turned up there hundreds of years ago and which the people worshipped. It was supposed to have belonged to some Saint or other, so it counts as a Holy relic, if you believe in that stuff." Paddy's tone of voice suggested he didn't believe. "His real name is the Infant Jesus of Prague. People put his statue outside their front door when they want good weather for something, like a wedding or a football match. At the same time, they say a prayer for their wishes. But the wee boy often gets left outside until someone remembers he's there and takes him back in again. Anyway, no Protestant would ever have one of those outside their house, because they regard all such statues as idolatry. Which means that someone with my accent won't have any trouble."

Paddy opened the car door and started to climb out. "You, on the other hand, better keep y'r gob shut and let me do the talking."

They walked along the path and waited at the front door for the landlady of the B&B to answer their knock. She introduced herself as Mrs McGillivray and assured the two of them that she had rooms available for the night.

"Would one of you just fill in the visitor's book while I show the other to their room." She bustled along the corridor with Danny Glass in her wake, while Paddy O'Driscoll picked up the cheap ball point pen lying beside the visitor's book and started to write his name in it. Glancing up the page he stopped in mid pen-stroke, his attention attracted by the names directly above his own.

110

The previous week, on the same day as Carter had gone missing, four men had booked into the B&B. Their names were Flannigan, Brannigan, Hannigan and Lanigan. That seemed unlikely to O'Driscoll, as did the four addresses in Derry that proclaimed them all to live at neighbouring houses in Foyle Street.

"You friend isn't very talkative." Mrs McGillivray said as she returned to collect him,

"No, he has a bit of a speech impediment that he's a little bit shy about. He only talks to strangers if he has to."

"Ah, God Bless him. I'll bear that in mind."

"I see you were a bit busy last week." O'Driscoll said, pointing towards the names in the book as he finished writing in his own and Glass's.

"Aye, I was that, but I'll tell yez, they were a strange foursome. They left without having their breakfast. I'd cooked a whole load of rashers and sausages which I had to throw away because there was no one to eat them. Good job I left frying their eggs until I realised they'd gone."

"Well, that is a bit odd." O'Driscoll agreed. "I've never met an Irishman that didn't like a good fried breakfast."

Mrs McGillivray was clearly in a mood to gossip, or at least to complain, because she began to warm to her theme. "Aye, after they checked in they just stayed in their rooms for a while, then went off saying they were going to the pub. I told them that Flaherty's was the place to go and to avoid Jacksons because it's used by the Prods. And that was the last I saw of them. Of course, I wouldn't have heard them come in because I don't sleep well at night since the bombings last year, so I have to take pills and after those another bomb wouldn't wake me up if it went off outside my door. So, I don't know what time they left, but it must have been before seven, because that was when I got up to make their breakfast. Pretty rude, I thought to me sel'."

"It was that, Mrs McGillivray." O'Driscoll sympathised as he followed her along the corridor.

111

"Well, this is your room. Your friend is next door." She pointed along the corridor where there were two more doors. "The far one is the bathroom. Please leave it in the same state as you find it. What time will you be wantin' your breakfast?"

"Eight o'clock should do it. Is there somewhere where we can get a bite to eat tonight?"

"Well, the café will be shut now, but there's places open in Derry if you don't mind driving." A thought obviously struck here. "And there's another thing. What are four blokes from Derry doing booking into a B&B in Claudy, barely twenty minutes' drive from their own homes? It's plain daft if you ask me. I'll tell you another thing, if they're from Derry I'll eat my Easter bonnet."

"What makes you think that? Apart from the fact that they booked in here instead of staying at home?"

"Because their vans had Donegal registration plates, that's why. And I know Derry well enough to know that nobody lives on Foyle Street. The river runs on the one side and on the other it's all businesses. I think they were up to something, but that's none of my concern."

It's about the only thing that isn't your concern then, thought Paddy, but he kept his feelings to himself.

"If you don't fancy driving out, I could do you and your friend a ham sandwich or two and just add it to your bill."

"Well, thank you Mrs McGillivray. I think that will be just the job."

"And I have some nice wheaten scone to go with it and maybe a few biscuits. Do you like Kimberleys[3]?"

"I love them Mrs McGillivray. You're really spoiling is."

After placing his overnight bag on the narrow bed, O'Driscoll went next door to see Danny. He told him what he had seen in the visitor's book and the additional information provided by their host.

"You think they may have been involved in Lucky's kidnap?" Glass asked.

"It has to be a possibility. Four men claiming to be from Derry, but driving Donegal registered vehicles, turning up here in the

112

middle of winter, then disappearing sometime during the night. It's probable that they booked in here just so they could wait until they were wanted and to make sure they didn't attract any attention by hanging around in their vans. After Mrs McGillivray has fed us, I'll take a walk to the pub to find out if they turned up there. If they were the ones who captured Lucky, they couldn't have spent the night in the pub as well, because of the time his car was found."

* * *

Paddy was back within the hour. "They didn't go to the pub, that's for sure." He reported. "I'm the first stranger they've had in there in weeks, according to the barman."

"Did he just come straight out and tell you that?" Danny asked.

"Pretty much. After he asked me what I wanted to drink, he said 'we don't get many strangers in here these days.'. So I asked him when the last time was, he asked one of the barflies and they said it must have been months. They didn't need to raise the subject at all, so I don't think they were trying to deceive me in any way. After all, why would they? If they knew of the four strangers, they don't owe them anything."

"They may have been threatened. Told to keep quiet. That's how the gangsters in London do it."

"Possible, but in that case, why mention strangers at all? It was them that started the conversation, not me."

"OK, I'll buy it. So, what now?" Danny asked.

"We head back to Donegal in the morning and see if we can pick up a trail there."

"Does that mean we're discounting Loyalist involvement?"

"Not completely. It could still have been them, but the use of this B&B, when there are Proddy owned ones in the village, suggests we're looking for Catholics."

"That's assuming that it has anything at all to do with those four names in the visitor's book. For all we know they could be a gang of itinerant brick layers."

"Yes, we could be on a wild goose chase. But the Irish were the original Wild Geese[4], so it's in our nature."

"We're basing a lot of assumptions on those four names." Danny Glass observed.

"Too much of a coincidence. They were probably only part of the team though. They'd have had one person keeping an eye on the informant's house, so they knew when someone turned up looking for him. He was probably just being used as bait to catch someone from the security forces. That would have been a more valuable prize for them."

"So, what's our next move? Danny Glass asked.

"Well, I don't think we'll find out anything more around here. We'll head back to Donegal in the morning."

"Why not tonight?"

"No one travels in the North at night if they don't have to. That was when they picked up Lucky, remember?" Paddy's attention was drawn to the small portable TV that sat on the dressing table. It was showing a news broadcast. "What's the big story?"

"Local news. Doesn't mean much to me." Danny replied. "apparently some blokes robbed an amusement arcade at gunpoint. The Falls Rad, they said."

"That would make it Loyalists then. The Falls Road is definitely Nationalist territory."

"I thought it was all part of UK" Danny grimaced.

"There's plenty in the North would disagree with that point of view. And that, my friend, is why these troubles are happening."

* * *

They took the most direct route back to Letterkenny, straight through Derry and across the border nearby. They were stopped at Army checkpoints at both ends of the bridge across the River Foyle and again on Letterkenny Road, the route that skirted around the Bogside. Finally, they were waved through the customs post at the border and into the Republic of Ireland.

"How would they have crossed the border without having their vehicle searched?" Danny Glass wondered aloud as he steered the hire car onto the N13 road.

"You can't think of the border as being any sort of barrier." Paddy replied. "What you have is about three hundred miles of places to cross. You just have to know the best place to do it without being seen. The River Foyle marks the border through County Derry and Tyrone and the Army has check points on the bridges right enough, so you can't cross there. Further south, in Fermanagh, there's Upper and Lower Loch Erne and the only way to approach the border would be through Enniskillen and that means crossing more bridges. But everywhere else all you have is open fields. You can walk across and no one would even see you. It's a bit like it was in Malaya in that respect, though nowhere near as hot.

There are hundreds of places where you can drive a tractor across and probably fifty or sixty where you can take a car or even a lorry. Smugglers have been using those unofficial crossings since 1922. The Army and UDR mount check points on them from time to time, but if you have someone watching the road you want to use, you'll know about them and know not to use them.

I would think that whoever took Lucky went south into Fermanagh and crossed into Monaghan somewhere around Clones, then turned west into Cavan and then Leitram, before carrying on up the west coast into Donegal, taking the same route as you used. It would be the safest route. That's if they went to Donegal at all. Let's face it, there's plenty places they could hide him in the North and no one would be any the wiser."

"But with the police and Army searching in the North, there's a possibility they might stumble on the hiding place by accident."

"That's true. The South would make more sense. But it still doesn't mean they went to Donegal. They could just have stayed in Monaghan or Cavan, maybe even County Louth on the east coast. We're only assuming they went to Donegal because of the number plates on the vans".

They drove in silence for a while, until the spire of Letterkenny's cathedral could be seen glinting in the distance, lit up by the bright winter sunshine.

Danny half turned to look at Paddy, sat slumped in the passenger seat. "I've been meaning to ask, ever since the other night in the hotel, why are you so keen to help Lucky? I'd have thought that with your new affiliations, you'd at least sit this one out."

"I could ask you the same question." Paddy responded.

Nodding his head in acknowledgement, Danny spoke again. "OK, you go first."

Paddy sat deep in thought for several seconds. "I think it goes all the way back to Achnacarry. A lot of the other soldiers on the march from Fort William were looking at me a bit surly, like.[5] You know, it was still close enough to the fight for Irish independence for the stories to have been heard by them, even though they would only have been babes in arms at the time they happened. We Irish still weren't that popular. Even less so with the ones from the six counties. A bit like today, in fact and for much the same reasons. But Lucky made a point of coming over to talk to me. It made a bit of a difference with the rest of the blokes, sort of told them that we were all in the same boat. Then, of course, there were all those operations we were sent on. Even though what we did was far more dangerous than it was for other soldiers, Lucky always made sure we didn't take unnecessary risks and, even when the risks were high, that we always had a good chance of making it back safely. He never asked us to do anything he wouldn't or couldn't do himself. He wasn't just a good officer, he was an exceptional one. If he had asked me to crawl over broken glass I'd have done it, because I would have known there was no other way to get the job done.

A man like that leaves a mark on you. Well, he did on me anyway. It helped to make me the officer I eventually became. At least, until I fell into a whiskey bottle. But if Lucky had been around, he probably wouldn't have allowed that to happen either." He fell silent for a moment, re-living old memories. "Now, what about you?

What made you ride to Lucky's rescue? You could have gone home days ago, yet here you are, large as life and twice as ugly."

"For me it goes back to that bridge we took in Sicily, you know the one?"

"I do. We couldn't hold it, so we had to disperse and work our way back to our own front line with all those Jerry paratroopers hunting for us.[6]"

"Well, you'll remember he fell asleep when he should have been keeping a lookout for Jerry patrols and we got taken prisoner. We could have ended up getting executed on the spot."

"Aye, I remember it well enough. But we didn't get shot. We got back to the lines safely, mainly thanks to Lucky."

"Yes, well, that's as may be, but I got the right hump with him for that. If either of us had done it, we'd have got kicked out of the commandos. But there was different rules for officers. Anyway, even though I respected him before that, I went right off him for quite a long time. Then we ended up in Holland, remember[7]?"

"Aye, I remember that sure enough. It was cold enough to freeze the balls off a brass monkey. The coldest I've ever been, before or since, and that town we were in didn't have a building with a roof left on and the water in the pipes was frozen solid all the time we were there. We even had to melt snow to make tea."

"Well, you remember there was a bloke got lost and drove a Jeep over a landmine. He got stuck out in no-man's land for three days until one of our snipers spotted him. He was just about to slot him when he realised he was one of us."

"Yeah, I remember. What was his name? Patterson? No, Patterdale, that was it."

"Yes, him. Anyway, Lucky didn't take a second thought, he just got in a Jeep and dashed out across no-man's land to pick him up. He faced machine guns, mortars and goodness knows what else.[8]"

"I was with him, remember! I was driving that Jeep." Paddy protested.

"Yes, and he still went out there, despite the added danger of you driving."

117

Paddy laughed to acknowledge the joke. He'd been a notoriously bad driver and no one in the commando had ever understood why Carter had selected him as CO's driver.

"Well, that was when my opinion changed again. If he would do that for Patterdale, who he hardly knew, he'd do it for me, you, or anyone in the commando. And that's why I'm still here. I know if it was me been kidnapped by the IRA, he'd pull apart every rock in Ireland to find me." He paused for a moment. "And so that's why I'm doing it for him."

They had reached the collection of industrial buildings that marked the boundary of the town before Danny spoke again.

"Where will I stay?" Danny asked. "I can hardly book into the Mount Errigal again. Someone else paid last time, but I couldn't afford a seat in the bar."

"I'll see if my landlady can find space for you. She won't charge you much just for a bed. We'll worry about food as and when."

From Main Street, Paddy directed Glass up the hill past the cathedral, then instructed him to turn right at a large modern school building. On the opposite side of the road were some neat little bungalows, which gave way to two storey houses further along. "This is Sentry Hill." Paddy told him. "Then we go into Ard O'Donnell. The locals call it The Burma, because one time it was famous for neighbours coming to blows. They said it was like the fighting out in Burma and the name stuck. But those days are past and it's a nice wee street now. The houses may look small, but there's been some pretty big families raised behind those doors.

Indicating where to park, Paddy got out of the car, Danny following close behind. O'Driscoll used a key to open the front door of the nearest house. "Only me, Mrs O'Connor." He called along the corridor.

A stout middle aged woman came bustling out, drying her hands on her wrap-around apron. "Is it yerself now Paddy? Good to see you back from your travels. You weren't gone long."

"No, just a little bit of business to attend to in the North, but it's all done now. But I'm looking for a wee favour. This is my old friend Danny Glass from my days in the Army. He's over to visit me but has nowhere to lay bis head. I don't suppose you'd be able to find him a wee corner?"

"You're in luck. Callum has gone back home for a few days to see his mother. She's poorly. She hasn't got long left, God Bless her …" She made the sign of a cross on her ample chest, "… so he won't be back for a wee while. You can have his room if you promise not to touch any of his stuff."

"I wouldn't dream of it, Mrs O'Connor." Danny assured her, extending his hand to be shaken, as though to seal a bargain.

"Mrs O'Connor's husband was out in Italy the same time as us. You remember that Irish Brigade, the 38th, that relieved us at Termoli? Well, he was with them."

"Paddy told me all about it. Youz had a tough fight there, by all accounts. My Jack didn't make it back though. He died at Monte Cassino."

"But your husband probably saved our lives in Termoli, Mrs O'Connor, and for that I'm very grateful." Danny said in a serious voice.

Behind the woman's back O'Driscoll gave a wink to show Danny that he'd said just the right thing.

"I'll show you the room, Mr Glass." The woman said, turning towards the narrow staircase.

"Call me Danny, please, Mrs O'Connor."

"Just before you do that, Mrs O'Connor," A thought had just struck Paddy, "you don't know anyone who's familiar with farms in the area. Or maybe if there are any disused factories."

"Now, why would you want to know about them? No, never mind. I suspect it's probably better I don't know." Glass wondered how much Mrs O'Connor knew about Paddy's activities and it sounded as though she at least suspected something. "You need to speak to Eileen O'Callaghan. She knows the county as well as anyone. She collects the rates from the outlying farms and businesses. If she canna help youz, then she'll know someone who

can. She gets home around six o'clock. Her bungalow is just a step
along Sentry Hill.

9 – Interrogation

Carter jerked backwards to avoid a spray of blood spattering across the room as Jerry staggered into a corner and collapsed. He had been badly beaten, Carter could see that. The door to their prison slammed shut and the sound of the padlock being secured could be heard through the metal doors.

Pulling his shirttail from his trousers, Carter tore a strip off and dipped it onto the plastic water bucket they had been given. He shuffled across and started to dab at the blood that ran in rivulets down Jerry's face. Jerry winced at his touch but didn't make any effort to stop Carter.

Jerry half raised his hand and his lips moved. "Don't try to talk." Carter said. "Let me clean you up a bit first." The strip of cloth was soon saturated and there was no way of rinsing it out without contaminating their water supply. Carter pitched it into the slop bucket and tore another strip from his shirt.

Once the blood had gone it revealed a number of splits to Jerry's eyebrows, cheeks and lips. He couldn't be sure, but Carter suspected that at least one of Jerry's teeth was missing and one was certainly broken.

"Did they ask many questions? Don't try to talk, just nod or shake your head."

Jerry shook his head. "No questions at all." His voice slurred through swollen lips.

"So, just a demonstration of what they're going to do to me if I don't answer their questions next time they ask."

Jerry's lips tried to form a smile, but he gave up. Instead, he just nodded his head a fraction. "Warning." He said.

It didn't make a lot of sense to Carter. He'd spoken freely, secure in the knowledge that nothing he told his interrogator would be of any real value. Maybe they thought that he was holding back on the really important information. But they hadn't needed to beat seven bells out of Jerry to give him that warning. That suggested a level of sadism; they'd done it because they could.

Jerry tried to move and winced in pain, clutching at his ribs. Not all of his injuries were visible, it seemed.

"Someone's going to pay for that." Carter said out loud, though he hadn't meant to.

"Just ..slight … problem…" Jerry started to say.

"We'll find a way out." Carter assured him, though he wasn't sure of it himself. But he had always believed that there was no problem that couldn't be solved if you let your mind work on it. Besides, he needed to keep Jerry's morale up after the beating he had taken.

They had no idea where they were, but that didn't mean that the police and Army wouldn't find them. With Prof Green holding such a prominent position, there was no possibility that the search would be called off until every last ditch and hedgerow, factory and farmhouse had been searched. All they needed was a bit of time, but the timetable wasn't being set by Prof Green or, indeed, by Carter.

* * *

They came for him a few hours later, half dragging him, half walking him, across the inside of the barn. He was wearing the hood again, which was reassuring. If they were going to kill him, they wouldn't bother hiding their faces.

Jerry, on the other hand, had the hood removed for his beating. That wasn't so reassuring. Though Carter assumed they would have been wearing their balaclavas and bandanas.

Carter was thrust into a chair once more and felt his hands and legs being secured to prevent any attempt at escape. Not that he intended provoking his captors in that way. If escape was going to become possible, Carter thought it unlikely to be during an interrogation session.

There was the sound of a chair being dragged a short distance, then the hood was removed from Carter's head by someone behind him. The figure sitting behind the table was probably the same one as had questioned Carter before, though he couldn't be certain. The eyes were the same ice blue and a wisp of fair hair was visible at the edge of the balaclava, but no more than that.

"We checked out that amusement arcade on the Falls Road." The man said. "We are considerably more wealthy as a consequence. I suppose we should be grateful for the information."

Carter stayed mute. It wasn't a question, so it didn't require an answer. But it confused him more than a little. The IRA didn't steal from themselves. Did that mean that these men weren't IRA? Were they Loyalists? It didn't change his situation, but it was important information, nonetheless.

The man stared at him intently. "Not very chatty today, are youz?"

"Maybe you could beat me until I say something, like you did Jerry."

"Oh, we will if we think it's necessary. But that was just a little demonstration for your benefit. Just so's youz would know what we might do to you if you don't play ball, G Man."

"If you want to know something, just ask. I don't know anything more than I have already told you."

"So, why were you at the house of a known informant?"

So, Belfast was right. Mayfly had been under suspicion, maybe he'd fled, after all. Or maybe he was already dead. "I've already told you the answer to that question. I was sent to try to locate him. He wasn't there, so I was on my way back to Belfast when you and your pals intercepted us."

"But that was what puzzled us, you see. What was an analyst doing out in the field? We couldn't work it out, so there was only one conclusion we could draw and that is youz're not an analyst. Youz're something else. You even told us youz were, once upon a time."

"That was a long while a go. I was in the Army commandos during the war. But I haven't done any active service in that capacity since 1955."

"That's what one of our sources told us, too." Carter tried to hide his surprise that the terrorist had been able to check him out in that sort of depth.

"Oh yes, G Man. We know all about you: decorated officer, hero of Honfleur, leader of men, commanding officer of 15 Cdo. What? Do you think we don't have our own spies? You'd be surprised at how many people over the water are sympathetic to the cause and willing to do what they can to help."

He paused, presumably to allow the information to register with Carter. Then he rested his elbows on the table and steepled his fingers under his chin. "But we don't think you have stopped working in the field. We think you've just put your uniform away and caried on doing what you did back then. That being the case, we intend finding out what you were really up to in Strabane. You're a killer, *Colonel* Carter, that much we know. So, who were you sent to kill?"

Stay quiet, Carter told himself. He realised that he couldn't prove a negative; he couldn't prove he wasn't working as a field operative. If the man was convinced he was, there was nothing he could say that would change his mind. So, how should he proceed? What could he do that would prevent himself getting beaten half to death like Jerry?

"I can see your mind working, Carter. How much punishment can you take before you tell us what we want to know? You'll have been trained to resist interrogation. But they'll also have told you that everyone talks in the end. But we're not going to beat you, Carter."

"Why not?" It seemed unlikely to him.

"Because we don't need to. Like I said, we've got sympathisers across the water. We know you have a family, and we know where they live."

Although Carter couldn't see the man's mouth, he could imagine the smug smile on his lips. He had the only aces in the game and he knew it.

"So why did you need to beat Jerry?" Was all Carter think to say. If they knew about Fiona, they hadn't needed to do that.

"That was so youz would know what your wife will look like if youz don't tell us what we want to know."

Carter felt his blood run cold. Up until then he had thought it was only a saying, but the chill running through his veins at that moment said otherwise. Fiona was alone in the farmhouse most of the time these days. The children were grown up and married, away making homes of their own. None of the farm workers lived on the farm itself. And it was sufficiently isolated for shouts for help, more likely screams, to go unheard.

The only thing Carter could do to prevent his wife from becoming a victim of these terrorists, was to tell them what they wanted to know. The only problem with that tactic was that he didn't have anything of value to tell them.

"Look, leave Fiona alone. I'll tell you whatever you want to know. But, really, I don't know anything. I really am not a spy, or an assassin, or whatever you think I am. I really am just an analyst."

"So, you keep saying, Carter. But we don't believe you. And one of the reasons we don't believe you is because you were in the Republic last year, asking questions. What were you doing there?"

What did they know? It was an old trick, Carter knew, to reveal a little bit of information, making it look like they knew more, in the expectation that the person being questioned would answer because it meant nothing if they already knew everything. So, did they know about Paddy? Of course they did. He was one of theirs, so they would know his name. But would they know about their meeting? If they suspected Paddy of being an informant, anything Carter said was likely to condemn Paddy to death. But if he didn't tell them, he'd be condemning Fiona to the same fate. Keep it as close to the truth as you can, he told himself, without giving away too much. That was the only answer.

"I was looking for an old Army pal. We'd lost touch but a mutual friend said he wasn't well. So, I went to see if I could find him."

"And your friend lives in Letterkenny?"

"That's where I was told he was. He's originally from Mayo."

"Did you find him?"

Dare he lie? If they knew about the meeting they would know it was a lie. If they didn't they may suspect he was lying but couldn't be sure. Sorry Paddy, Carter said to himself, but I have to think of Fiona.

"Yes, I found him. His name is Paddy O'Driscoll."

"And what did you and Paddy O'Driscoll talk about when you found him?

"Not much. I suspected he was involved with your lot, so I tried to talk him into giving it up and going back to Mayo. He told me to get lost and that was the extent of our conversation."

"You expect us to believe that?"

"What you choose to believe is your concern, but it's the truth. We were hardly together for ten minutes before he walked out."

"How did you know where to find him?"

"Like I said, from a mutual friend; from our Army days."

"And how did he know?"

"You'd have to ask him. I have no idea." It was a lie, but one that would be hard to prove.

"So, last year you're in Scotland and take a fancy to visit an old friend in Donegal, then the next year you're in Belfast. And you expect me to believe those two things aren't connected?"

Carter shrugged his shoulders. There was nothing he could say. He knew the two events were unconnected, but he also couldn't prove it. "Like I said, it's up to you what you believe. I'm working … was working … in Belfast because someone had a skiing accident. That's the truth. He is expected back at work in a couple of weeks' time, and when that happens I was supposed to go back to my real job in Scotland. You can probably check up on the skiing accident victim, if you have such a good intelligence network."

"Oh, don't worry, we will. What's his name, this unfortunate skier."

"Arbuthnott. First name Colin."

The man nodded, as though he had committed the name to memory. "OK, tell us which other businesses are involved in the money laundering."

126

The sudden switch of direction wrong-footed Carter for a moment. He had to pause to gather his thoughts.

"There's a betting shop in Armagh we're looking at. O'Toole's, I think the name is."

"What about Proddy businesses. Or were yez just picking on the Cat'lics again?"

Carter shrugged. The names of the businesses and their locations didn't mean a lot to him. He knew that the Falls Road was a Nationalist area, and that the Shankill was Loyalist, and that The Bogside and Creggan in Derry were both Nationalist, but that was because of the news coverage, not because of his work. The addresses he was given didn't specify the political divisions of the cities they were in.

"Give me some street names and I might have an idea of what we were looking at the last time I was in the office." Why were they so interested in the money laundering operations, Carter wondered. Then he recalled what the man had said earlier in the interrogation. 'We are considerably more wealthy as a consequence.' That was what this was about. It was money, not politics. All the rest was just camouflage, to make Carter think he was dealing with terrorists. Whereas he was actually dealing with criminals.

Maybe they had been politically motivated when they had started out. They probably had been connected to the Provisional IRA at some point. But now they were in it for themselves, he felt sure.

Which meant they were probably holding him for ransom. It fitted the situation. If they had just wanted to get information out of him before killing him, as the Provos would, he would be lying in a shallow grave already. But at the moment he was of more value alive than dead.

Jerry, on the other hand, wasn't of any value. He was just being used as leverage to get Carter to talk more freely.

His mind raced, connecting scraps of information garnered from when he had been asked to go and try to locate Mayfly, until that moment.

But was he fooling himself? Was he trying to make the facts fit the scenario, rather than seeing if the scenario fitted the facts?

The man was speaking again. "What about Sandy Row?"

"I can't say I heard of any businesses there that we were looking at."

"What about The Shankill?"

"Nothing specific, but I was told that a taxi company we were looking at was close to Shankill Road. Billy's taxis on Conway Street."

"That figures. Our side uses taxi companies as a cover for all sorts of things, so no surprise that the Prods would do the same."

Carter felt movement behind his chair. "OK, that'll do for today. We'll take a look at that taxi company and if it checks out, your wife will be safe for a wee while. But you best keep thinking, because we aren't finished asking our questions."

Carter was tempted to thank the man, but that would be to admit that he was worried and that would give him more leverage. He was worried, of course, but he didn't have to give the man more ammunition. The figure behind Carter stepped around so that he was to one side and started to drag the hood back over Carter's face. There was a fraction of a second where Carter was able to take in more detail about the man. He couldn't see his face, but he was wearing a tweed jacket, which Carter didn't associate with terrorists. He also caught a glimpse of a metal badge on the jacket's lapel.

Finally, it began to make sense.

* * *

Carter's guard pushed him through the door back into the wooden cube with a parting shot. "This isn't over yet, G-man." A locking bar slammed into place and there was the rattle of a padlock before silence fell.

"How was it?" Jerry croaked through battered lips. "I see they didn't beat yez."

"They didn't need to." Carter replied. "In fact, they didn't need to beat you either. I think they just did that for fun."

He told them what had happened, including the revelations about the discovery of his family's location.

"Well, I suppose ye co-operated."

"I did. I'm not proud of it, but there are no secrets worth my family's safety."

"Don't worry yersel'. I'd have done the exact same thing."

"But I'm pretty sure now that this has nothing to do with The Troubles. At least, not directly. I'm pretty sure that whoever this lot are, they're in it for themselves and not for any cause."

"What makes ye think that?"

Again, Carter explained. "Then they asked me about Loyalist businesses that might be being used for money laundering. If they were Republicans, I could understand them wanting to take money off Loyalists, but he'd already admitted that they had robbed the amusement arcade being used by the Provos. So, either they are some sort of third force, or they're in it for themselves."

"I can see your reasoning. I'd draw the same conclusions."

"And I'm pretty sure I know who's behind it." Carter suppressed a smile of triumph.

"Oh, how did yez work that out?"

"Have you ever heard of the Foyle Valley Fishing Club?"

"Can't say I have. Probably some local outfit and I'm from Belfast."

"I didn't think you would be familiar with them. But who do we know who is a keen fisherman?"

"I'm not sure I know … hang on, do you mean Mayfly? The tout[1] we were sent to find?"

"None other. I saw a badge on the jacket of the guard who was behind me which had the name of the fishing club on it."

Jerry looked thoughtful. "That puts a different complexion on what we saw at Mayfly's house."

Carter nodded agreement. "We saw what we were meant to see. Our conclusion was that he had been grabbed by someone, probably the Provos. If the Provos went into the house looking for him, they'd have drawn the same conclusion, but they would know it wasn't them that had done the snatching. He couldn't have been picked up by the police or Army, because when they turn up at the door it's like a three ring circus arriving in town. Someone would have been bound to have noticed. But the Provos would maybe think he had been picked up by a Loyalist group.

I think Mayfly knew he was on thin ice with the Provos, so he's gone into business for himself. Probably trying to raise enough money to start a new life somewhere else; America maybe, or Australia. I think he knew that if he stopped communicating, someone would be sent to look for him and Belfast duly obliged. We were snatched for ransom I think. But then Mayfly discovered what work I was involved in and decided to use that information to his own advantage."

"The government wouldn't pay a ransom anyway. It would set too much of a precedent. If they paid to get you and me back, they'd have kidnappings by the dozen. They're probably a lot safer than bank robberies as a way of funding the terrorists."

"That was my thought too, but Mayfly wouldn't necessarily know that. Maybe a ransom demand has already been made, but we don't know it."

Jerry nodded his head. "Maybe. But if you're right, they don't need the ransom money now. They just need you to keep coming up with business names they can rob."

"Each business will be worth a few thousand when they rob it, no more. It will all add up, but it probably wouldn't be the size of pay cheque Mayfly needs. And there's the people helping them; they'll want paying too. So when I run out of addresses, what happens?"

"I don't think you really want me to answer that. But if they can't get ransom money from the government, they may try your wife. Do you have money?"

"Not the sort of money that would pay a ransom. But they know about the farm. They'd demand Fiona took out a mortgage on it to pay for our safe return."

130

"Your safe return, you mean. I'm not part of this deal. If they let you go, they'll probably let me go too, but I'm not counting my chickens."

"If I get the chance, I'll ask for you to be released with me."

"Thanks, but I don't think they'll listen to you. They'll do it if they think that it would be harder to cover their tracks if they kill me and have to dispose of my body. But, as I'm sure you know, I wouldn't be the first member of the security forces to disappear without trace. Ireland has a lot of peat bogs. You could bury an army and no one would ever know."

They fell into silence. Their food, cold meat pies still in their packaging, was served and Carter was escorted to the corner of the barn to empty their slop bucket, before the lights were switched off to leave them in darkness.

It was the early hours of the morning when Carter was woken by the sound of the metal of their prison being scratched. He was lying along the wall where the door was positioned, while Jerry used one of the side walls. They both wanted to keep as much distance as possible between themselves and the noxious slop bucket, which stood in the corner furthest from Carter.

"Jerry," hissed Carter. "Jerry, are you awake?" To reinforce his words, Carter reached out a hand and shook Jerry's leg.

"I am now." the Irishman replied groggily.

"I think there's someone outside."

"So what? Probably one of the guards checking we haven't chewed our way out through the woodwork."

"No, it sounds more like someone is testing the door to see if they can get it open."

Carter fell silent as he heard a hissed voice dimly though the thin metal of the door.

"Lucky? Are you in there?"

"Who's that?"

"It's me, Danny Glass."

.

10 – McSweeney's Farm

Eileen O'Callaghan's bungalow was impossible to miss. In the centre of the front garden stood a four foot high statue of the Virgin Mary, surrounded by a variety of woodland creatures rendered in plaster of Paris or concrete. They had once been brightly painted, but the Donegal weather had faded most of the colours to beige, where it hadn't been worn away completely.

"Come in, come in, will yez." She was of a similar age and build to O'Driscoll's landlady and Glass wondered if there was a factory somewhere near Dublin that churned out little old Irish women. She was even wearing a wraparound apron just like Mrs O'Connor's.

She ushered them into the front parlour and disappeared with the words "I'll just fetch yez a cuppa tea."

"Fair warning," O'Driscoll whispered. "A cup of tea means a full blow meal in this part of the world."

"But we've just …"

"I know." O'Driscoll cut across him. "But she'll be mightily offended if you don't eat something. Just do your best."

"They don't do that back home." Glass commented. "You're lucky to get offered a biscuit."

"I know, as I discovered the first time I went to England. But it's something to do with the famine[1]. If you had food, you shared it as you had no idea when the last time was that someone ate. And whatever morsel you could give them might save them from starvation."

Glass took in the small parlour. Every available bit of wall space was covered in religious pictures and artifacts, from simple wooden crucifixes to garish representations of the Sacred Heart. There was no doubt that this woman took her religion seriously.

An ancient TV set sat in one corner, the sole concession to secular life as far as Glass could see. The furniture was a functional three piece suite covered in pink fabric with giant red roses for a pattern. Embroidered antimacassars[2] were draped across the backs of the chairs and matching doilies lay on the arms. A Formica topped coffee table, banded in mock brass, took up most of the remaining space. The room sweltered in the heat being thrown out by the peat fire that smouldered in the fireplace.

Eileen O'Callaghan returned a few minutes later with a tray laden with plates of cakes and biscuits, before leaving only to reappear a few seconds later with plates of sandwiches and buttered brown bread, or wheaten scone as it was known locally. Finally, she arrived with a large rose decorated tea pot, with matching milk jug, sugar bowl, cups and saucers.

"I'm sorry it's such poor fare, but I haven't a morsel in the house. I haven't had time to shop today." She seemed genuinely dismayed by the idea that she hadn't provided enough to eat.

Glass surveyed the spread, which covered the coffee table and was enough food to feed a platoon, while Paddy O'Driscoll did his best to assure her that there was plenty there and they'd just had their dinner anyway.

She picked up the teapot and started pouring, using a tea strainer to prevent the leaves from getting into the cup. "Mrs O'Connor didn't say what yez were wanting, so I'm abuzz with curiosity. It's not often I get people wantin' to see me, not even me own family." When she had handed out the tea and had finally poured her own cup, she settled into a well-padded chair.

"Mrs O'Connor said that you worked for the Council, collecting rates or something." Danny Glass said through a mouthful of wheaten scone.

"Aye, that's right. I go around the farms and small businesses and collect their rates."

"Why don't they come into town and pay them in person?"

She gave a small smile. "That's a relic from the days when you British ran the place. The Irish didn't much like paying you their taxes back then, so tax collectors went out to get what was owed. If the farmers said they didn't have any money, they took goods instead and to make sure there was no argument about it, they took soldiers with them.

134

Well, when we became independent it turned out that the farmers were no more keen on paying what was due to the Irish government either, so we had to carry on going out doing the collecting. It's only the rates that are collected that way nowadays. Taxes have to paid by post and I only take cash or cheques, because no one wants to be messing about trying to put a pig into the back of a car, like the old days." She laughed at her own joke.

"So, you know the farmers pretty well then? And all the small businesses. You'd know if there were any strangers hanging around?" O'Driscoll interrupted.

The woman gave O'Driscoll a shrewd look. "I don't know why you would be interested in strangers, and I don't want to know. I'm as loyal an Irish woman as any, but I don't hold with what's happening in the North, no matter who's doing it. So, I'll need some sort of explanation before I say anymore. I'll not be part of anything illegal, do I make myself clear?"

"You do, Mrs O'Callaghan." Paddy assured her.

"It's Miss, but call me Eileen." Her expression softened a little.

"Thank you, Eileen. I assure you we mean nobody any harm. It's just that a friend of ours has gone missing and we think he may be in Donegal. Not entirely of his own free will, if you get my meaning. We're just trying to find him."

"Why haven't youz reported this to the Gardai? That's what they're there for."

"We aren't absolutely sure if our friend is even in Donegal, Eileen." Danny explained. "We think he is, but we can't be sure. So, we don't think the police will take us seriously. If we can locate him, we'll tell the Gardai straight away, of course. We don't want to break any laws." If we can avoid it, he didn't add.

"Is he in any danger, this friend of yours?"

"We think he is, Eileen." Paddy continued. "We think he may be in very serious danger. Your help may be vital to save his life."

The thought that she might be saving someone's life seemed to persuade the woman. "OK, that sounds fair enough. But you must realise that I only cover a small part of the county. There's a few of

135

us and we each have our own area where we collect. I can tell yez, I haven't seen any strangers around any of the farms or businesses that I go to."

"Where is that?" O'Driscoll asked.

"Around the middle of the county. Stranorlar and Ballybofey are the main towns, then east towards Raphoe and the border with Strabane. To the west and south of that is covered by Donegal Town. I know some of the collectors over that way, but I don't see much of them.

"Is there any way you could find out if any of your colleagues has seen anything?"

"I can ask. But that's about all I can do. Now, what do you think o' that wheaten scone? I made it m'self."

"It's probably the best bread I've ever eaten." Danny Glass replied truthfully, picking up another slice.

Eileen's face beamed with pride.

* * *

There wasn't a lot that Danny and Paddy could do while they waited for news from Eileen O'Callaghan. Paddy took them to a couple of bars out in the countryside where elderly gossips whiled away their retirement, but they didn't pick up anything of use. Most of what they heard were complaints against Liam Cosgrave's Fine Gael[3] government, Donegal being a Fianna Fáil stronghold.

"Look who's here to see you" Mrs O'Connor said as the two men entered the house.

"I've a Vigil Mass I want to get to this evening." Eileen O Callaghan's voice drifted out from the parlour. "So, I thought I had better come over and see youz boys as soon as I got in from work."

Danny Glass had to suppress a smile at being referred to as a 'boy'. At fifty three years of age he was barely any younger than Eileen herself, though the woman's lack of makeup and old fashioned style of clothes made her appear much older.

"Good evening to you, Eileen. You have news then?" Paddy asked eagerly.

"I think I have."

"I'll get you some tea. " Mrs O'Connor said, leaving the three of them in the front parlour. Danny groaned inwardly, knowing he was about to be subjected to another barrage of carbohydrate based snacks. And he'd then be expected to eat dinner, the delicious aroma of which had set his nose twitching as soon as the front door had opened.

"So …" Eileen settled herself in the most comfortable chair, taking it as a right because she was to be the centre of attention. "I asked around this morning, when I got to the office before starting my round. Nobody could think of anyone that was out of place. You must understand that here in Donegal lots of people get visitors from across the border. The families are related from generations back, before that border even existed. So, there's always aunties and uncles, cousins and second cousins coming and going. Especially nowadays with all the trouble in the North. People like to get away somewhere safe for a few days when they can."

A warning glance from Paddy O'Driscoll encouraged Danny Glass to resist the temptation to try to hurry Eileen along. She had her own way of telling her stories and it was unlikely that any urging from him would be well received.

"But then, this evening, Liam … that's Liam from out on the Port Road, Maggie's eldest … oh, you probably won't know Maggie O'Donoghue. Anyway, Liam O'Donoghue is one of my colleagues and he covers the area north of Letterkenny, from Rathmullen all the way up to Fanad Head. It's wild country, with lots of remote farms out that way. Some beautiful scenery, but as someone once said, you can't eat the scenery.

As it happens, most days Liam stops for his lunch in a little pub … well, it's a shop really … in Port Salon. That's a little seaside place on the side of Loch Swilley. It's got a lovely beach that goes on for miles with never a being on it. Good golf course too, or so I'm told. I'm not a golfer me'sel, you understand. Oh, where was I now?" She had clearly lost her thread.

"Liam was having his lunch in a shop in Port Salon." Prompted Danny.

"Of course, yes. He goes there most days. Anyway, this young man comes in and starts loading up his arms with meat pies, bread, cheese and so on. 'Are yez havin' a picnic?' Liam asks him, joking like. 'Mind your own business,' The young fella says, not very friendly at all, and Liam such a nice wee man too. Wouldn't hurt a fly.

Anyway, when he'd paid up and gone, Liam asks the barman about the fella, him being so rude and all. Now, it isn't unusual to get strangers around Port Salon, you must understand. There's plenty of people with holiday homes there. But that wasn't the story. Callum, that's the boy who owns the shop, he says the young fella's out working on McSweeney's farm and the food is for there."

"Does Liam think that's significant?" Paddy asked.

"Not in itself, but he told me about it anyway. And then I thought, I know Theresa McSweeney. We did a pilgrimage to Lourdes together a few years back. I know for a fact her husband is up at the hospice, because I see him when I go up there for Mass. I don't have to go up there, of course, not with the cathedral just being a step away, but my friend Mrs Galbraith has her husband in there, so I go up with her and help her to get John into the chapel because he prefers it to the priest giving him communion at his bedside. But I always stop for a word with Sean McSweeney if I see him as well. And he was telling me not so long ago that when he got sick he sold all the animals on the farm, because Theresa wouldn't be able to take care of them."

"So, no animals means they don't need anyone to help on the farm." Paddy surmised.

"That was my thought exactly, Mr O'Driscoll. Then I thought a bit more and I remembered the trip to Lourdes. We were on the bus for a long time, and on the ferry too, of course. So, we spent a lot of time talking. Anyway, Theresa McSweeney told me most of her life story. I suppose I did the same me'sel to her. Anyway, Theresa isn't from Donegal. She was from Tyrone, some little village just outside

Strabane. She also told me she had a brother there. He was the black sheep of the family and spent a bit of time in prison during the fifties[4] because he'd got himself mixed up in the IRA. Not the Provos, you understand. They weren't around back then. No, the old IRA. Say what you like about them boys, but they'd never have planted a bomb where women and children could get kilt."

She paused, a look if distaste on her face. "Anyway, I racked my brain for the name of the brother. I can't be sure, but I think it might be Michael and Theresa's maiden name was O'Neil."

"And you think that Michael O'Neil might be up at the farm staying with his sister, along with the younger man."

"I think that's possible. Liam said the young fella's accent was more northern than it was Donegal. It's only a few miles, but if you have a good ear you can tell which side of the border someone was born. And as for Belfast, that lot sound like the heathens they are."

"Well, that gives us a lot to think about." Paddy replied as Eileen paused to take a sip of her tea. "Thanks for that and please thank Liam for us.

"Ach, it was nothing, just a wee bit of gossip and I do enough o' that already, God forgive me." She made a sign of a cross on her breast, before picking up a slice of buttered brown bread and taking a bite.

"This is lovely wheaten loaf, Mrs O'Connor." She offered her opinion.

"Ach, it's not a patch on yours." The other woman replied. "Everyone knows that you bake the best wheaten loaf in the county."

* * *

"Well, what do you make of that?" Danny asked Paddy, after Eileen O'Callaghan had taken her leave.

"Circumstantial, at most." Paddy replied. "Not enough to take to the Gardai, that's for sure."

"Yeah. 'there's an old IRA man at a farm and e's buying a bit more food than he really needs' wouldn't persuade me to do much."

139

"Exactly. But it's more than we had an hour ago." He picked up the last slice of wheaten bread and bit off half of it. "But if Michael O'Neil is involved in Lucky disappearing," he said through a mouthful of crumbs, "then Prof might be able to tell us something, if only that he is or isn't active in the IRA these days.

You're right." Danny replied, getting to his feet and going to the parlour door. "Mrs O'Connor," he called towards the back of the house, "may I use your phone? I'll pay for the call."

"Aye, go ahead. There's a box alongside for the money." Her disembodied voice replied.

The phone sat in solitary splendour on a small table near the front door. Danny checked his wallet, finding a small piece of paper. Dialling the number written on it, he waited for a reply

"Drinkwater." After many rings, a voice finally answered.

"It's Danny Glass …"

"Where the devil have you been?" Drinkwater cut across him. "We thought you'd gone the same way as Carter."

"I've been working with Paddy O'Driscoll, trying to find some trace of Carter. And we may have a lead."

"Well, what have you got?" Drinkwater didn't sound mollified, but he was at least willing to listen.

"Does the name Michael O'Neil mean anything to you?"

"Not off the top of my head. Why? Should it?"

"We don't know. That's why I'm phoning you. He certainly had links to the IRA twenty years ago. He's suddenly appeared on this side of the border and we're wondering if it has anything to do with Lucky's disappearance."

"Lucky? Oh, Col Carter. Well, I can make a few calls and see what I can find out. Ring me back in two hours." With that the line went dead.

The wait seemed longer than the specified two hours and the two men did nothing but exchange small talk. The TV couldn't hold their attention and there was little else in the house to occupy them.

At the appointed time, Danny Glass rang the number again.

"OK," Drinkwater said without preamble, "You may be on to something. Michael O'Neil was the man Carter was sent to try and find in Strabane. It was assumed that he had fled or was killed for being an informant. That doesn't mean he had anything to do with Carter's disappearance, but it's too much of a coincidence to ignore."

"OK, that's all we needed to know. We'll see what else we can find out and we'll get back to you. May I carry on spending and using the hire car?"

"It's a little bit late to say no, but keep it within reason. Are you still at the Mount Errigal?"

"No, I'm in the same digs as Paddy O'Driscoll. I don't know how much I'll be charged, but it will be cheaper than the hotel."

"OK, that's fine. But don't go buying any aeroplanes or anything."

The line went dead and Danny relayed Drinkwater's revelations to Paddy.

"OK, let's see what we've got now." Paddy said. "Lucky goes to Strabane to try to locate O'Neil and then goes missing. We suspect that he was then brought to Donegal, based on the registrations of two Ford Transit vans seen in Claudy the same night as Lucky went missing, but which may have nothing to do with anything. And, finally, Michael O'Neil is now thought to be at Theresa' McSweeney's farm, but we don't know that for sure. We only know that a young fella from the North is buying more food than two people would need."

Danny shook his head despondently. "Still not enough to go the police."

"No. We need to see things for ourselves. It's too late for today, but we'll take a look tomorrow. I'll see if Eileen will introduce me to Liam so I can get directions to that farm, then we'll get you kitted out in something a but more suited to crawling through the heather."

* * *

141

Danny drove them north along winding coastal roads that offered beautiful views across Lough Swilley, glittering in the winter sunshine. As they rounded a bend the view opened up to reveal a golden beach stretching away from them, backed by a golf course behind the dunes, before the road started to descend. They continued through the small village of Port Salon, then climbed again into the hills beyond.

"It's about four miles along here." Paddy informed Danny. "Look out for a ruined stone cottage on the right and the farm is the next turning on the left." He pushed his hand into the voluminous pocket of his waxed canvas jacket and drew it out holding a pistol. "I hope we won't need this, but better to have it and not need it than to need it and not have it."

Taking his eyes off the road for a moment, Danny gave the pistol a cursory glance. "I won't ask where you got that, because I'd rather not know. What make is it?"

"It's a Makarov nine millimetre."

That's Russian isn't it? I thought the IRA got its weapons from the Yanks."

"They get them from wherever they can. Think about it. Across the border there's ten thousand British troops tied down by The Troubles. That's the equivalent of a full division. Now, who do you think benefits from that?"

"I see where you're coming from. So my enemy's enemy is my friend, is that it?"

"It is. It might be Brezhnev in the Kremlin now, but it was the same back in the fifties when it was Stalin and Khrushchev. That's probably when this weapon was given to us."

"I thought you didn't get involved in the killing part of things." Danny said, failing to sound non-judgemental.

"I don't, but I give The Boys some basic weapons handling training, just so they don't shoot themselves in the foot when they're given a gun for the first time."

"But they obviously get more than that somewhere. They're known for sniper attacks these days."

"When they start to climb the ladder in the organisation, they're sent off to training camps in Libya. It's a strange word we live in; on one side of the camps are the Provos and on the other side are the UVF or UDA[6]. Not just them, of course. Pretty much every European and Middle Eastern terrorist group you've ever heard of does their training there and a few more you may not hear about for years yet. That Colonel Gaddafi isn't fussy about who he trains so long as he sees them as an ally against his enemies. And his enemies are whoever snubs him this week. He's not paying, of course. The Ruskies hold the purse strings. So long as Gaddafi's enemies and the Kremlin's enemies are the same, there's no shortage of money, even for a nutter like him."

"And here was me thinking we'd put a stop to all that when we kicked Hitler's arse for him."

"Ah, well, you see, so long as one country or political philosophy seeks to dominate another, you'll have someone on the other side willing to fight them over it. And before you think that doesn't apply to your own dear nation, just remember what happened in Aden, Cyprus, Kenya and Malay in the fifties and what's happing barely thirty miles away right now. Now, I think that was the ruined building, so the farm must be close. Just drive straight past and we'll find a place to pull over and approach it from a different direction."

A damaged stone wall gave way to a sagging gate in need of repainting, attached to which was a rectangular sign with scrawled lettering declaring it to be the gate of McSweeney. Danny did as instructed and drove past. The road climbed a short hill and a track turned off and curved behind a stand of stunted pine trees. Danny drove the car behind the trees and stopped it, turning off the engine.

"OK, what's the plan?" Danny asked.

"We work across country and find a place where we can see the farm, but no one on the farm can see us."

"Just like the old days then." Glass observed with a smile.

"Pretty much. There's even the risk of getting killed if we're discovered."

"Always the optimist." Glass chuckled.

143

They got out of the car and Paddy handed over the Makarov, pulling a second one out of another pocket for himself, along with a small pair of binoculars. "Not the most powerful, but good enough for our needs." He said. Turning towards where they knew the farm must be located, they set off across the unkempt fields.

That morning they had visited a country sports shop and kitted Glass out with strong boots, thornproof and water resistant trousers and a waxed jacket similar to O'Driscoll's. It was better suited for their purposes than anything that the British Army had ever issued them with. Even the colours were more suited to the terrain.

The fields were broken up by badly maintained dry stone walls which hardly offered any sort of barrier. Despite his poor physical appearance, O'Driscoll seemed to be taking the rough terrain quite literally in his stride. After about fifteen minutes, Glass stopped and sniffed at the air.

"Smoke." He declared. "I think we must be getting close."

"The wind's in the right direction for it to be from the farm." He sniffed for himself. "Peat." He declared. "It's what they burn up here instead of wood or coal. We'd better be a little bit more tactical from here."

They bent from the waist and continued until they saw two columns of smoke spiralling upwards until the wind caught them and whipped them away to the east. Dropping to their hands and knees, they continued onwards until they reached another tumbledown wall, this one with a metal five bar gate interrupting it halfway along its length. Grass grew to a height well above the lowest bar, suggesting it hadn't been used for a while. They changed direction to make their way towards it and crawled in behind the wall, one on either side.

O'Driscoll raised the binoculars to his eyes and scanned the view in front of them, focusing them on the collection of buildings clustered in the valley about two hundred yards distant. Without the binoculars Glass could only make out the larger buildings that made up the farm. It was arranged in a U shape. The single storey stone farmhouse made up the left hand arm, a chimney stack at each end sending out the smoke that had alerted them to its presence. The roof was made up of grey slates, though Glass had expected to see thatch. Perhaps the roof was newer than the cottage itself.

There was no doubt that the barn on the other side of the U was at least a hundred years newer than the house. Its corrugated iron was streaked with rust and the ground in front of it had been churned up by the passage of thousands of animal hooves. Now it was dotted with large puddles, though there was evidence that a path had been picked through the dryer parts between the house and the barn.

The third side of the U, the side closest too them, was made up of another low stone building, but that, like the barn, was roofed in rusted corrugated iron. An equipment shed, Glass assumed. On the far side of the yard the U was closed off by another wall, with a gate halfway along, a rutted track leading off in the direction that Glass knew the road lay. Two Ford Transit vans, the white paintwork smeared with mud, sat near the gate, one on either side of it. It was all the evidence that Glass needed to confirm to him that Carter was there, probably locked inside the barn.

The farmyard was empty, suggesting that whoever was in the house thought they had no need to mount sentries.

"Take a look through these." O'Driscoll hissed to Glass, swinging the binoculars on their strap before releasing them to land in the grass alongside Danny's head.

Glass grabbed them and raised them to his eyes, fiddling with the focus wheel to adjust them for his eyesight. Details swam into view.

The farmhouse windows were covered in net curtains, defeating any effort to see if anyone was inside. The door in the middle of the wall stood shut, keeping the heat in and the cold out. A television aerial was mounted on a long pole attached to the furthest chimney, the aerial itself pointing southeast, suggesting it was picking up TV stations in the North rather than from the Republic. The pole shook as occasional gusts of wind caught it.

On the drier ground near the two vehicles, half a dozen chickens pecked at the ground.

Turning his attention to the barn, Glass made out two large sliding doors that formed the end wall. In one of them there was a Judas gate. As far as Glass could make out, the gate wasn't locked.

As they watched, a man appeared from the farmhouse carrying a bucket in one hand and a paper bag in the other. A second man followed him out, a rifle in his hands. A quick look at the weapon told Glass it was an AK-47: a weapon he had become too familiar with during his time in Malaya.

Paddy beckoned for the binoculars. Danny passed them back to him. "That one looks familiar". He commented. "The one with the rifle. Ruari I think his name is. I thought he was a danger to himself and I'd say he still is." He passed the binoculars back to Glass.

The man with the bucket stopped outside the Judas gate and the armed man stepped past him and swung it open. Raising the weapon to his shoulder he stepped over the raised bottom edge and disappeared inside. He was back in moments, shaking his head and stepping out of the barn. He had obviously told the bucket carrier that there was no threat, because the man stepped through the door. The rifleman leant against the wall for support, aiming within the building. If anyone tried to make a break, they were bound to pass through his sights.

There was only a brief gap before the bucket carrier returned, the bucket itself appearing to be lighter as he swung it in his hand. There was no sign of the paper bag. The Judas gate was slammed shut and the two men meandered back to the farmhouse.

O'Driscoll crawled across the gap and took cover behind the wall on Glass's side of the gate, sitting down with his back to the wall, making it easier for them to talk without raising their voices.

"I think that just about clinches it." Paddy said, talking in a whisper even though they were only inches apart and too far away to be heard. Old habits die hard. "I don't think they were feeding the chickens."

"I agree. You don't need to provide armed cover inside an empty barn. So, what now?"

"I'll stay here and keep an eye on the place. You go back to Port Salon. I saw a telephone box near the shop. Call that mate of yours in Belfast and see if he can persuade the Irish authorities to carry out a search."

"He's no mate of mine." Glass grunted. "But he can pull some powerful strings. I'll get back as soon as I can."

"Take your time. I don't think anything much is going to happen. You don't feed prisoners you're going to kill."

Glass handed back the binoculars then wriggled backwards away from the wall until he judged it safe to crawl, then to walk bent almost double. Once he judged he was at no risk of being seen from the farm and could move upright he broke into a jog, feeling satisfied that despite his sedentary occupation, he still had some of his old fitness.

Finding a parking space not too far from the phone box, Glass heaved the door open on its heavy spring then let it swing shut against his back as he lifted the handset and pushed coins into the slot, using the largest denominations he had because a cross border call was likely to be expensive.

The call was answered on the first ring, suggesting that it was anticipated. "Drinkwater." came the single word greeting.

Glass brought him up to date on what he and O'Driscoll had observed. "Can you persuade the Irish government to send the Irish police or the army up there to carry out a search?"

"Ah, we might have a problem there. We're not in the best of places to ask for favours of the Irish right now."

"Why, what's happened?"

"Have you not heard the news today? No, obviously not. Well, there was a cross border incident last night. A UDR patrol opened fire on what they thought were arms smugglers but turned out to be a Gardai patrol on the other side of the border. The Army swears they were on the British side and, naturally, the Gardai claim they were in the Republic. But the really damaging bit was that two Gardai officers were wounded, one seriously. There is a riot going on between Westminster, Dublin and Belfast right now and I don't think that asking for a Gardai search will go down too well. It will also not be seen as a priority in terms of trying to restore normal relations between North and South." He paused for breath before continuing. "However, I know our mutual friend will move Heaven and Earth to try to get a search carried out. I just can't promise anything right now."

"Well, do what you can. In the meantime, we'll keep an eye on the place. If anything happens, we'll let you know."

"OK, but don't do anything without checking with us first. We can't afford another international incident right now."

Glass grunted non-committedly. He couldn't give a monkey's for Anglo-Irish relations. He cared only about his friend and he would do whatever he considered necessary to get him back safely.

Feeling a little peckish, and knowing that O'Driscoll would probably be feeling hungry too, Glass went into the shop to see what sort of snacks they had to offer. As Eileen had explained, it was a pub at one end, but through a narrow doorway there was a shop selling the basics that would keep people fed if they couldn't get to better stocked shops. There was sliced bread on shelves above a crate of bottled milk. Tinned goods were arrayed on shelves. In a small chilled cabinet there were lumps of cheese, labelled "Irish cheddar", packets of ham and a single meat pie. Judging by the space available, there had probably been more and Glass suspected that the contents of the paper bag he'd seen being carried into the barn probably accounted for some of the stock that might have been there earlier. He took the pie and a chunk of cheddar, picked up a loaf of bread and a bottle of lemonade and went back through to the bar to pay.

"Are yez on holiday?" The man, probably Callum if he remembered the name mentioned by Eileen O'Callaghan correctly, asked cheerfully. Glass had been in Ireland long enough not to find the question intrusive. Everyone seemed to like to chat.

"Sort of. Just trying to find an old friend."

"Does he live up here?"

148

"No, but he may be staying up here." Glass said, not wanting t say too much. Then a thought struck him. "Do you know the McSweeney farm?"

"Oh aye; I surely do. Sean McSweeney was in here almost every night for a wee drop, before he went into the hospice. Why do you ask?"

"I heard my friend might be staying there."

"Ach well, that's possible. There seems to be quite a few staying with Theresa McSweeney at the moment. At least half a dozen, I'd say. They come in here to buy food and also for a drink in the evening. We only ever see one or two at a time, but when you add them all up you know, it must be half a dozen fellas."

"Are they young or old?"

"Oh, definitely young. Not Michael though. He'd be closer to your age."

"Michael?"

"Aye, Theresa's brother. He's been coming here for years, of course. Ever since Theresa married Sean I suppose, but that was before I bought this wee shop."

"Are they all Irish?"

"Oh aye, but not from around here, I'd say. More likely from across the border."

"Thanks, but that doesn't sound like any of those men would be my friend. For a start he's English, like me."

"Ah, then I can't help yez. You're the first Englishman I've had in here this year. We get a few over for the golf and the beaches, but it's the wrong season for them."

"Well, thanks for your help anyway." Glass counted out the amount of money that was shown in the window of the old fashioned black till.

"No bother. You have a good day and I hope you find your friend."

Half a dozen, probably including O'Neil, Glass thought as he drove away from the village. That sounded about right to carry out a kidnapping on the road at night. Two in front to stop the car, one to cover the back once the car was stopped. Two to drive the vans and one inside the back of one van to take control of the victims until they could be secured. It could be done with less, but it would be more difficult. It was a valuable piece of intelligence, because if he and O'Driscoll were forced to mount a rescue attempt, they would need to know the strength of the opposition.

Glass hoped it wouldn't come to that, but it as best to be prepared.

* * *

It was getting late in the afternoon, the winter sun dipping towards the top of the hills to the west, though it had never been that high in the sky all day. A car bounced along the pot-holed track to the farm, its headlights dancing over the buildings. From the front it was only possible to identify it as a Gardai vehicle because of the blue lamp on the roof that glowed when the weak sunlight struck it.

"Looks like the cavalry has arrived." O'Driscoll reported. It was his turn to keep a watch on the farm while Glass dozed in the lee of the wall. He had never lost the knack of being able to fall asleep anywhere, no matter how uncomfortable.

"How many?" Glass asked, shuffling into a position from where he could also see.

"Just one car at the moment."

The car stopped while the driver got out to open the gate, before climbing back in, driving through, getting out to close the gate and then driving a few more yards to stop at the short paved footpath that led to the front door of the house. No doubt it was a routine he practices whenever he visited a place where farm animals might be able to escape through a gate left carelessly open.

Through the binoculars O'Driscoll watched the front door open and a small, bent woman appeared in answer to the Gardai officer's knock. She was followed out by a black and white border collie whose barking carried over the distance to be heard by Glass and O'Driscoll, until the woman calmed it with a few words. The dog snuffled around the police officer's feet then did the same around the car, before returning to lie at the woman's feet.

There was a discussion, questions asked and answered, with the Gardai pointing to the various buildings. The woman didn't seem to say much, mainly nodding or shaking her head in response to the questions. Her body language suggested to O'Driscoll that she was under stress, but that may have been a symptom of her age. From time to time, she half turned towards the house, as though looking for someone, but managed to resist the temptation to turn completely and faced front again.

After a while the officer nodded to the woman and set off to walk around the yard in an unenthusiastic manner, going only where the mud and water was least threatening to the shine on his shoes.

Which meant he avoided the barn almost completely.

"I don't know what this eejit's been told," O'Driscoll said, "but he doesn't seem to be very motivated. If I didn't know there were armed men in that house, I'd stand up and shout at him."

"I'll bet you a fiver that he leaves without even going inside the house."

"I won't be taking that bet. Look, he's on his way back to the car already."

O'Driscoll was correct. After taking a cursory glance inside what Glass thought might be the equipment shed, he was already halfway back to the car.

Raising his hand to the peak of his cap by way of farewell, the officer drove back to the gate and went through the routine of opening and closing the gate once more. A minute later the car's taillights had disappeared from view.

"I guess that means we have to do it for ourselves." Glass observed.

"Looks like it. But we'll need to wait until everyone in the house is asleep. We'll go back to Letterkenny, get something to eat and grab some sleep, then come back later."

The woman watched the car disappear and was joined by a man of around the same age. Some sort of argument developed, with shouting on both sides. The border collie rose into an aggressive

151

stance, probably growling at the man. The argument ended when the woman put her hands to her face and ran inside.

"I don't know what he said to her," O'Driscoll muttered more to himself than to Glass, "but he's made the poor biddie cry."

The man stalked across to the gate, threw it open, then climbed into the nearest of the Ford Transit vans and drove off down the track.

"My guess is he's worried by the Gardai's sudden interest in the farm and is off looking for a new hiding place."

"Do you think they'll move him tonight?"

"More likely tomorrow. It will take time to arrange, but they may start off while it's still dark, so we either get in tonight, or we have to try to follow them to wherever they go."

"Not easy to do on country roads. Too little traffic to confuse the issue. He'll pick up our headlights straight away."

"I agree. Tonight it is."

Without waiting for a reply, O'Driscoll wriggled backwards, away from the gate. Glass followed close behind him.

* * *

Prof Green replaced the telephone's handset in its cradle and breathed a sigh of relief. Calls from Downing Street were never easy these days, with so much carnage happening on the streets of Northern Ireland, but having to explain why a single missing Civil Servant couldn't' be found, to someone who had no knowledge whatsoever of Ireland's toxic mix of politics, religion and segregation, was the hardest conversation Prof could have had.

Downing Street seemed to think that all the police had to do was to knock on doors and put out appeals until they were given the information necessary to locate Carter, wherever he was being held. The reality was that appeals would be ignored and any police officer knocking on a door in many parts of Northern Ireland had a fifty-fifty chance of getting shot. It was almost a one hundred percent chance of the door being slammed in their face.

He had spoken directly to the Chief Constable of the RUC and was satisfied the man was doing everything he could to locate Carter, as was the General Officer Commanding the Army in Northern Ireland. The problem was that there was precious little they could actually do. Without information their task was hopeless and whoever was holding Carter was making sure that there was no information to be had.

A light knock sounded on the door of his office, as though the person on the other side was reluctant to actually enter. But the door opened, and a man's head appeared in the gap. "Is now a good time, Minister?"

"It's never a good time these days, Allan, but come in anyway." Prof replied with a rueful smile. "All my life I've dreamed of becoming a government Minister. But now I'm reminded of the old line from Aesop's Fables[7]. 'Be careful what you wish for, because your wishes may come true'".

"The poisoned chalice of politics, Minister." Drinkwater replied.

"Now we're mixing metaphors, Allan. So, what news?"

"Your friends in Donegal think they've located Colonel Carter. I spoke to the Chief Constable and asked him to liaise with his opposite number in the Gardai to get a search done. From what Mr Glass told me, a Gardai officer did visit the farm, but the search was only cursory. I'm guessing he's a local man and knows the owner of the property and thought the whole thing to be a wild goose chase."

"So, what does Danny intend doing now?"

"That's why I'm here Minister. Mr Glass has suggested that an Irish Army patrol is sent to do what the police didn't. There's a unit stationed in Letterkenny. They could be there within a couple of hours. But I think the request would have to come from you."

"I think it would probably have to come from Downing Street, but I'll see what I can do first. If I have to involve London, I will. How sure is Danny about Carter's location."

"Judging by what he has told me, there's definitely something funny going on at the farm. They've seen armed men, so it looks like they are guarding something worth killing for."

"OK. I'll make the call and see what happens. But I'm not hopeful, not after that debacle on the border the other night. Get me the Defence Minister in Dublin."

Drinkwater left the office to connect the call and a few minutes later Green's phone bleeped to attract his attention.

"The Irish Defence Minister, Sir."

"Thank you. Stay on the line please and take notes. If things go wrong I'd like to have a record of what was said. We can be pretty sure they'll be doing the same in Dublin."

"Very well, Minister. Connecting you now."

There were clicks, a brief crackle of static and then a broad Tipperary accent greeted him.

"Good afternoon, Minster Green. To what do I owe the pleasure of this call." The tone of voice used suggested it was anything but pleasurable, but that was the nature of diplomacy.

"Minister, you've no doubt heard about a man we have missing up here. A non-combatant Civil Servant by the name of Carter."

"I've certainly heard the rumours. Including a rumour that he isn't a non-combatant. Civil Service maybe, but probably from the Intelligence branch".

The Irishman's sources seemed to have kept him well informed. The fact that Carter worked for the Security Service wasn't known outside of his office and Carter's onw department, so far as he knew. Now Green would have to tell a direct lie.

"Just a Civil Servant, Minister. Nothing sinister about his work. But that is why I have called. We've received information that suggests Colonel Carter is being held on a farm in Donegal. The Gardai have checked the place out, at our request, but they don't seem to have been very thorough."

"And what has this to do with me?"

Green guessed that the man had already worked out what it had to do with him. Green had met him at cross-border security conferences on a number of occasions and the man was nobody's fool. He just wanted Green to beg.

"I was wondering if you would consider sending an Army patrol out to do a more thorough job."

"And would my soldiers be in any danger?"

Green knew he couldn't lie about the risk. To send soldiers on a mission without disclosing all the facts was tantamount to murder if anything should go wrong. "According to my sources, armed men have been seen at the farm".

"And who are your sources? Have you got security forces operating on Irish soil, Minister?"

"No!" Green blurted the word out a little too emphatically. "I'll be honest, I do have some friends in Donegal, but they have nothing to do with our security forces."

The Irish Minister grunted, as though not entirely believing Green. "How reliable are these 'friends'?"

"I've relied on them both for my life before today."

"Ah, friends from the old days. I've read your career history, Minister. You had a good war, from all accounts."

"No war is good, Minister." Green replied. "It's why I'm so worried about Colonel Carter. I have no idea if he is alive and if he is, for how long he is likely to stay that way. Without him I might not be here to speak to you today. The same goes for my friends in Donegal. I owe them all a lot."

"And you want me to help you to repay your debt. I think not, Minister. I'll contact my own people in Donegal and see if they can tell me if anything untoward is happening. If there is, I'll consider sending an Army patrol out. But I'd prefer to leave it to the Gardai if I'm being honest."

"Without wishing to seem rude, Minister, I'd rather not leave the fate of my friends in the hands of some country coppers. Would you?"

The Irishman chuckled. "I take your point, Minister Green. But I'm not about to send some soldier off to risk his career by chasing after ghosts. If there's no evidence to back up your suspicions, the answer will be no."

With that the line went dead.

Green sat for a few moments considering his next move. He could go to the Secretary of State and ask for him to intervene. With his direct access to the Prime Minster and the PM's access to the Taoiseach, it was likely that the Irish Defence Minister could be overruled.

But the same problem remained. All he had by way of evidence was the unsubstantiated word of an old soldier in Donegal. It wouldn't be enough to persuade the British government to risk embarrassment by asking for Irish troops to be sent running around the hills of Donegal.

But he had no doubt about what Danny and Paddy would do. They would crawl across broken glass to save Lucky Carter, he was sure. Which meant that they would risk raiding the farm themselves if the Irish Army failed to act.

And, even if he wanted to, there was no way he could stop them.

If he could, he would head over to Donegal as fast as his legs would carry him. But his position prevented that. If a British intelligence officer was a highly valued prize, a senior British politician was a prize beyond value.

But he wouldn't be true to himself if he didn't try to do something, he had to acknowledge. He picked up the telephone handset and dialled a number.

"Good afternoon, Elizabeth" he addressed the Secretary of State's private secretary. "May I have a few moments of the Secretary of State's time?"

11 – The Banshee's Scream

O'Driscoll suggested that Glass report back to Drinkwater on events at the farm, so they stopped at the telephone box in Port Salon so Glass could make the call.

"The Gardai were useless." Glass said without preamble. "We were watching from close by and they wouldn't have found an elephant in an empty room."

"Probably just local boys." Drinkwater replied. "They'll think it was a wild goose chase. Did they make any attempt at a search of the buildings?"

"Not so much as a peep inside."

"I don't know what to suggest then."

"How about getting the Irish Army involved. I think they'd do a better job if they think there's something to be found."

"Hang on a minute."

Glass heard the clunk of the handset being placed on Drinkwater's desk, then nothing but a few unidentifiable noises. He had to pump more coins into the box to maintain the connection while Drinkwater was doing whatever it was that he was doing. At last Drinkwater picked up the handset again.

"The nearest Army unit is Letterkenny, apparently. How far is that from the farm?"

"About fifteen miles. They'd need time to put a patrol together and brief them, but they could be here within two hours."

"OK, I'll get our friend to put in a request to Dublin, but if the police have already reported back that there's nothing of interest, I'm not confident of getting anything more done."

The phone went dead and Glass returned to the car.

"So, where does that leave us?" he asked Paddy after giving a report on the conversation.

"We go ahead and plan on doing it ourselves." O'Driscoll replied. "If the army do take action and go to the farm, they'll be sure to find

157

Lucky. Then it becomes a police matter. By the time we get back here there'll be a police presence on the gate by the road and if we go back to our OP[1] we'll see them in the yard. If there's no one there, we go ahead with our own plan."

"Which is?" Danny asked.

Paddy smiled. "Let me work on that. There's a lot to consider. We don't want to go off halfcocked and end up in the same fix as Lucky – or worse."

O'Driscoll guided them back to Letterkenny via the small town of Milford, which was apparently a better road to use in the darkness. Glass decided that 'better' was probably a relative term. The road might be flatter and straighter, but it was still narrow.

The key was in the front door of the house, which Glass had noticed was common for most family homes in the street. A waft of cooking smells greeted them as O'Driscoll called out a greeting to Mrs O'Connor. "We'll be in for a few hours, then we're going out at around midnight." He announced as they entered the kitchen. Mrs O'Conner started serving food, which had obviously been ready for a while.

Glass's eyes lit up with anticipation as he recognised one of his favourite meals, steak and kidney pudding. Mrs O'Connor achieved angel status in his eyes.

She placed the heavily laden plates in front of the two men as they sat at the kitchen table, not saying a word. Glass recognised a troubled look on the woman's face. They ate in silence, not wanting to discuss their plans in front of Mrs O'Connor. The less she knew the better, they had agreed.

After she had cleared away the plate. she started to serve up apple pie.

"I heard the cry of a banshee last night." She observed as she poured steaming thick yellow custard onto the pie.

"I've heard far worse than a banshee in my time, Mrs O'Connor, and I'm still here to tell the tale.

"You shouldn't take such warning lightly." She retorted, banging a dessert plate down in front of O'Driscoll. She placed Glass's dish

158

with greater care. She gave O'Driscoll a dark look but said no more before she left the room. As she did so, Glass noticed her make the sign of the cross on her ample bosom, though whether she was blessing herself or muttering a prayer for Paddy, he had no idea.

"What's a banshee?" Glass asked when she had gone.

"Irish mythology." O'Driscoll replied. "It's the spirit of a witch or a fairy or some such. Legend has it that when you hear one scream, someone in the house is going to die. It's a lot of nonsense, used to scare kids. For a start, even if she did hear one it wouldn't mean anything to us. You only hear it if the person that's going to die is a relative, which doesn't apply to us, so far as I know."

"So why did she say it then?" Glass asked.

"She's worried about what we might be up to tonight." Paddy grinned, "Trotting out that old yoke[2] is supposed to warn me off, I think."

"Still, maybe we should …"

"Ah, Danny, not you too." Paddy interrupted, "I didn't have you down as superstitious."

"I'm not." Glass replied, "It's just that when you're on an operation, it doesn't do to ignore intelligence."

O'Droscoll laughed. "Intelligence me arse. There's no such thing as a banshee, any more than there's any such thing as a leprechaun. Besides, as I said, we're not related to Mrs O'Connor, so even if there were banshees and she actually heard one, it wouldn't be wailing for us. That she's carin' about us enough to be worried about our welfare is flattering, but we know how to look after ourselves." He smiled at Glass, "Now, better get some kip. We'll leave at midnight, and I'll brief you on the way."

* * *

Paddy heard the chair being dragged back and Ger's body slumping into it. A cup rattled in its saucer as it was placed carelessly onto the café table.

"No burger tonight, Paddy." Ger observed.

Paddy lifted his head from his study of the foam ring on the rim of his empty coffee cup. "Not really feeling hungry. Mrs O'Connor fed me a while ago and one of her dinners will keep me going for a week."

It wasn't just a lack of appetite that had prevented Paddy from ordering his usual meal. He'd much rather be getting a few hours of sleep before his and Danny's late night venture, but to miss his Thursday night in the Four Lanterns would provoke curiosity from those who expected to see him there. Not knowing if Ger would show up or not meant Paddy had no option but to attend, even if the visit turned out to be fruitless.

"You've got a new bunch of volunteers for me then." It was a statement, not a question.

"No." Ger replied. "We've a few we're trying out with message carrying and looking after guns and such like, but none that we think are ready to move up a notch. At least, not yet. Maybe March or April."

"I was hoping to be back in Mayo by then." Paddy said morosely.

"Maybe you will be. Maybe you won't."

"So, to what do I owe the pleasure of your company, Ger? You're not the sort to drive down here just for a bit o' craic."

"There's no pulling the wool over your eyes, is there, Paddy? No, I do have another reason to be here. You've been seen in the company of another Brit, apparently, and the boys in the North want to know who and why. Rumour has it he looks like a soldier. Well, if it wasn't for his age, perhaps."

"Rumour can be wrong." Paddy replied.

"But is it?"

"No, it isn't. It's another old friend from my Army days. More than a friend, in fact. He was Best Man at my wedding."

"So, what is he doing here? Yez'll understand that you having two Brit visitors in the space of a few months is causing a bit of worry on the other side of the border."

160

"There's nothing for anyone to worry about. He just fancied a bit of a holiday and thought he'd come and pay me a visit. There's nothing strange about that."

"Ah, but ye see, there is. This part of the world is a little bit dangerous for visitors these days. Unless someone has relations here, it's just not worth the risk."

"It would take a bit more than a few bombs to put Danny off, I can tell you that. A tougher commando there never was. Maybe never will be again. He doesn't scare easily. Besides, we aren't in the North. We're in Donegal and there's no danger here."

"Now, you know as well as I do, Paddy, that if we don't want someone to be around, then we can make sure they don't stay. We're happy enough to let a few Brits live here and spend their money, but we aren't keen on Brit soldiers wandering around."

"He isn't a soldier, not anymore. He's a lorry driver and a pal who's come to visit."

"OK, so where have you been visiting? You were seen driving out along the Ramelton Road today. What is there out there that would be of interest to your friend?"

Paddy was surprised to find that his movements were being so closely observed. Or maybe Carter's visit the previous summer had made his movements of more interest than they had been.

"Just a bit of sightseeing. He's a keen golfer," Paddy lied, "I was showing him some of the courses out that way. You know: Port Salon, Rossapanna and a few others. If the weather stays fine he might play a few holes. I'm not a golfer m'self, you understand, but Danny loves a game."

"I understand the Guards were sent to a farm out Port Salon way this afternoon. You didn't happen to see them, did you?"

"Why should I have seen them? I don't think I've seen a Guard anywhere for weeks. I behave m'slf and they leave me alone. I like it that way."

Ger gave Paddy an appraising stare, weighing up what O'Driscoll had said, but decided to let it drop.

"You called a couple of the lads earlier in the week, asking questions about goings on around Strabane. What was that about?"

O'Driscoll wondered how news of that had reached Ger's ears, then realised that his questions would have been noted by the men he had spoken to and reported up the chain of command. Someone would wonder why he was asking them, and Ger had been dispatched to find out.

How far could he stray from the truth without being discovered? He wondered. What did Ger already know, or how much had been guessed? There was only one way to find out.

"A relative of a close friend of mine has gone missing in the North. She asked me if I could ask a few questions, maybe find out if anyone knew anything?"

"Would this friend have a name?"

"They would, but not one I'd be willing to tell you. The people I spoke to said they didn't know anything, so I'm guessing that it's nothing to do with The Boys. That being the case, there's no need for anyone in the North to worry about it."

"So why has he gone missing?"

"He's the sort that borrows money and doesn't always remember to pay it back. I think he's probably lying low until he has enough cash to get his creditors off his back. And if he can't get enough cash, he'll probably take the boat to England rather than risk staying in Ireland. Of course, I can't tell his mother that, so I had to go through the motions of making a few inquiries for her. The matter's closed as far as I'm concerned."

Paddy hoped that would satisfy Ger's curiosity. If The Boys, as the Provos were sometimes referred to, discovered they had a senior British intelligence officer close by, it would become a race to track him down. Paddy had no idea why Carter had been kidnapped, but if the Provos did manage to get their hands on him before he and Danny, it wouldn't go well for Carter.

That was assuming that it wasn't the Provos holding Carter already of course. In the smoke and mirrors world of terrorism, it

162

was possible that the left hand didn't know what the right hand was doing.

"OK, Paddy. But you tell your friend that he isn't welcome here and that if he's still here at the weekend, it will go badly for him."

"You'll have to go through me first." Paddy said, defiantly.

"Oh, don't think we won't, Paddy. You want out. That makes you expendable. There is more than one way to retire from our organisation, you know."

With that, Ger pushed his chair back, stood up and strode from the room, trying to look like a bad guy but only succeeding in looking as though he was in urgent need of a toilet.

Paddy watched his retreating back. The lies seemed to have done the trick for the moment, but Paddy doubted they would satisfy keener minds on the other side of the border. At best he had bought a little bit of time for himself and Danny.

Ger was right about one thing, at least. If the boys in the North decided he was a liability, then putting him in a shallow grave out on a remote Donegal hillside was an attractive option for them.

With that in mind, success that night became more of a necessity than it had been. He was determined that no harm should come to Danny on his account. So, come hell or high water, Danny had to be out of the county by the morning.

With or without Lucky Carter.

* * *

In response to a tap on the door of his room, Danny Glass emerged into the corridor and followed Paddy O'Driscoll down the narrow staircase. They took care to make as little noise as possible, trying not to wake Mrs O'Connor.

The hire car was parked at the kerbside where they'd left it. Paddy picked up a sack from behind the garden wall. There was the soft clatter of metal striking metal.

"Tools" he whispered. "I've managed to find some bolt cutters and a hacksaw. I'd have liked more, but there wasn't much to be had at short notice."

Danny took his place behind the wheel of the car, while Paddy quietly laid the tools on the back seat, then eased his bulky frame into the front. Starting the engine, Danny steered the car away from the curb and headed down Sentry Hill towards the cathedral. Glass noticed O'Driscoll make a sign of a cross as they passed the building but decided not to say anything. There are no atheists in foxholes, he reminded himself[3].

The darkness was broken only by paler pools created by the street lighting. There was no one around, not even on Main Street when they reached it.

Once they were out in the countryside, Danny spoke for the first time since they had left the house.

"OK, what's the plan?"

"Well, hopefully we've got a wasted journey ahead of us and we'll find the Irish Army crawling all over the place." Paddy shrugged, "But if they're not, we park up behind the trees as before, then approach the farm by the same route as we did yesterday. If the barn is the same type as I've been seeing all me life, it will have a pair of doors at the far end, as well as at the end next to the farmyard, so that the animals can be let straight out into the field. We go to that end, let ourselves in then see what we find inside. I've torches in the bag, but we won't use them unless we have to. Lucky is bound to be secured in some way. That may mean he's just tied to a post, or it could mean there's some sort of structure inside that's been turned into a prison. Either way, we release Lucky and the driver that was with him and then we get out by the same route."

"And if we're discovered?" Danny looked worried. "I can't see that lot in the farmhouse just letting us walk away, and they've got at least one assault rifle."

"We'll try to get to one of the vans." Paddy replied. "Can you hot wire one?"

In the darkness of the car Danny Glass's teeth glinted as he gave a smile.

"I was hot wiring cars when you were still sucking on your mother's tit, Paddy. Can I make a suggestion?"

164

"Sure."

"While you scout out the back of the barn, I'll check out the vans." Danny suggested. "You said people up here don't lock their front doors, so maybe they leave the keys in their cars too."

Paddy nodded, "It's certainly been known."

"OK, so I'll open the doors of the van if they're not locked, and I'll open the gate too. That way we can make a quick getaway. I'll disable the other van so they can't use it to come after us." Danny added, "I'll drop you at the gate on the road. You make your way up the hill to this car and collect it."

O'Driscoll thought for a brief moment. "There's probably a car too, parked in one of those sheds we couldn't see inside. No one would live way out there without some sort of transport and McSweeney would have needed to get in and out of town for market day and his wife to do her bit of shopping, even if she only went as far as Port Salon."

"Yes, but getting it out of the shed will take time and they'll be looking for the headlights of the van and they'll see them hightailing it down the road towards Letterkenny. So they won't think of looking for you walking up the hill."

"In a car they might catch up with the van." Paddy pointed out.

"Yeah" Danny agreed, "I'll have a pretty good head start on them though. They might close the gap, but if it looks like they're getting too close I'll find a turning and pull off the road and they'll drive past with a bit of luck. If they spot me … well, they'll never make it out of the car."

"That's a bit drastic," O'Driscoll replied, "but it's a plan alright. Best we try not to get discovered in the first place. The first thing they'll hear will be the van's engine and by the time they get out of bed and out of the farmhouse, we'll be well away."

"What do we do about the dog?" Danny asked, "It seemed friendly enough with that police officer, but even a friendly dog barks."

"Not much we can do." Paddy said. "Hopefully it will be inside the farmhouse. That means it won't smell us, at least."

Danny wasn't convinced. "But it might hear us."

"True." The big Irishman agreed, "All the more reason to make sure we don't make any noise."

"Let's hope you're right." Danny realised there was nothing they could do about it. "OK… Hopefully they may not try to follow us. They won't want to risk the police coming after them if we do get away, so I think they'll head for somewhere safe where they can wait for things to cool off. The problem is, the only short road out of this part of the world is the one we'll be using. That or the Knockalla Road, but they come together in Ramelton because there's only the one bridge over the river. So whether they're chasing after us or running towards safety makes no difference. They'll be following us either way.

Paddy turned to face him, "If they're Provos, there's plenty of safe houses on both sides of the border. I'm surprised they didn't use one of them in the first place, instead of the farm. Strangers stand out, as we know. In fact, that's how we found them ourselves."

Danny was nodding slowly, "I've been wondering about that. You said your Provo contacts knew nothing about this. So, assuming they didn't lie, why wouldn't they know?"

"A good question and one I've been thinking about meself." Paddy agreed. "They definitely aren't Loyalists, that's for sure. Not out here in the house of a good Catholic woman. You won't find many Protestants out here. They mainly live in the towns. There aren't all that many anyway. A lot moved to the North back in 22. No, I'd have to lay me money on this lot being a splinter group of some sort."

"Which means they'll also be working to a different set of rules to the Provos." Danny said.

"I'm not sure the Provos have a rule book of their own," Paddy responded. "The old IRA had some sense of honour. They would take care not to do anything that might hurt women or children, even if they were on the other side. But the Provos aren't nearly so fussy."

Glass noted the disapproving tone in O'Driscoll's voice and was just about to remind his old friend that he had thrown his hand in with the Provos of his own free will, but thought better of it. If there was one thing he had learnt in his short time in Ireland, it was that Irish politics was complicated. Politics made strange bedfellows sometimes. He knew that from his war service, where capitalists and communists had fought on the same side against a common enemy.

He drove on, the silence broken only when Paddy reminded him to take a turning. The road wasn't easy to follow, and the junctions appeared almost without warning. They hadn't seen any vehicles since leaving the Letterkenny and the houses they passed were all in darkness. Country folk went to bed early, it seemed.

"Slow down." Paddy instructed as they approached the gate at the side of the road that gave access to the farm. It was dark and silent. "So, no police and no army. Looks like your man in Belfast didn't succeed."

"It was always a long shot." Danny explained. "Relations are strained at the moment and the spirit of co-operation doesn't seem to be strong in Dublin."

"It rarely is." O'Driscoll said. "Pull over."

Glass slowed down and stopped in the road, not bothering to pull into the side; there didn't seem to be any point. Paddy got out of the car and trotted back to the gate. He was back moments later. "May as well have the gate open. It will save you smashing the van's headlights by crashing through it later."

Half a minute later Glass turned off the road, switched off the car's headlights and they bumped along the track to the stand of trees where they had concealed the car the previous day.

"You take care of it." Danny instructed, handing O'Driscoll the keys. "If you smash it up it's going to be me that pays the bill."

"Ach, sure, if we get Lucky back, I think the least the British government can do is pay for any damage."

"Well, I'm not relying on them doing that, so don't you drive like a mad thing, like you always used to."

They got out of the car and O'Driscoll retrieved the tools from the back seat. The wind had got up since they left the town and flurries of snow flew into their faces.

"That could complicate matters." Danny whispered.

"Don't worry, it won't lie. The Gulfstream comes in with the tide and that helps keep the air warmer down here. It will settle on the slopes of Errigal and Muckish, but not this lower lying land."

Glass was just about to ask where Muckish[4] might be, but decided he didn't really want to know.

Danny drew the Makarov pistol from his jacket pocket and pulled back on the slide, releasing it to rack a bullet into the chamber. Then he held the hammer under control and pulled the trigger, allowing the hammer to lower itself until it was in a safe position. If he needed to use the gun, using his thumb to pull back the hammer again would be quieter than racking a bullet into the chamber and noise was their greatest enemy at night. O'Driscoll did the same with his gun, before tucking the weapon into the waistband of his trousers.

There was no need for any more words. They knew what they were going to do, so they moved forward in silence to do it.

12 – The Farm

They crouched behind the wall, carefully examining every inch of the farmyard that was visible. A bright light, mounted on the wall of the barn above the doors, provided a lot of illumination and a smaller light, above the farmhouse door, lit up the path.

From their day spent in the field they knew that a strip of worn grass formed a path from the gate beside them to another one almost directly below them, which gave access to the farmyard, adjoining what they assumed to be an equipment shed. To the right of the gate was a fence which ran for a few yards before making a right angle turn to continue until it met the side of the barn.

Paddy turned to Danny, "We'll cut to the right and get around the back of the barn, then you carry on around until you get to that front wall, where the vans are parked. I'll wait for you there while you deal with the vans."

Nodding silently, Danny slithered through the gap under the gate where the ground had been worn down by the passage of the feet of thousands of animals. He heard Paddy grunt as he struggled to squeeze his bulk through the same space. 'Why don't you make a bit more noise?' Danny thought silently.

But there was no sound of a barking dog, so he guessed they were still too far away for the animal to hear the small sound. Rising to his feet he walked carefully forward. He knew there were no large obstructions in the field, but that didn't mean that there wasn't anything lying hidden in the long grass. There might also be rabbit holes. If he tripped and fell the noise might just be enough to wake the dog. If he hurt himself and cried out involuntarily, it would definitely raise the alarm.

The blessing of the lights in the farmyard was that they would effectively blind anyone who went out there. Their eyes wouldn't be able to see anything beyond a few feet from the edges of the pools of light, because their eyes wouldn't function properly. If Glass had been assigned to guard the farmyard, the first thing he would have done would be to take the bulbs out of those two lights to prevent their use. A night-blind sentry was little better than no sentry at all.

Which appeared to be the state of play in the farmyard. The kidnappers seemed to be so confident of not being discovered in this remote location that they didn't have a guard posted, as far as Danny could see.

OK, there could be someone in the equipment shed, but that seemed unlikely. They might also have someone inside the door of the farmhouse, ready to react to any noise outside. But if they did, it was probable that they would have dozed off. One of the reasons that guards marched up and down was to keep them awake. A guard sat down in a warm farmhouse was almost certain to succumb to slumber.

Another flurry of snow blew across the field, stinging Glass's skin and obscuring the barn. That was good. Snow would keep the guard, if there was one, tucked up snug inside. He saw the flakes being driven through the patch of bright light. It seemed to be getting quite heavy.

Keeping deep in the shadows cast by the lights from the farmyard, Danny and Paddy slipped along the side of the barn and then turned the corner to make their way along the rear. Using his fingers, Paddy located the Judas door set into the barn's large double doors. The rear of the barn was identical to the front, except for the fact that the light above the doors wasn't lit. Whether that was because no one thought it needed to be lit or because it wasn't working, they couldn't know, but they were grateful as the lack of light meant their night vision wasn't impaired.

Receiving a gentle push from Paddy, Danny continued his journey around the rear and the side of the barn. Reaching a wire fence, glinting in the farmyard's lights, Danny stopped. Covering one eye to protect his vision, he risked a look around the corner. Seen from this side, the farmyard looked as deserted as it had from the top of the hill behind.

170

From this side the equipment shed could be seen, though much of the interior was in deep shadow. What was visible was the front end of a car, an ancient Ford Anglia by the look of it, and the front end of a tractor. The farm vehicle tilted to one side, suggesting a flat tyre or damaged suspension. The car was the bigger threat though. In that they could be followed.

Glass pondered the pros and cons of crossing the farmyard to disable the vehicle. Or he could go around the back of the barn once more and come at it from the other side. It would take time, but they had that to spare. Dawn was still several hours away at this time of year.

On the other hand, any delay risked someone coming out and finding him, perhaps to check on the prisoners. It also presented more opportunities for him to stumble over something and make noise which might set the dog barking.

On balance, the risk felt too high. The vans were the greater threat and would also be of greater use.

The fence was about four feet high and consisted of four strands of rusting wire strung tightly between posts that were spaced about three yards apart. He pushed down on the lowest strand and up on the one above it, widening the gap between them so he could slip through. Fortunately, whoever had built the fence had decided not to use barbed wire, so there was no risk of Danny snagging his skin or clothing on it and causing it to rattle.

Twisting his body, Danny eased the tension on the wire and let it settle back into place. So far, so good.

The vans were parked as they had been in the afternoon, one either side of the gate, pointing towards it but with their noses close up to the front wall of the farm. It would mean them having to be reversed backwards before they could be driven through the gate. A small delay, but an important one if there were shots being fired.

Tip-toeing to the nearest van Danny opened the driver side door, the one nearest to him. He cringed as there was a clunk as the mechanism released. He stopped, his ears straining to hear the sound of a barking dog, but the farmhouse remained silent.

In the ignition a key fob swayed back and forth with the gentle motion caused by the door opening. Glass allowed himself a silent celebration. That made their whole escape a lot easier.

He left the door hanging open and made his way to the rear of the van. The doors there were also unlocked and he left them standing wide, ready to receive passengers. They might be able to squeeze three people in the front of the van, but not the four that were expected to leave the farmyard if everything went to plan. He considered opening a side cargo door, but decided it wasn't necessary. Getting everyone in through the back doors would be quicker than someone going around all the way to the other side.

He went back along the driver's side to the front of the van and passed between it and the wall. The second van formed a barrier between him and the front of the farmhouse, preventing him from being seen from either the door or the windows. Glass shook his head in silent amazement. No one had paid even cursory attention to sightlines and routes by which the farmyard could be approached. If he needed to, he was sure he could get an entire company of commandos into the yard without anyone being any the wiser.

Bloody civvies. He said to himself. Not a clue.

He had considered the best way to disable the van. His preferred method would have been to remove the distributor cap from its housing, disconnect the cables from the spark plugs and then throwing the whole assemble as far as he could out into the fields at the front of the farm.

But he discounted that idea. Opening the bonnet of the van without making any sound probably wouldn't be possible. Unlike the door hinges, they were less likely to be well greased. He drew his small penknife from the pocket of his trousers and unfolded the blade. Stabbing hard into the rubber of the front tyre he heard the immediate hiss of air escaping as the tyre punctured. Moving to the back of the van he repeated his actions. The van now leaned over drunkenly. Just for good measure he opened the van's front door, removed the ignition key and hurled it out the field.

The van wasn't actually disabled. If he could hotwire it then someone else might also be able to. But with punctured tyres it wouldn't be able to follow at speed. And once on the hard tarmac of the road the tyres would quickly shred, leaving the vehicle to run on its steel wheel rims. It wouldn't go far and certainly not at any speed.

The last thing he had to do was to open the front gate. That was where the greatest risk of noise came from. He had never heard of a farm gate that didn't groan like a wounded bull when it was opened. Admittedly he was a city boy and most of his knowledge of farmers came from film and TV, but he knew it was a risk.

But he didn't have to actually open the gate, did he? He reminded himself. He just had to leave it so that the van could get through it without major damage. So long as the gate was off it's latch, the weight of the van nudging against it would do the rest and by then, noise wouldn't matter.

Now the bright light of the farmyard worked in his favour. He could see that the gate was constructed from metal tubes, five of them welded between two uprights, with a diagonal bar running from the bottom hinge to the top of the free end. It was held shut by no more than a frayed length of rope looped over the gatepost. He lifted the rope up and let it hang slack over the top rail of the gate. The fence post leant against the end of the gate itself, applying friction that kept the gate in place. It would only take a shove to open it, but in the meantime the gate stayed closed.

Taking another look longingly at the car in the equipment shed, Danny felt temptation tugging at him. It would be good to try to get to it and disable it as well. But he shook his head dismissively. Too much risk.

He made his way back through the fence and around the barn to find Paddy.

"There's a car as well. But I didn't want to risk trying to get to it." he whispered.

"Good thinking." O'Driscoll whispered back. "If we can get everyone into the van without raising the alarm, we can put a couple of bullets into radiator before we go. It won't matter by then if we

173

make any noise and it won't get far before the engine seizes up with the heat."

"OK," Glass agreed, "But first we have to find Lucky and the other bloke."

O'Driscoll nodded, "Well, there's no lock on this door, but it feels stiff. I don't think the hinges have been greased in a while. No need, I suppose, with the animals all gone. The front door opened outwards, so this one probably does as well." He reached for it, then turned to Danny, "Give us a hand here."

Curling his fingers around the edge of the door, Glass braced his feet, ready to start pulling.

"On Three." Whispered O'Driscoll. "One … two …three."

The door moved, but with a loud groan of hinges that hadn't seen lubrication for a while. They got it half open then stopped.

"That's enough." O'Driscoll said. "The wider we open it, the more likely it will be heard by that feckin' dog.".

They paused, listening intently. They could hear no sound of an alarm being raised, but it was possible the bulk of the barn could muffle the noise of a dog barking. The wind rattling the corrugated iron of the structure would no doubt help to disguise the groan of the hinges. Up close it sounded like a steel band whose members were all playing different tunes.

O'Driscoll eased himself into the gap and Glass followed close behind. Without either of them speaking, they both pulled the Makarov pistols from the waist bands of their trousers and eased back the hammers. The soft clicks of them locking into place was more than covered by the rattling of the barn.

They waited, getting their eyes adjusted to the deeper darkness inside. Glass was already at a disadvantage, having been exposed to the exterior lights. He'd done his best to protect his night vision by keeping one eye closed, but it had opened involuntarily from time to time. Back in the commandos they had worn an eyepatch to help them, but he'd had nothing at hand here and hadn't thought to make a trip to a chemist's shop to buy one.

O'Driscoll fished inside his sack and pulled out a small torch. Flicking it on he directed the beam at the ground, sweeping the rough surface in front of their feet so that they didn't trip over anything. The torch's light wasn't bright, but it would be seen from outside if it passed over any of the many holes in the rusting walls of the barn. It was those holes that were allowing the wind to blast through, increasing the interior air pressure to flex the walls from the inside, causing all the noise.

The floor had once been a sheet of concrete, but over the years it had cracked. Frost had undoubtedly got in to force the cracks wider and then the passage of farm machinery had broken the surface up some more. Thousands of cloven hooves had mixed with animal urine to churn up the mud beneath and now it was difficult to make out what was dried mud and what was concrete. They'd have to watch their footing. It would be easy to twist an ankle.

The smell of decades of manure assaulted their nostrils.

"Smells like home." Paddy observed. "Well, what have we here?" O'Driscoll allowed the torch's beam to settle on a large metal object standing in the middle of the barn's floor. The word "Coughlan's Animal Feeds, Sligo" were visible in peeling paint along the sides, above a telephone number. Rust streaked the side of the container too, but there didn't appear to be any holes in it, unlike the barn.

"A shipping container." Glass supplied the answer, though the question was probably rhetorical. "It makes a good holding cell."

"There's another one there." Glass pointed. It was just as dilapidated but only half the size. It's door hung open, so it wouldn't be the one where anyone was being held prisoner.

O'Driscoll led them to the far end and the torch picked out the bright metal of a padlock holding the long vertical locking bars in place. Unlike the container, the padlock looked as though it had only just been bought. He lifted the lock and pulled at it, but it was locked firmly. He lowered it back into place, where it swung back and forth for a moment, scraping at the metal surface of the door.

"Maybe we should see if there's anyone inside before we spend a lot of time trying to cut through that padlock." O'Driscoll suggested.

Glass pressed his ear against the cold metal of the door.

"I can hear voices." He reported. "Lucky? Are you in there?"

"Who's that?"

"It's me, Danny Glass."

"What the…" The voice said back, not bothering to try to conceal itself. "Never mind. Just get us out of here."

"We're on the case, Lucky."

"We? Is Prof with you?"

"No, It's Paddy." O'Driscoll spoke for himself. "Bet you didn't expect to hear from me again. Now, Stay back from the door while we deal with the lock."

Reaching into his sack once more, O'Driscoll pulled out a large pair of bolt cutters. Forcing the jaws over the shackle of the padlock, he began to squeeze the handles, pressing hard. Glass heard his gasps for breath as he exerted himself.

O'Driscoll was a big man, but he wasn't in the peak of physical shape. Glass, on the other hand, spent his working days heaving full beer kegs on and off the back of a lorry. "Let me have a go." He said, pushing his friend to one side.

He was rougher than intended and O'Driscoll lurched against the container, releasing the bolt cutters to fall to the ground with a loud mechanical clattering.

"Feckin' eejit." O'Driscoll hissed. "Yez'll wake the feckin' dog."

"We better get a move on then." Glass said, knowing he may have given away their presence. He picked up the cutters and set to work again. It took him almost a minute of squeezing and bending, levering the cutters back and forward, but at last the jaws snapped closed, and the body of the padlock swung away on one side to hang loosely in the hasp of the locking bars.

As Glass lowered the cutters to the ground, O'Driscoll removed the useless padlock and swung the doors open.

Lucky was through them straight away, grabbing Glass's hand and pumping it up and down in a handshake of congratulations. "Am I glad to see you two." He said.

"Quiet." Glass warned. "There's a dog in the house. Too much noise and it will wake up whoever it is that's in there."

Carter released Glass's hand and seized O'Driscoll's instead. "Paddy," He lowered his voice in response to Glass' warning. "You're a sight for sore eyes."

"Save the chit-chat until we're safely out of here." O'Driscoll said. "Are yez alone?"

"No. Jerry was with me when I was grabbed." He stuck his head back inside the container. "Jerry, do you need a hand?"

"I'm coming." Jerry's broad Belfast accented voice replied.

Carter heard a groan and the thump of a body hitting the side wall of the container.

"Give me hand, Danny." Carter ducked back inside, Glass following close behind. Between them they helped to support Jerry, one under each armpit, and he was able to make his painful way out of the large metal box.

They all froze as they heard the dog bark. It was too loud for it to have come from inside the farmhouse, which meant that someone had let it out into the farmyard. There was a thud against the front doors of the barn, then the scrabbling of nails against the corrugated metal, accompanied by more whining interspersed with more barking.

"Shit!" Glass said. "Now we're in trouble."

"We'll go out the same ways as we came in." O'Driscoll said, leading the way towards the rear doors. Between them, Carter and Glass half carried, half dragged Jerry with them.

The barking of the dog was now accompanied by raised voices, demanding to know who was there. There was a clattering as the front Judas door swing back on its hinges. Light flooded through from the exterior, silhouetting a man.

"Silly boy" O'Driscoll muttered, levelling his pistol.

"Don't kill him." Carter hissed. In this time of crisis, he found he was still able to keep a clear head. The consequences of killing a man in a foreign country were unfathomable, even claiming self-defence.

O'Driscoll raised his arm a fraction and fired the Makarov. By chance the bullet must have smashed the light bulb after it penetrated the corrugated metal wall, because the barn was plunged into darkness as the sound of glass tinkling to the ground could be heard.

That was good, Carter thought. Anyone out the front would have no night vision, while theirs was reasonably intact.

With no further need for caution, O'Driscoll pushed the Judas door wide and they clambered through it into the field beyond. Moving to their left, they followed the rear wall of the barn until it turned the corner, then crept down the side to the point where the fence met the barn wall.

Peering around, O'Driscoll could see shapes moving around in front of the barn, lit dimly by the light that was still on over the farmhouse door. There were at least four of them and two of those were carrying rifles. By the shape of them O'Driscoll though they were probably assault rifles of some sort.

The dog ran up and down the yard, prancing on its front feet and barking, thinking some sort of game was in progress. What attracted its attention they would never know, but it suddenly stopped, lowering its head towards the ground and stared straight at O'Driscoll. Perhaps it had just caught his smell on the night air, or perhaps some slight sound had attracted its attention, but it was now alert to their presence.

The men at the front of the barn, however, were still unaware of that. They were arguing, trying to decide whether to enter or stay outside. Their broad Northern Irish accents could be made out, though only the occasional word and that was usually an expletive.

O'Driscoll ducked back around the corner to confer with his companions.

"We've got a choice." He whispered. "We can either make a dash for the van and hope for the best, or we can work our way back around the barn, up the hill and back to the car we have up there."

"I'm not sure I can travel far." Jerry replied, gasping for breath. "I think I may have a broken rib."

"What if Danny and Lucky are supporting you?"

178

Jerry shook his head. "I'll slow you down too much. I think the van is the best option. How far is it?"

"Straight line. Maybe ten, fifteen yards at the most." Paddy told him.

Jerry shrugged, "If you can keep the gang's heads down, Danny and Lucky can probably get me there."

"OK, van it is then." Paddy agreed, "We'll have to do it like we did in the war, with someone holding the wire apart while everyone else crawls through. Once we're all on the other side, we do our best to get to the van without being spotted. If they do see us, we'll have to open fire and keep their heads down. But they've got a lot of fire power."

"If we don't then we're all dead already." Jerry said, morosely. "They'll be worried that you've told someone they're here, so they'll kill us all, dump the bodies then find somewhere safe to hide up until the chase goes cold."

"In that case, we've nothing to lose." Carter said. "Check to see if the coast is clear and we'll see what happens."

Crawling back to the fence, O'Driscoll eased his head between the two lowest strands of wire, only to be met by the dog's tongue, licking at him in welcome. He stifled a cry of disgust and the urge to wipe the dog's saliva from his face. Instead, he tried to calm the dog down.

"There's a good boy. Good doggie. Now, you stay nice and quiet now, while we just come by, is that OK?"

By way of an answer, the dog tried to lick his face again. "Well, at least you're friendly enough." O'Driscoll whispered to it. He grabbed the animal by the scruff of its neck and pulled it through the fence. The dog must have thought this was some sort of new game, because it didn't struggle.

"Here, keep this mutt quiet for a minute while I take a look see what's happening." O'Driscoll pushed the dog back into Danny Glass's waiting hands then turned to look around the corner of the barn once more.

There were only two men visible now. The other two must be inside. Which meant they would find the back door of the barn open within seconds and know where they were. With two at the front and two coming around the back, they would be caught if they didn't move quickly.

The two at the front were too intent on what was happening inside the barn, both peering in through the Judas door. It was now or never.

Rolling onto his back, O'Driscoll grabbed at the lower two strands of wire and forced them apart. "Come on." He hissed.

To help Jerry, Glass had to let go of the dog and it immediately ran through the gap O'Driscoll had made in the fence. It stood, its head cocked to one side, giving O'Driscoll a curious look. As Carter and Glass pulled Jerry through the dog started prancing about again, and let out an excited bark.

""Shit! Get a move on." O'Driscoll called hoarsely. He needn't have bothered trying to keep quite.

"Stay still or I'll shoot." A broadly accented voice shouted from the front of the barn. O'Driscoll let go of the wire and took careful aim with the Makarov, firing a single shot. Sparks danced off the side of the barn and the two men dived for cover, locking shoulders in the barn's doorway before falling inside.

"Go, go, go!" shouted O'Driscoll.

Carter and Glass needed no urging. They dragged Jerry bodily through the fence and continued towards the van. Jerry's body bouncing over the ground.

This was no time for a good bedside manner. Jerry let out a wail of pain.

The dog barked and danced around them excitedly, wanting to join in the game.

Automatic fire opened up from the barn door, but it was undirected, the rifle having been poked through and turned in their general direction. Bullets smacked into the farmyard wall and a ricochet whined away into the night.

Taking careful aim again, O'Driscoll fired another shot. He was no longer worried if he killed anyone or not. This was life and death and he was determined the death wouldn't be his. The rifle withdrew. O'Driscoll fired again, just to make sure the message was understood.

"Paddy, let's go!" Glass called from the rear of the van., slamming the doors shut. He ran to the driver's side door, swinging it open and started to clamber in. Seconds later O'Driscoll heard the engine cough into life.

Clambering to his feet, O'Driscoll sprinted towards the van and around the back to the passenger side. He should have dived through the back doors, but Carter was still wrestling Jerry through them and the space looked too crowded. The dog danced around his feet and they became tangled up, bringing O'Driscoll heavily to the ground.

Struggling to get upright again, the sound of more automatic rifle fire ripped the night apart. The dog let out a shriek of pain and fell to the ground.

Watching events in the van's wing mirror, Danny saw Paddy fall to the floor a second time, this time he didn't try to get back to his feet.

"Lucky, I think Paddy's been hit."

The sound of bullets hitting the vehicle made Glass duck his head, not that the driver's seat offered much protection again an assault rifle. He heard the side door slide open and watched as Lucky jumped out, grabbed Paddy under the arms and pulled him towards the side door.

Winding down the side window, Glass aimed his Makarov back towards the barn, firing blind with his left hand, hoping that it would distract the terrorists long enough for Carter to get O'Driscoll on board.

'No man left behind', he reminded himself of the old commando saying; not that it had been true. They had left plenty of men behind in Italy.

Bending over, Carter heaved O'Driscoll up and over the door sill, rolling him inside and throwing himself in after him as another volley of shots struck the van.

"Go". He shouted as he slid the side door shut again.

Glass threw the gearstick into reverse, backed the vehicle up a few feet, turned the steering wheel and drove forward, aiming the nose of the van at the centre of the gate. It shot open under the van's weight, bounced against something and slammed back against the side of the van as it sped through.

"There goes the no claims bonus." Carter quipped from the rear of the vehicle.

Glass didn't respond. With his eyes switching between the two wing mirrors, to see what was going on behind, he slammed his foot down hard on the accelerator pedal and the van leapt forward.

Seeing the twinkle of muzzle flashes, Glass started weaving the van back and forth across the farm track, trying to put the rifleman off aim. A second rifle joined the first as another man opened fire from the corner of the barn where they had all been lying just a few moments before.

More bullet struck the van and Danny felt the wind from one as it sped past him and smashed the windscreen. A spider's web of cracks appeared where the bullet passed through, but it still held together as a single sheet

The rush of cold night air through the bullet hole made Danny's eyes water, but he was able to make out the bend where the track turned towards the road, then the gate where the two met.

Common sense told him to turn right and try to put distance between him and their pursuers. But he thought again.

Instead, he turned left and headed up the hill, away from Port Salon. With no lights showing from the van, any pursuers wouldn't know which way they had gone.

He slowed as he reached the summit, searching out the turning towards the stand of trees where the car waited.

"I'm going to lie up and hide." He called over his shoulder into the interior of the cargo compartment.

"I don't think we have time for that." Carter's voice came in reply. "Paddy's been hit and he's losing a lot of blood. Jerry doesn't sound too good either."

"In that case, let's at least give them some first aid. It'll be easier if I'm not trying to dodge bullets."

"Have you got a first aid kit?"

"Nope. We'll just have to make do with whatever we have. Start with Paddy's shirt, seeing he's the one who's bleeding all over the place."

Finding the turning, Glass steered them to the stand of trees where the hire car was parked and brought the van to a halt. The sudden silence after he switched off the engine was deafening, until O'Driscoll let out a groan of pain that sounded like the lowing of a cow in labour.

Glass got out of the van and went around the rear, opening the back doors and clambering inside. He thought about switching on the cargo bay light, but decided against it. Although they were some way from the farm, there was no guarantee it wouldn't be seen and give away the fact that they hadn't left the area.

The floor was slick with blood, which Glass knew wasn't a good sign. In his experience, no one bled that much and lived to tell the tale.

"One bullet through the back and out through the gut." Carter announced, as Glass crouched down beside him.

O'Driscoll let out another groan and opened his eyes.

"Lucky, is it yourself? Fancy seeing you here."

Carter couldn't tell if he was attempting a joke or just trying to use humour to ease the pain, as they had all done before. Or perhaps his brain was blocking out what had just happened to him, and he really didn't recall their escape.

"Aye, Paddy, it's me."

"And is that Danny Glass as well?" O'Driscoll groaned, "Would you look at the big eejit, sitting there looking like he'd found sixpence and lost a pound."

"Are you OK Paddy?" Danny asked.

183

"I've been better, I think. What happened to me?"

"Time for explanations later, but you've been shot. We'll patch you up as best we can and then we'll get you to a hospital." Carter said, trying to sound unconcerned.

"I wouldn't waste your time, Lucky. I think this is it for me."

"Don't talk rubbish, Paddy." Carter admonished gently.

"It's OK. I've always known I wouldn't make old bones. I'm ready for it in me heart."

"You'll outlive me, you old reprobate." Carter replied.

O'Driscoll decided not to argue with him. Instead he said "Do youz remember the great times we had, back during the war?"

"They weren't all great." Carter reminded him.

"Ach, sure, but there was some good times amongst the bad. Do your remember the time we met those two nurses in the Sally Army club in Suez?"

"I don't think I was there." Carter replied.

"Ach, sure you weren't, you bein' an officer and all. You weren't allowed out on the tear like the rest of us." Paddy agreed, his memory clearing a little. "It was just me, Prof and Danny. But Prof decided not to stay. Then the two nurses took us off to this nightclub. It was full of officers, and they all seemed to know the two nurses. We thought we'd lose them to the toffs, for sure, but they loved our green berets, so they did."

"I remember it, Paddy." Danny confirmed.

O'Driscoll chuckled, then gasped with pain. "That's because you got the ugly one. You'd be bound to remember that."

"She wasn't ugly." Glass denied the accusation, "She just wasn't classically beautiful."

"She had legs like feckin' tree trunks, so she did. But that wasn't the best part. They took us back to the hotel they were billeted in." Paddy chuckled painfully, "Then their officer must have heard us, 'cos next thing we know she's banging on the door demanding to be let in and we had to jump out the window. Stark bollock naked we wuz. Do you remember that, Danny?"

184

"I certainly do." Danny told him, "I left a boot behind, and we'd missed the last transport back to El Ataka. I had to limp all the way back. Miles it was. I don't think my left foot has recovered from it yet."

O'Driscoll broke into a fit of coughing.

"Hold still while I tie this bandage." Carter protested.

But O'Driscoll had fallen silent.

"Is he OK?" Danny asked.

In the darkness Carter felt for a pulse, trying O'Driscoll's neck then his wrist.

"I think we've lost him." He said, quietly.

"No, no, he can't have gone." Glass protested, scrabbling about, trying to find somewhere he could take a pulse. Feeling O'Driscoll's slack jaw covered in blood that had spewed from his mouth, he realised the truth.

"Oh Paddy, what did I get you into?" He asked plaintively.

"You didn't get him into anything, Danny." Carter rested a blood soaked hand on Glass's shoulder. "If anyone is to blame here, it's me. I shouldn't have been running around Northern Ireland playing spies. If I hadn't got myself caught, Paddy would still be alive."

There was movement from the other side of the van. "Bloody hell, I'd forgotten about Jerry." Carter blurted out, turning to look at the man lying along the side of the vehicle.

"I didn't want to interrupt such an enchanting reunion." Jerry gasped.

"Are you fit to travel?" Carter asked him. "It might be a bit bumpy, even if we ditch this and use the car."

"I think I'll be OK. Got a hell of a pain from my ribs. I keep feeling a sort of grinding whenever I move. I think it's the bones rubbing together."

"I didn't realise you'd taken that much of a beating. I could see where they'd battered your face, but I didn't know about your ribs."

"Aye, they were thorough all right. I took a couple of boots to the ribs when I fell off the chair. They seemed to be enjoying themselves, so I didn't want to interrupt."

More dark humour, Carter thought. It seemed that the police did the same as the Army when things got difficult.

"I'm sorry about your friend." Jerry said. "You seemed close."

"As close as you can get. We fought side by side many times. You get to know a man when you do that." Glass replied. He slightly resented Jerry still being alive when O'Driscoll was dead. It was unreasonable, he knew. It wasn't Jerry's fault that Paddy had been killed. But it didn't stop him wishing that Jerry was the one who had died.

"I think you'd probably be more comfortable in the car." Carter broke into the silence. "What sort is it, Danny?"

"An Opel Kadett; what we'd call a Vauxhall Viva."

"OK, we'll stretch you out on the back seat, Jerry." Carter told him.

"What about Paddy?" Glass protested. "We can't just leave him here."

"There's no room for him in the car, unless we put him on the boot."

"He's not going in the boot." Glass's tone brooked no argument.

"It's either that or we leave him here. The Irish police can come and get him tomorrow."

"No man left behind. remember?"

"Yes, I remember Danny, but the priority now is with the living, not the dead. We can leave Paddy here or we can put him in the boot of the car. Or we can take this van and risk losing Jerry as well. I'm not your officer now. I'm not going to make the decision for you this time. What's it to be?"

"I'm not leaving Paddy behind. OK, much as I don't like it, I guess it'll have to be the boot."

It took them several minutes to fold O'Driscoll's body into the spacious boot of the hire car, then to help Jerry out of the van and into the back seat of the Kadett. Jerry groaned as the vehicle lurched along the track back to the road, but he settled easily enough once they were on the smoother tarmac. Glass kept the speed down to make the ride less violent.

They we almost in Milford when they spied headlights coming towards them at speed, with blue lights flashing on two of the three vehicles.

"Here comes the cavalry, late again." Carter drawled. The lead vehicle was a police car, followed by a Mercedes truck bearing Irish Army markings. The final vehicle of the three was another police car.

"Stable doors." Glass grunted. "The terrorists will be well gone by the time they arrive. Just an old woman and a dead dog left behind, I would think."

"They're not terrorists, at least not now." Carter replied.

"Well, they certainly looked like terrorists to me." Glass snapped back.

"Oh, they probably were at one time," Lucky said, "but I'm pretty sure they're in it for themselves now. Once they found out what I was doing in Belfast, all they were interested in was the addresses of places that were handling a lot of cash and they weren't bothered whether they were Nationalist places or Loyalist places. I know for a fact they turned over an amusement arcade that was fronting for an IRA money laundering operation."

"But how did they know what you were doing?" Glass asked. "Come to think of it, what were you doing in Belfast? No, never mind, you probably shouldn't tell me that."

"No, I shouldn't," Carter told him, "but I will, seeing as I've already told the ones who kidnapped me. I was analysing financial data on various businesses to see if we, the authorities, could identify businesses that were fronting for money laundering operations. Then we could go after the money, which is the life blood of any modern terrorist organisation. No money means no way of buying guns or explosives."

Danny nodded. "But how did they find out about you?"

"They didn't." Carter replied. "All they knew was that someone would be sent to try to make contact with an informant who had dropped off the radar. It could have been anyone. With me they just got lucky." He grunted. "Ironic considering the nickname I've had for the past thirty odd years. Anyway, the objective was to demand ransom money, which they probably did anyway. But the information I had meant they could get what they wanted regardless of whether the government paid up."

"What happened to the informant?"

"I'm pretty sure he was the ringleader. I'm guessing he at least suspected that the Provos knew about his existence, if not by name at least by location. It would only be a matter of time before they found out who he was. That meant he had to get out, but he needed money to do that. So he recruited a few others who were fed up risking their lives for little reward in the Provos and they came up with this plan. No doubt they were all dreaming of a nice retirement in Spain, or maybe America."

"So now they'll head that way anyway?"

"I think they'll try, but when I tell Belfast what I know, they'll tell the Irish authorities and they'll have a hard job getting out of the country. They'll need fake passports and they probably haven't made enough money to pay for those.

I'm guessing they'll probably try to knock over a few of those businesses I told them about to raise more cash, but we'll have them under surveillance within hours of me getting back to the North. They'll be picked up if they go within a hundred yards of any of them."

"Or maybe we'll just get the word out to the Provos and the UDA and let them do the dirty work." Jerry piped up from the back seat.

"That's an option too." Carter chuckled. "I certainly wouldn't want to be them if the Provos get their hands on them."

They fell silent as the streetlights on the outskirts of Letterkenny appeared in front of them. "I'm not sure how to get to the hospital from here." Danny said. "We'll need to find someone to ask."

"No, head straight for the border." Carter instructed. "Will you be OK if for a while longer Jerry?"

"I should be. This is a lot smoother ride than that Transit van."

"I've left my bag at Mrs O'Connor's" Glass said wistfully.

"I'm sure a grateful nation will reimburse you for your losses, Danny. And if they won't, then it would be the least I could do by way of thanks. Part of the reason I don't want to go looking for this hospital is because the gang know where Fiona lives and I wouldn't put it past them to go after her, so I need to get a call through to my Glasgow office and get the police onto it."

"I'm sorry, Lucky, but they don't know where she lives." Jerry said.

"What do you mean. They told me they have people in Scotland …"

"They were bluffing. They wanted information about you and they were beating the crap out of me, so I had to tell them a few things. Those long chats we had in that container thing gave me enough to go on. I'm really sorry. They know your wife's name and they know you live in Scotland. That's all. I never gave them the name of the town or anything that would lead them to her."

Carter gave a sigh of relief.

"I'm sorry, I really am, but…"

Carter gave another sigh. "Don't worry about it. Given the circumstances, I'd have probably done the same. I probably should have guessed. Once I'd worked out what was really happening, it should have been obvious that they wouldn't be going near any sympathisers in Scotland. But I'm still worried about Fiona. There was probably something in my wallet that had my home address on it."

They drove on towards the border in silence, each caught up in their own thoughts.

After climbing out of the passenger side door of the Opel Kadett and raising his hands in compliance with the young soldier's orders, things had escalated quickly. A police Landrover had arrived carrying four armed constables, followed by a Sergeant, who summoned an Inspector who was closely followed by a Lieutenant Colonel and a police Superintendent.

Before he knew it Carter was in an RAF helicopter on his way to Belfast, Danny Glass sitting alongside him. Jerry would have been there too, had he not been in need of urgent hospital treatment. He had been whisked away to Londonderry's Altnagalvin Hospital.

The helicopter vibrated as if every rivet holding it together was trying to break loose. Conversation was impossible. Even the crewman, perched in the open doorway, communicated with them only with hand signals.

The helicopter took them to Army Headquarters in Lisburn, where Intelligence Corps officers and plain clothed civilians started to bombard Carter with questions.

He crossed his arms defiantly. "Let's talk about Paddy O'Driscoll's funeral first. Then I'll be happy to answer all your questions."

13 – Lecanvey

The little seaside village of Lecanvey looked pretty enough as the car carrying Carter and his wife drew up outside the small village church. The bulk of Croagh Patrick mountain loomed behind them, while the sea glittered brightly to their front.

Carter couldn't help but feel that the village would see more activity on this day than it had in a long time. He opened the car door and got out of the rear, walking around to open the door on the other side for his wife, but one of the large men in the front seat beat him to it. The other large man got out from behind the steering wheel. The two of them looked uncomfortable in their sombre suits and dark overcoats, more used to Gardai uniforms that funeral garb. The bulges under their armpits where their holstered weapons were concealed didn't help their appearance as respectful mourners.

A second, almost identical car drew up behind and Danny Glass climbed out of the rear of that one, his wife Edith getting out the other side. She looked a little dazed, as though she was wondering how she had been plucked out of her little house in Shepherds Bush and transported to what seemed like the ends of the Earth. They, too, were accompanied by Gardai officers in plain clothes.

Scanning the area, an old habit from his wartime days, Carter picked out several cars with far too many aerials sprouting from them to be domestic vehicles. Security was high and he was able to hazard a guess as to why. He looked into the churchyard and saw the reason for all the additional precautions confirmed. Standing by the church door, talking to the priest, was Prof Green. Dotted around were more sombre suited men, all with their backs to the church and their eyes on village and its surrounding countryside.

A senior British politician couldn't just arrive in the Republic of Ireland without the rest of the circus arriving with him. No doubt there were Irish diplomats hovering somewhere close by, making sure that their country was putting on a good show for their visitor.

It had been only three days since Glass had driven them into the vehicle search area of the Army checkpoint on the Letterkenny Road in Derry, or Londonderry as it was officially called. Not that anyone really used the name, not even the Loyalists.

It was the practice in Ireland to bury the dead as quickly as possible. Certainly it was unusual for there to be more than two days between the death and the burial. Apparently, it was because it was normal for the deceased to be kept at home for all the neighbours to come and pay their respects. Funeral parlours with their own chapel of rest were almost unknown. In hot weather it could cause all sorts of problems. Not that the late January sunlight was much of a threat. But rules were rules and the arrangements for Paddy O'Driscoll's funeral were made swiftly.

Carter took Fiona's arm and led her through the gate and along the path to the door of the church. They stopped as Prof Green turned to greet them. Green almost shrank back under the hostile look that Fiona gave him. He wasn't the only one in the doghouse, of course. Carter and his wife had barely exchanged a word since the car had picked her up at Belfast's Aldergrove Airport that morning.

"So, the government agreed to you coming, then." Carter greeted him, extending his hand to be shaken.

"It took a lot of persuading. I had to twist a few arms. Officially I'm on a trip to consult my opposite number in Dublin on cross-border relations. Just to make it look good I'll be whisked away after the service to have a few photos taken in Dublin, of us shaking hands, before I head back to the North again. The Irish Air Corps have a very nice helicopter that's reserved for the use of the Taoiseach and the President and it has been placed at my disposal for the day."

"Alright for some. We had to make do with a car from the airport and it's a very long drive."

"And how are you, Fiona. It's a while since we last met." Prof did his best to put on a welcoming smile, but Fiona's frosty look wasn't encouraging.

192

"I'm fine, Prof. Apart from my husband being kidnapped by terrorists, everything is just grand."

"Strictly speaking that wasn't down to me…" Prof attempted to explain.

"No, it's down to my husband, who agreed to come to work in Northern Ireland, but that is a conversation for later." She turned and gave Carter a look that would have had lesser men running for their lives. "But you are here, so you stand in place of all the people that were unable to mount a rescue. You had to leave it to a lorry driver and a recovering alcoholic to do it instead."

"Erm, yes, I see what you mean."

Prof was saved having to say anything else by the arrival of the hearse, followed by several black limousines carrying members of the late Paddy O'Driscoll's family.

"If you would like to make your way inside …" the priest waved a hand pleadingly towards the door. Prof led the way, closely followed by Carter, Fiona, Danny and Edith Glass.

Inside, the small church was filled to capacity. The whole village of Lecanvey seemed to be there, along with reinforcements from the surrounding area; townlands as they were known.

One of the Gardai waved a hand and the crowd parted to let the five of them through to take seats behind the three front rows of pews, which stood empty and were reserved for the family.

The priest led the way down the aisle, the coffin carried by eight men. Four were uniformly dressed, suggesting that they were professional pall bearers, while the others were in in a mixture of suits and overcoats. Family members, Carter guessed. Such was O'Driscoll's bulk that it needed eight men to carry him.

They lowered the coffin gently onto a pair of trestles, bowed and backed away from it, genuflecting to the alter before turning to either walk to the back of the church, or to take their places in the congregation.

The coffin looked barren to Carter. In Britain a green beret with O'Driscoll's regimental badge would have been found from somewhere to lay on it, along with his several wartime medals and those he had no doubt won fighting for the Australian Army. The Royal British Legion would have provided a standard bearer from its local branch and there might also be a bugler to play the Last Post. Some regiments even provided a facsimile version of the regimental colour to drape over the coffin, or the national flag would be used.

But O'Driscoll's coffin wasn't even adorned with any flowers. It was the wrong time of year, Carter supposed.

The Republic of Ireland had been bad at honouring the men from its shores who had crossed the water to Britain to join the fight against the Nazis. On their return they had been treated more like traitors than as heroes, with those who had abandoned the Irish Army to go to Britain being denied some state benefits and banned from government employment[1].

The family took their place, filling the first three rows of pews. Carter hadn't realised that O'Driscoll came from such a large family. There were at least four generations there, including two he guessed to be no more than ten years of age, looking around them curiously.

The service was a simple one. The priest spoke warmly of Paddy, who he had known since he was a child, but no one else spoke. Paddy's mother sat in the front pew, twisting her hanky in her fingers as she fought, and failed, to hold back her tears. Paddy's father stared stoically ahead, his mouth moving in response to the prayers but making no other sign of his feelings.

Carter felt for them. They were in their late seventies and never dreamed they'd have to bury their son. No parent ever imagines doing that.

"Has Paddy's wife been notified?" Carter whispered to Prof, as the congregation lined up in front of the priest to take communion.

"We've got the High Commissioner's office in Canberra pulling out all the stops, but she hasn't been found yet. We think she may be living under a different name. Paddy and she were never officially divorced, but that wouldn't prevent her taking another name if she was living with someone, especially if she wanted to appear to be a respectable married woman. You know how conservative they are over there when it comes to that sort of thing. They'll put a notice in all the New South Wales newspapers, asking for her to contact the authorities, but she may never find out about his death if she doesn't try to make contact with Paddy herself."

After the conclusion of Mass, the whole congregation moved out into the churchyard for the burial. Paddy was to be interred in the family plot, which sat on a slope at the rear of the church.

"He'd have preferred a sea view." Glass whispered. "He always said the best part of an operation was the sea voyage to get there."

Mrs O'Connor had made the journey down from Donegal. She caught Danny Glass's eye and sidled up to him as the priest said the final prayers over the grave.

"Did I not tell him I'd heard the cry of the banshee?" She whispered. "But he wouldn't take heed and now look where it's got him."

"It would have taken more than a banshee to stop either me or Paddy doing what he felt he needed to do, Mrs O'Connor." Glass whispered back. "When a man's life depends on you doing something, you do whatever it takes. Paddy knew that and it could have been me lying there instead of him. I know that as well."

"You men are forever fools when it comes to danger." She responded. "It makes me wonder how any of yez make to adulthood. Hah!" her sudden outburst made people turn to see what was going on. "Adulthood indeed. You're all a bunch of kids playing cowboys and Indians, like them ones in the fillums." She nodded towards Mrs O'Driscoll, who had now swapped her delicate woman's hanky for a much more substantial man's one to wipe away her tears. "But it's always the women who are left to do the grieving when your adventures go wrong."

She moved away, back to the side of a young man with long hair, who Glass took to be a relative, or maybe a neighbour pressed into service to drive her to Mayo.

After the service, Carter and Glass wanted to go back to the family home to pay their respects, but the Gardai officers were adamant that they leave straight away.

"It's your own government's orders, Sir." The senior man said.

195

Carter tried appealing to Prof Green. "Sorry Lucky, but the full story of what happened to you is being kept under wraps, with the agreement of both London and Dublin. We don't want it being blurted out after one too many whiskeys. The family have been told that Paddy died as a result of being caught up in crossfire between an IRA ambush and an Army patrol. He's to appear as an innocent victim and we think that's the best we can do for all concerned. Even your disappearance hasn't been made public. I had to go against London's wishes just to tell Fiona what had happened to you. She was getting anxious that she hadn't heard from you and was giving your boss in Glasgow, Hamish, a hard time. She had to be told because she was threatening to go to the police and newspapers."

"Newspapers first, police afterwards" Fiona said, a defiant tone in her voice. "Hamish wouldn't tell me anything, so I had to threaten to do something."

"Now, I have to get off to Dublin, so I'll wish you goodbye for now." He shook hands with both Carter and Glass and gave Edith and Fiona a peck on the check. Fiona was reluctant to let him, but in the end manners prevailed.

"I'll be coming to this year's Honfleur reunion, come hell or high water." Prof declared, "I'll resign from the government if I have to! We'll give Paddy a proper soldier's farewell there." He climbed into the rear seat of a car to be driven off to the field where the Irish Army helicopter sat waiting for him.

"They've reserved us a room in a hotel in Belfast." Carter said as they were driven along the narrow rural roads of County Mayo.

"I thought you'd be coming straight home." Fiona replied.

"I will be, in a couple of days. But I'm still being debriefed. They didn't want me to come to the funeral at all, but I told them if I wasn't allowed to, I'd come anyway, even if I had to crawl on my hands and knees. They can't keep me prisoner, because I'm the victim in this, so in the end they had to agree. But as you've seen, security is tight."

"Do they think you might be attacked again?" Fiona gave a nervous look out through the car's side window, as though there might be a rifleman behind every hedgerow.

"Just the usual stable doors being slammed shut." Carter reassured her. "I'm pretty sure the people who took me are long gone by now. Not only are the police forces of two countries looking for them, but both the IRA and the UDA are as well. They'll have to go a long way to find a safe place to hide."

Fiona stayed silent for the rest of the trip and Carter feared the worst as he left her in their hotel room to be escorted to the office block where he was to continue telling his story.

* * *

Edith Glass was delighted to find they had been lodged in the finest hotel in Belfast and decided explanations could wait until later. "I've never seen anywhere so posh." She gushed. "I feel like one of them movie stars."

"There was that place we stayed on our honeymoon." Glass reminded her.

"The Bide-a-Wee B&B in Eastbourne can't be compared to this, Danny, and you know it. Have you ever stayed anywhere like this before?"

Glass had to admit he hadn't. The best he had experienced was the First Class cabin on the ship that had taken he and Carter to Australia and even that would have fitted comfortably inside the bedroom they were now in, with room to spare.

"You enjoy it love." Danny said as he gave his wife a farewell peck on the check. "The government's paying, so see how much of my tax you can get through before we have to leave. I think you might enjoy the champagne in the hotel bar."

Edith giggled girlishly. "I've never had champagne. Not the real stuff anyway. I don't know what you've been up to Danny Glass, but if this is how you're rewarded, then you can do it again."

"It got Paddy killed, Edith, so I think I may let others risk themselves next time."

On that sombre note he went down to join Carter for the short drive to the office block where the de-brief was to take place.

* * *

Carter was back in front of his interrogators, telling them everything he knew. In another room Danny Glass was going through a similar quizzing.

After two days going over the same ground time after time, checking every detail and cross referencing it with what Glass had said and the information the security forces had garnered for themselves, Carter was finally allowed to leave.

A Corporal escorted him along a corridor and showed him into an office where a soldier waited. Carter recognised the Colonel that he'd last seen in the corridor outside his own office, after he'd been shouting at Carter's own boss.

The officer stood and leant over the table to shake Carter's hand.

"I'm sorry you had to go through all that. Not just the interrogation, of course, but the kidnapping. That fool McAnally should never have sent you."

"If it hadn't been me it would have been one of my less experienced colleagues."

"It shouldn't have been any of you." The Colonel replied. "McAnally was told to get someone to check out Mayfly in Strabane. The idiot was supposed to use a trained field operative, not a clerk. No offence intended, but you aren't trained for field work."

"I'm better trained than some." Carter demurred.

"Yes, but field work in Northern Ireland is tricky." The Colonel said. "A trained operative wouldn't have tried to drive back to Belfast. He'd have gone to a safe house and made his report from there. Not your fault, of course, you were doing what you thought was right. You could have reported in from a police station or an Army post, then we'd have got you back to Belfast in an armed convoy if we'd had even the slightest suspicion you were in danger. All the signs were there and your driver, Jerry, had picked up on them. Of course, he was a fool as well for not suggesting a better way of doing things, but he was taking his lead from you."

Carter decided a change of subject was in order. He didn't like allotting blame at the best of time and as far as he was concerned Jerry had done nothing more than his job.

"So, what's happening about Mayfly now?" He asked.

"Well, Mrs McSweeney has been questioned by Irish Special Branch officers, but it is pretty clear she was acting under duress. She's given them the names of the five lads that were with her brother and they've been passed on to us."

"You're sure it was her brother?" Carter asked. "Danny and Paddy only assumed it was him because her farm had been chosen as the place to keep us."

"The fact that she hasn't named him is the giveaway." The Colonel explained. "She owes no loyalty to the five tearaways, but family is different. Her car was found abandoned down near Sligo and three others were reported stolen in the area. I suspect they'll turn up at a ferry port in due course. Strange as it may seem, you don't have to produce a passport to get on a ferry to Britain."

Carter nodded. "Not even a fake one." He quipped. The officer wasn't telling him anything he didn't know.

The Colonel continued, "They'll disappear into the Irish communities on the mainland and re-emerge with fresh identities and tickets to Spain or somewhere else where there are no extradition treaties[2]. We'll keep an eye open for them, but with the amount of cross channel traffic that goes through the Channel ports it would be like finding a needle in a haystack. We don't even have any photos of them that are reliable."

"What about me?" Carter asked.

"I've arranged air tickets for you back to Glasgow tomorrow morning, so the make the best of your hotel tonight." The Colonel smiled, "You won't be coming back to Northern Ireland again, for any reason. I have that on the highest authority." He pointed a finger upwards to where Carter assumed Prof Green's suite of offices lay.

"But the stuff I was working on …" Carter hated leaving a job unfinished.

"Don't worry about that." The Colonel said, "What you've told us is going to be a great help. We've always suspected that a few of the Provos, and the Loyalists, are in it more for themselves than they are for ideological reasons. What you've told us confirms that. All we have to do is identify the ones who are gangsters more than they are idealists and they could be pretty useful to us. A gangster will sell his own granny if you offer the right price, so they could help us a lot with our intelligence gathering. As for the financial analysis, trying to identify the money laundering operations, any accountant can do that. We're planning to bring some specialists across from London to do the job." He smiled again, "Now, I'll let you get back to your wife."

"The interrogation I'm going to get from her is probably going to be a lot more severe than the one those terrorists gave me." Carter said ruefully.

The Colonel chuckled. "If you need a flak jacket[3], let me know." He stood and offered his hand again, making it clear the meeting was over.

*　*　*

Fiona waited until they were back in Troon before she made her ultimatum to her husband.

"I want you to retire, give up government work and stay home with me on the farm." She told him, her tone flat, neither angry nor demanding. It was just a statement of her feelings.

"But what will we live on, Darling?" He protested. He was only going through the motions, however. He had seen her in this mood before and it was unlikely she could be persuaded to change her mind. Her mother might have talked her round, given time, but Mary Hamilton had died three years earlier and now no one could make Fiona do anything she didn't wish to do; especially not Carter himself.

200

"There's one of those big farming conglomerates have been trying to buy the land for years. It was only the thought of leaving it to the twins that stopped me selling up. I'm getting too old to work the farm now and they have no interest in farming, so it is just a millstone around our necks if I keep it. We'll sell the land, live in this house as before and you can retire."

"But ... but ..." he floundered, trying to think of something, anything, that might get his wife to change her mind. "What will I do all day? I've never been one to sit around, twiddling my thumbs, you know that. Even when I took my holiday time from work, I'd help you here on the farm."

She laughed. "You can do what every other man does when he retires. Take up golf or fishing. Write your memoirs, do jigsaw puzzles. But I'm not having you gallivanting off and getting into danger. Not anymore."

"But that wasn't my fault." He protested. "You know that. I didn't set out to get kidnapped, you know."

"Not this time, maybe," She conceded. "But what about the other times? What about Malaya for example?"

Carter felt his jaw drop open. How did she know about that? He had never said anything and he was sure Prof, Danny, or Paddy wouldn't have said anything on the few occasions when they all got together.

"You didn't know I knew about Malaya, did you?" She smiled triumphantly. "I was clearing out that old bureau a couple of years back, you know, the one that had all my father's papers in it. I found your old passports. I scanned through them, looking at all the places you'd been to, after the war of course. You didn't need a passport to invade France. Anyway, I found the entry and exit stamps for Malaya. I didn't know what they signified, of course, but the fact that you were supposed to be in Australia at the time and that you hadn't told me about going there, meant that you'd been up to something dangerous."

"Why didn't you say anything at the time?" Carter asked, his voice husky as his throat closed up with embarrassment.

"I think I didn't really want to know. You came back safely, that was what was important. If you wanted me to know what you were doing, you would have told me. I assumed it was something secret for the government, so it was probably better that I didn't know. Just like your wartime operations. Well, was it dangerous?"

"Yes, it was." He admitted. "But that wasn't my fault either …"

She raised her hand the palm flat and facing him, to cut him off, "Fault doesn't come into it. And it wasn't just Malaya. You went to Prague, Moscow, Belgrade and a whole lot of other places behind the Iron Curtain. None of those you told me about and none of them could have been safe. You told me you were in Paris and Bonn[4]. You put yourself in danger because someone always asks you to. I think you miss the excitement of the war. I know a lot of old soldiers that seem to wish they were back in uniform. But it has to stop and the only way I can make sure it does is if you're here in this house with me. You can go on your reunions with your old Army friends. You can tell your war stories. I don't mind that. But I don't want you doing anything that would risk you not coming back again. Even if it's by accident."

Running out of objections, Carter had to admit defeat. Fiona had obviously thought it through. They wouldn't be short of cash. When he turned sixty five they'd even have a Civil Service pension on which he could draw. Fiona hadn't said how much the land was worth, but she was good with money, so if she thought they could manage then she was probably right. The twins were both financially independent so they wouldn't impact on their finances.

So that was that.

"Can I buy a boat?" Carter said, more in jest than anything.

"No." she said, surprisingly emphatically. "Boats are dangerous, as too many widows of fishermen could tell you. But you can fish off the end of the harbour wall anytime you like."

* * *

Carter cocked his head, sure he had heard a sound. He stood up and crossed the living room and turned down the volume on the TV set. "Did you hear something?" he addressed the room's only other occupant.

"I didn't." Fiona replied. "Are you sure you're not imagining things?" She said with a slightly mocking smile.

"My eyesight may be going," he said, taking off his glasses and waving them at her, "but my hearing is as good as it ever was." He cocked his head once more. "There, did you hear that? Like something being dragged across the farmyard?"

"Actually, I did. It sounded like the dustbin being moved."

Troon wasn't a high crime area, Carter knew. They had their bad boys, the same as any town, but they didn't tend to move away from the areas they knew. They had never had any prowlers in the farmyard, not even during the war when food shortages had made farms the targets for egg and livestock thieves.

"You stay hear, I'll take a look outside."

"Take care, Steven." His wife said, concern in her voice. "Maybe I should phone the Polis."

"No need to bother them for what is probably no more than a fox looking for its dinner." He chuckled as he left the room.

Behind him Fiona rose to her feet and followed him as far as the hall, concern etched on her face as he reached the front door. He flicked the light switch for the exterior light and then unlocked the door.

With the confidence of a man familiar with his surroundings, he swung the door open and stepped into the pool of light.

"Who's there?" He called into t darkness. No reply came back.

He called again. This time there was a rattling sound away to his left.

Carter stiffened, his senses alert. His memory sped back nearly 30 years to an operation in Jersey[1] and Prof Green throwing pebbles to distract a sentry, so that he could creep up behind the man and kill him.

It hadn't been the first enemy soldier Carter had killed, but it had been the first time he had killed at such close quarters.

"Who's there?" He called once more. He moved into the darkness, away from the sound of the pebble. If there was someone there, whoever it was wouldn't be where that sound had come from. Knowing the layout of the yard, he knew that the noise had been where the corner of the house met the wall of the yard. So, the stone or whatever it had been had probably been thrown from the other side of the gate, near the barn.

A shiver ran through him. It might have been late April, but the evening air wasn't yet warm enough to be out without a coat and he had come from the warmth of his fireside, which accentuated the feeling of cold.

But he knew that the shiver had nothing to do with the cold. It was fear of the unknown. Despite all his years of training and warfare, he was still as vulnerable to fear as any man who had never served.

The man who knew no fear had yet to be born. What made him different was his ability to conquer his fear and move towards danger, rather than running away from it.

The rattling sound came from the same place. Now that he was away from the pool of light outside the door of the house Carter felt less vulnerable, though he knew that the night vision of whoever, or whatever, was out there had been longer established. They would also have been able to see him as he left the house and started across the yard, which gave them an advantage.

Carter reached the front of the barn and turned to make his way towards the gate, where he suspected the intruder now stood. Stones on the ground pressed through the thin soles of his carpet slippers, hurting his feet. On the one hand his footwear meant he made no noise, but on the other hand there was a risk of him letting out a sudden noise if he stepped on something sharp.

He made his way slowly along the front of the barn, passing the doors that stood wide open. The building was only used to keep their car inside now, so there seemed to be no point in closing the heavy doors. He had just reached the far side of the looming darkness of the gap when he heard a step behind him and then the cold hardness of something metal pressing into the back of his neck.

"If you want to stay alive, G Man, don't do anything stupid now." A familiar voice said, the strong Northern Ireland accent unmistakeable.

"I thought you'd be a long way away by now, Mayfly." Carter said, trying to keep all trace of fear out of his voice.

"Wrong. He isn't Mayfly." Another voice came from in front of him. "I am. And, yes, we should be a long way away by now, but we have unfinished business."

"I presume you're no longer interested in information about money laundering in the North." Carter said.

"You presume right. We need money and we could think of no one better than you to get it for us."

"You're barking up the wrong tree. I live on my pension. I'm not a wealthy man."

"No, but your wife has money. She sold this farm for a pretty penny, or so I've been told."

The sale of the farm's land had been common knowledge and there had been plenty of speculation about how much it had fetched. Many a small famer in the area, scraping a living, was interested in selling out to the big farming conglomerates that had started to buy land across the whole of Britain.

Carter was unsure what to say. Mayfly, the only name by which he knew the man, had clearly been talking to someone, but there were plenty of people in the pubs of Troon who knew them and would be happy gossip, especially if someone else was buying the drinks.

It seemed that Jerry's revelations while in captivity had left them at more risk of attack than Carter had realised.

"Do you think she keeps the money under the mattress?" he said at last. "The money is safely in the bank."

"Which is where she will go tomorrow morning to withdraw he lot and bring it back to us here. If she does that, you get to stay alive. If she doesn't, she will make a very attractive widow. That's if we don't kill her too. Now, it's getting a wee bit cold standing out here, so let's go inside and make your wife's acquaintance and tell her the plan, shall we?

The gun pressed harder into the back of Carter's neck, and he stepped towards the house.

They crossed the yard quickly and entered the front door. Carter turned to the left to lead them towards the kitchen, trying to keep them away from Fiona in the living room. It would only delay the inevitable meeting, but in the back of Carter's mind was the thought that Fiona might realise what was going on and perhaps be able to make and escape.

The two men followed him. There was a crack, a gasp of pain and the pressure of the gun disappeared from Carter's neck, followed by the thud of a body hitting the ground.

Carter whirled around to see a figure lying on the ground, unconscious or dead Carter didn't know. More likely unconscious as Fiona wouldn't be able to exert the same amount of force as he would have.

Fiona reversed her grip on her father's old shotgun, so that the barrels now pointed directly at the other man in the hallway, the one Carter knew as Mayfly.

Carter realised he had never seen the man's face before. He was remarkably nondescript. Perhaps the same age as Carter, maybe a couple of years older. His face was thin, his hair greying and sparse. He was wearing the same tweed jacket as Carter had caught of a glimpse of before, with the fishing club badge pinned to the lapel.

"Don't do anything stupid." Fiona said. Carter recognised her tone of voice and knew that Mayfly shouldn't ignore the warning. "Drop the gun."

Mayfly had levelled his pistol to aim at Fiona. Carter stepped to one side, removing himself from Fiona's line of fire. Unfortunately, it also took him away from the place where the unconscious man's gun had landed when he fell. Any move towards it was bound to bring a shot from Mayfly.

"Well, well, the little lady seems to be quite resourceful." Mayfly mocked. "But I think it is you who should be putting the gun down, Mrs Carter. Or maybe I should call you Fiona."

"I'd do what she said." Carter advised. "She isn't bluffing."

"If it was you holding the gun, I'd be doing that, no fear, Carter. But she's not going to shoot me. But I don't think your lady wife is a killer."

Carter saw his wife's knuckles whiten on the trigger of the shotgun. "You don't know how wrong you are." Carter said. "I really would put that gun down if you want to live."

Undeterred, Mayfly kept his aim steady. "I'm going to count to three, Fiona. If you don't drop the gun, I'm going to shoot your husband." To confirm the threat, Mayfly swung his arm around so that he was aiming directly at the centre of Carter's chest. From a distance of no more than four feet, there was no way he could miss.

"One …Two…"

He never got to three. The shotgun blast sounded like a bomb going off in the confined space of the hall and blood spattered up the wall as Mayfly crumpled to the ground.

"We're going to have to redecorate." Carter said as he picked up the gun dropped by the unconscious man and kicked Mayfly's weapon along the hall, out of reach if the man regained his senses.

"I never liked that wallpaper anyway." Fiona replied as she broke the shotgun to eject the spent cartridge. "Can I call the Polis now?"

14 – Loose Ends

The two figures held a large bouquet of flowers between them and they bent to lay it on the grave. The woman, Danielle, made some adjustments to the way they lay, then they straightened, holding hands once again.

It was a ceremony they carried out every year on their parents' wedding aniinversary. Thier mother, Fiona had died first, in 2002. Her bowel cancer had been diagnosed too late for any treatment to save her. Their father, Steven, hadn't taken her death well. He suffered depression for several years before making some sort of recovery. One of the few commitments he maintained after his wife's death was the annual 15 Commando reunion trip to Honfluer. It was while he was returning from the 2010 trip that he had suffered a massive heart attack. By the time the ambulance had got him to Royal Sussex County Hospital, he was already dead.

After standing in silence, heads bowed, for several minutes, they turned and made their way slowly back along the path towards the cemetary gate. Despite the signs of aging, anyone could tell that they were brother and sister. In fact, they were twins.

"Lunch?" Patrick asked.

"Only if you're paying." His sister said, laughing.

"We'll go halves as usual and I'll choose th restaurant." He replied, nudging his sister with his shoulder.

"How's the research going?" Danielle asked.

After finding some tape recordings that his father had made, telling his war stories for the National Army Museum's archive, Patrick had decided that he would write a series of novels based on the stories. "Oh, you know …"

"Slowly." She chuckled. It was what he always said.

"All the members of 15 Commando are dead now, so I have to rely on what I can find on the internet, or in old books."

"All of them dead? I thought there was still that one … oh, what was his name? Dad's radio operator."

"Henry James; No, he died in 2020 apparently. There was a guard of honour from the Royal Marines at his funeral, according to his local paper. I guess there are a few from other commandos still alive, maybe the younger ones who joined later in the war, but they won't know much about the operations dad took part in. And they especially won't know anything about those hush-hush ones that don't appear in the 15 Cdo war diary. You know, the ones dad went off and did with Danny, Prof and Paddy."

"Do you know anything about those?"

"A Bit. Prof Green referred to them in his memoirs and I was able to contact a cousin of his who had his original diaries. They were able to tell me a bit more."

"So, they're all gone now."

Patrick opened the gate and led the way to the carpark, opening the passenger door for his sister before taking his seat behind the steering wheel.

"Yes, all gone now."

Danielle fell silent, wrapped in her memories of her father's oldest and best friends. Prof Green, who had hidden his sexuality for so many years, who had risen through the ranks of the Labour Party to become a Minister of State, before standing down as an MP and being rewarded with a Peerage and a seat in the House of Lords. He still held the record for being the oldest man in the UK to enter into a same sex marriage, when it became legal in 2014. He'd died a year later.

Then there was Danny Glass. They had moved out to the Costa Del Sol when Danny hit it big on the National Lottery. Edith had died in 2010 after a short illness, then Danny 2 years later. Unconventional to the end, he had fallen off the roof of his Spanish villa, while trying to fix his satellite dish.

"Did you ever find out about Paddy's wife, Rosie?" She asked.

"Yes, just recently in fact, from one of Paddy's nephews. About two years after Paddy was killed, Rosie wrote to Paddy's mother, trying to track him down to get some divorce papers signed.

Apparently she had met a bloke when she was working in an ex-servicemen's club, close to Randwick where Paddy was based. He swept her off her feet and gave her the one thing Paddy was never able to give, his undivided attention. He was just passing through, doing some work locally, and when he went back home she went with him. She decided not to tell Paddy where she had gone, because she was worried that Paddy might come after the new bloke. Knowing Paddy, I think it was probably a wise precaution. She never saw any of the newspaper adverts that the High Commission put in the newspapers, trying to trace her whereabouts. I'm not surprised, having seen a few of those 'public announcements' in the newspapers that have to be placed for legal reasons. They're always in tiny print so, unless you're looking for them, you'd never notice them.

So, she found out she was a widow and that meant she could get married without any legal complications."

"Do you think dad was happy after he retired?" Danielle asked. It was a question she had pondered on many times over the years. "I know he missed the Army after the end of the war.

Patrick nodded his agreement. "I know he loved his golf, even though he was never that good at it. I think a lot of the other golfers his age were ex-soldiers, so they had a lot in common. There were a few former commandos amongst them too, that had married local girls and settled up here after the war. Then he was coaching the youth rugby team and he was very active in the Royal British Legion. He was branch chairman for about ten years. He certainly kept himself busy."

"Oh yes. I forgot about that. I must admit lost track of things a bit when Alex and I moved up to Glasgow. But busy isn't the same as happy."

Well, you know what happened after mum died. I don't think he ever got over it."

"No, he he never did." Danielle agreed.

Deciding a change of subject might be a good idea, he asked "How is Alex? Has he settled into retirement?"

211

"I think he's a bit bored. He keeps talking about researching his family tree."

Patrick grunted. "You can do most of that on-line these days."

She gave a short, barking laugh. "Not Alex, you know what a technophobe he is. No, if he does it at all he'll do it the old fashion way, going around the parish churches, trawling through their old records. What about Moira? How is she taking having you at home all day?"

"I hardly see her, to tell the truth. She's on so many committees and involved with so many charities it's hard work keeping track of where she is half the time. And when she's not doing that she's down in the shed with her pottery. We have so many vases and bowls in the house there's no room to swing a cat."

"So, when are we going to see the fruits of your labour? When does the first book come out?"

He laughed. "When I've written it. But I've decided to turn those recordings of dad's into a biography first. That will help me when it comes to deciding what bits will make a good adventure story and what won't."

He turned the car off the road and into the car park of a restaurant. Now, this place is expensive, so no ordering the lobster." He chided as the two of them climbed out of the car.

* * *

They shall grow not old, as we that are left grow old.
Age shall not weary them, not the years condemn.
At the going down of the Sun, and in the morning,
We will remember them.

(For The Fallen, by Laurence Binyon).

The End

Historical Notes

It is difficult to set a story in Northern Ireland in 1973/4 without taking sides with regards to the rights and wrongs of what happened there. In this book I've tried to be as impartial as possible, but as in every such conflict, one person's terrorist is another person's patriot, though in the case of around half of the population of Northern Ireland, that patriotism wasn't directed towards Great Britain and the patriotism displayed by the other half was towards a country that wouldn't recognise their vision of the United Kingdom.

The greatest tragedy is that The Troubles, as they were euphemistically known, were avoidable. Perhaps it could be argued that all wars are avoidable, but it is particularly pertinent in the case of Northern Ireland.

The cause of The Troubles could be said to go all the way back to the arrival of the Earl of Pembroke in 1169 AD, at the invitation of the then King of Leinster, to support him in an armed struggle to assert his claim to become High King of Ireland (overall ruler over the four kingdoms that historically make up Ireland and provide the names for its present day provinces). From that act King Henry II laid claim to Ireland. Henry made his youngest son, John, King of Ireland; all he had to do was claim his inheritance, which he never did. Instead, he became King of England on the death of his brother Richard the Lionheart.

But that didn't prevent successive English (later British) monarchs from claiming Ireland and, from time to time, enforcing that claim with military force until James I finally defeated the province of Ulster to complete the conquest of the island. Ulster had held out against British rule for the longest and to prevent a re-occurrence of opposition, James transplanted Scottish Protestants into Ulster, granting them land seized from the native Catholic population. It is known in Irish history as The First Plantation, although there had been smaller plantations in earlier years.

Following the bloody suppression of a rebellion in Ireland after the English Civil War, Oliver Cromwell granted land to 12,000 of his soldiers in lieu of wages. Even today Irish people have been known to spit when Cromwell's name is mentioned. Those puritan protestants became the major land owners and power brokers in Ireland for three centuries.

Ireland became the battle ground for William of Orange as he laid claim, on behalf of his wife, to the British throne and that war ended with the Battle of the Boyne (1st July 1690). This led a to a further influx of Protestants into the north of the country.

Other uprisings and rebellions followed, up to the famous one of Easter 1916. While that rebellion was no more successful than earlier ones, the way the British treated some of the rebels, executing them out of hand, turned the stomachs of the population and led them to support the guerrilla war that went on until Ireland won its independence in 1922.

However, in modern terms the start of the conflict is hard to establish, but I would date it to the civil rights marches of 1968, when Catholics in Northern Ireland began peaceful protests to demand equal rights with the Protestants, whose Unionist Party formed the government of Northern Ireland.

The difference in the treatment of the two communities goes back to the partitioning of the country into Northern Ireland and the Republic of Ireland in 1922, when the parliament at Stormont was established under the Unionist politician William Carson. All the laws emanating from that period favoured Protestants, including voting rights, rights to social housing, public sector jobs, and social welfare. In a United Kingdom where, by the 1960s, discrimination against Catholics was a thing of the past everywhere else, the Catholic communities of Northern Ireland felt rightly aggrieved.

Had those protests been treated sympathetically by Stormont and if talks had been entered into to change the laws, The Troubles would undoubtedly have been nipped in the bud. But the Ulster Unionist Party's government dismissed the protests out of hand, despite the entreaties of then Prime Minister Terence O'Neill.

O'Neill would eventually resign in frustration at the attitude of his own party and the Ulster Unionist Party would eventually split into hard-line and more moderate factions with the hardliners, led by the Reverend Ian Paisley, dominating.

The protests erupted into violence when Catholics, Loyalists, and police clashed in what became known as the 'Battle of the Bogside' between 12th and 14th August 1969. That and other clashes between Catholics and Protestants resulted in the Army being deployed to try to keep the two communities apart. Essentially it was a peace keeping mission, but it didn't stay that way.

The Army was being directed by the Northern Ireland government, which favoured the Protestant Loyalist factions. Soon they were being used to suppress the Catholics and into this mix stepped the IRA, ostensibly to protect Catholic communities but actually to further their agenda of Irish nationalism – the reunification of Ireland into 32 counties.

The mainstream IRA didn't want to get involved at that time, but a splinter group, mainly made up of young men from the northern counties, established the Provisional IRA and its political arm, Provisional *Sinn Fein*.

Initially the IRA didn't have a lot of support from the Catholic communities, but the events of Bloody Sunday (30th January 1972) in which 26 people were shot by paratroops, of which 14 died, changed that. Whether or not there were any armed IRA members present on that day may never be established, but it is now known that none of those killed were found to be armed. British paratroops proved to be the unwitting recruiting sergeants for the Provisional IRA and they gained massive support from across the Six Counties[1] and the Widgery Inquiry, which whitewashed the Army's actions, further hardened feelings.

Unsurprisingly, the Loyalists, as they called themselves, formed their own paramilitary groups to counter the threat they saw being posed by the Provisional IRA.

What followed was nearly three decades of terrorism, military action and sectarian violence that took the lives of 3,532 military personnel, police and civilians from all sides in the conflict and shattered the lives of thousands more, including those that just wished to be left to live in peace. The end of The Troubles eventually came in 1997 with the signing of the Northern Ireland Peace Agreement (aka the Good Friday Agreement), which established power sharing in Stormont. But the old divisions linger on, and trouble still breaks out from time to time.

It is still the stated aim of *Sinn Fein* to achieve a united Ireland and they hold considerable political influence on both sides of the border. At the time of writing, they now form the largest political party at Stormont but are unable to form a government because of a refusal to share power from the Unionist side. Sinn Fein have also done well in recent local government elections, possibly because disillusioned Unionist voters stayed at home out of frustration with their party.

Sinn Fein also hold the joint largest number of seats in the *Dáil,* The Parliament of the Republic of Ireland, and the only thing preventing them from forming the government there is an inability to find parties to join them in a coalition.

Keen political historians will know that in 1973 the Conservative Ted Heath was Prime Minister of the UK, but followers of the Carter's Commandos series of books will know that Prof Green was a committed socialist. I apologise to all parties for twisting history to my purpose by placing a Labour government in Westminster when, in reality, it was a Conservative government. If it makes any difference, it was a Labour government in power when British troops were deployed onto the streets of Northern Ireland to try to keep the two warring communities apart, a policy that remained in place under Ted Heath's government.

It was the Heath government that instituted the direct rule of Northern Ireland from Westminster in 1972 and established the Northern Ireland Office, in which I have made Prof Green the junior Minister, to replace the administrative functions of the Stormont government.

It was the role of the Northern Ireland Office to liaise with the other departments of the British government in order to meet the needs of the people of Northern Ireland. Understandably, security in Northern Ireland was the major issue of the day. Today the role is more about the oversight of the Northern Ireland Peace Agreement to ensure that its requirements aren't breached. You can tell how successful that has been by the fact that as I write this book, there is no functioning government in Northern Ireland because the two sides have, once again, failed to find a way work together.

The issues that divide them would require another book to explain, but post-Brexit trade with Europe is the one that is used to justify the divisions. My own local MP is the current Secretary of State for Northern Ireland, and I don't envy him his job. But, like Prof Green, I do wonder who he has upset in his party (he is the former Chief Whip under Boris Johnson, so the answer is "probably everybody").

Ted Heath was the architect of the Sunningdale Agreement of 1973 which created a power sharing political structure in Stormont, but it was wrecked in 1974 by a general strike called by the Ulster Workers' Council, which was backed by Loyalist paramilitary groups. It took until 1997 to create a new power sharing agreement which, ironically, was very similar in structure to the Sunningdale Agreement.

Letterkenny has changed a lot since I first set foot there in February 1972, on a journey to meet my future in-laws for the first time. It was only days after the terrible events of Bloody Sunday in the nearby city of Londonderry, or Derry as even the Loyalists call it when the Nationalist aren't listening. To say that the British weren't popular at that time would be an understatement.

But I have to say that I was given the warmest of Irish welcomes and was continually assured that while what Britain had done only 20 miles away was terrible, no one was holding me personally responsible. Even though I was a serving member of HM Armed Forces, I never felt threatened in the town, though I was careful to keep information about my occupation to myself. I wasn't an author at the time but when I needed a backdrop against which to set a novel that involved both Northern Ireland and Lucky Carter, Letterkenny and its surrounding countryside sprang to mind at once.

It was always rumoured that the Provisional IRA used Letterkenny and the surrounding area as a safe haven and even stronger rumours that some of the businesses that sprung up in the town during The Troubles were used to launder the proceeds of the bank robberies and protection rackets that funded the Provisional IRA. If the Irish government had any indication of it, they didn't act.

But such was the nature of The Troubles, that The Republic's politicians were very ambivalent about what was happening across the border and did only what was necessary to prevent their neighbour from causing a fuss. Some politicians, such as Neil Blainey, were far more vocal in their support for the Nationalist cause.

That is not a criticism, just an observation. I think it likely that the same would happen in any country that sympathised with the aims of a rebellious neighbour. Since the 1922 independence treaty between the UK and the Republic of Ireland, the Republic has continued to claim the six counties of Northern Ireland as its own, and any Irish politician that doesn't support that claim can expect to have a very brief career.

It is safe to say that Letterkenny did well out of the troubles. First the textiles giant Courtaulds moved its factory out of the troubled North and into the town, bringing new jobs. Other businesses followed. The people of Derry and Strabane wanted somewhere safe to enjoy their leisure time and Letterkenny offered that. New bars and nightclubs opened to cater for the weekend revellers. Now large hotels and new shopping centres dominate the town and have changed its character. Along with the new jobs came new people, mainly from the North but also from the EU and from other parts of the world. The influx of migrants that Britain has experienced is happening in Ireland too. That has also changed the character of the town.

The town became a centre of education with the existing technical college being expanded to provide further education to the whole of the northwest of Ireland, with halls of residence also being added. This gives the town a very 'young' feel, especially after dark when the students go out to party.

When I first arrived in Letterkenny, the most exotic food you could buy was a hamburger from the Four Lanterns café. Now you can eat cordon bleu standard cuisine from around the world.

In 1972 the town was as I described it: a main street lined with shops and pubs, with houses spreading up the hills on both sides and out along the side of Loch Swilly towards the neighbouring town of Ramelton. Where once there were fields there are now new housing estates and shopping malls line the banks of the river behind Main Street. It now has traffic lights at the junction where the Court House stands (the building no longer serves that function) and roundabouts and more traffic lights litter other junctions. The N13 road from Derry becomes a dual carriageway for its last few miles into the town. Thanks to EU money potholes are no longer a problem. Main Street finally became one-way in the 1990s.

From 1969 Letterkenny held an annual folk festival to try to boost its profile in the world. It truly was an international affair, with performers travelling from across the globe to appear, including the ones that stand out most in my memory, a troop of Russian folk dancers, which was a big deal during the Cold War. I still possess a recording (vinyl of course) of an Italian male voice choir that appeared and regular attendees were a Morris Dance side from the Bath area. The festival even launched the career of the folk group Clannad, from which the singer Enya developed a solo career.

Performances were held in the market square and in the town's cinema as there was no theatre, a deficiency that has since been rectified.

But the festival received no funding from either the Dublin government or from *Bord Failte* (Irish Tourism Board, now called *Failte* Ireland) and the national broadcaster, RTE, covered the event only once, in 1984 after questions were asked by local politicians.

Struggling for finance the festival grew smaller and smaller in scale until it disappeared. However, it did return for a 50th anniversary event in 2019.

The Fiesta is long gone, replaced by modern college buildings. The Golden Grill is closed and waiting for its present owners to do something with the site. Dillon's supermarket is now the Courtyard shopping precinct and the Gardai "barracks" (as they are called) on Lower Main St is now The Wolfe Tone Bar, with a newly built and much larger barracks at the other end of the town.

The Gardai strength has multiplied from half a dozen uniformed officers to a current strength of 124. At the time this story was set the location of McSweeney's farm would have been covered by the Gardai station at Kilmacrennan, a sub-station of Milford, which even today has only a single officer. As the local officer he would undoubtedly have known Theresa McSweeney, had she existed, and would have no reason to believe she was harbouring kidnappers, willingly or unwillingly, hence the cursory nature of his fictional search.

Crime rates were low in Donegal back then and people really did leave their keys in their front doors (and in their cars) even when they were out of the house. Visitors opened the door and called a greeting. If they didn't get a reply they'd know you were out and would just shut the door and call back later. The influx of strangers from the North put an end to that but it is still seen today in some of the more rural areas.

Letterkenny now aspires to city status and an ambitious new regeneration programme has been launched with its eyes on 2040 for completion.

Eleven months after my initial visit, my wife and I were married at St Eunan's Cathedral and our wedding reception was held at the Mount Errigal Hotel. We still return to the town to visit family whenever time, and our budget, allows and we were last there in January 2023.

For visitors, the county of Donegal is an undiscovered gem. There are long, empty, sandy beaches that aren't commercialised the way

220

they are in Britain or mainland Europe There is some stunning scenery which attracts hill walkers and cyclists and some of the finest links golf courses in Europe, which are almost deserted on weekdays. I'm not being paid to recommend Donegal as a holiday destination, I do so freely and willingly.

Some of the characters who are residents of Letterkenny named in this book are based on real people or are composites of real people. They are included out of a fondness for them but, of course, their words and actions are entirely fictitious.

With Carter and his surviving friends in their mid-fifties at the end of this book and Carter's wife Fiona threatening to divorce him (or worse) if he gets involved in any more dangerous activities, it is time for them to take a back seat in the events of the world. I have briefly described how their lives progress and they have no more adventures for me to tell you about. So, there will be no more Carter's Commando books. But, as alluded to in this story, Paddy O'Driscoll may have some stories of his own to tell, but we shall have to wait and see.

But as Siegfried Sassoon said, "Old soldiers never die, they just fade away."

I hope that the loyal readers of the series, of which I know there are many, will now consider transferring their allegiance to the other books that I have written.

When you go home,
Tell them of us and say,
For your tomorrow,
We gave our Today

(Inscription on the Kohima Cemetary War Memorial, Myanmar (Burma))

---

[1] Northern Ireland is not the same as Ulster. The historical province of Ulster is made up of nine counties. Six are in Northern Ireland: Antrim, Armagh, Down, Fermanagh, Londonderry and Tyrone and

the other three: Cavan, Donegal and Monaghan, are in the Republic of Ireland.

FOOTNOTES

Footnotes for Ch 1

[1]. Genesis 4:17. The Land of Nod was the place where Cain was exiled after slaying Abel. It was reputed to be to the east of Eden.

[2]. See Book 8 of the Carter's Commandos series, Operation Banyan.

[3]. For younger readers, The News Of The World was a Sunday newspaper well known for printing "kiss and tell" stories and other scandals. It was bought by Rupert Murdoch's News International Group in 1969 and maintained its low editorial values until it ceased publication in July 2011 after revelations that its reporters routinely hacked telephones in order to get stories.

[4]. Aristotle Onassis was a Greek shipping magnate whose name became a byword for conspicuous wealth. He was the Jeff Bezos or Elon Musk of his day. He married Jaqueline Bouvier, the widow of assassinated American president John F Kennedy, in 1968 which probably accounted more for his fame than did his wealth.

[5]. Mutually assured destruction, MAD for short, was the philosophy behind the nuclear arms race of the Cold War, in which both sides stockpiled so many nuclear weapons that any side that was the first to use them to destroy the other side, was itself assured of destruction by the weapons of its opponents. Its acronym was appropriate.

[6] The slang name for the Free Presbyterian Church, a very strict religious group one of whose ministers was the prominent Unionist MP the Rev Dr Ian Paisley. They have a relatively large congregation in Northern Ireland. They take a particularly dim view of homosexuality.

[7]. An own goal was slang for a terrorist being killed by his own bomb, usually because the construction of the device was faulty or because it was being carried while armed. In the early 70s such deaths were common amongst the Provos, as they were known, as their knowledge of bomb making was in its infancy.

[8] Pack drill was a minor punishment in the British army, originating from the late 19th century, in which the subject carried out hours of military drill while carrying full equipment. It was very tiring and in hot climates could result in heat exhaustion. It was abolished in 1935 but its reputation lived on in military lore and the expression is still in use. "No names, no pack drill" meant not snitching on offenders so they avoided punishment.

Footnotes for Ch 2

[1]. Similar to Scotland, Northern Ireland banks print their own banknotes, which are backed by the Bank of England. At this time the Republic of Ireland was using the Irish Pound or Punt, which sometimes varied in value against the Pound Sterling, stimulating cross border trade as people took advantage of the exchange rates. Sometimes it was better for Northerners to shop in the Republic and vice versa. This practice continues today, with shoppers from the Republic travelling to the North in order to benefit from the beneficial exchange rate between the Pound and the Euro and differences in the rates of VAT. Naturally, this is damaging businesses in the border counties of the Republic, which are losing trade.

[2]. Like the Hebrides, Donegal is famed for its tweed, though nowadays production is mainly aimed at the tourist trade.

[3]. Neil Terence Columba Blainey represented the north eastern constituency of Donegal in the *Dáil Éireann* (Irish Parliament) from

224

1948 until 1996. He is credited with doing a considerable amount for his native county but had to fight hard to get money spent there (hence the state of the roads noted by Carter). He was also suspected of having links with the Provisional IRA and was implicated in financing arms smuggling for them. He was sacked from his office of Minister for Agriculture and Fisheries in 1970 along with future *Taoiseach* (Prime Minister) Charles Haughey, but no charges were ever brought. He was expelled from the *Fainna Fáil* party and stood at future elections as an independent Republican, retaining his seat until his death from cancer. As a Member of the European Parliament following the 1979 elections, he managed to get money from the EU allocated to Donegal for infrastructure projects and the condition of the roads improved dramatically. As well as being a politician, Neil Blainey and his family had significant business interests in Donegal, especially pubs and hotels.

[4]. Poteen (pronounced pocheen) is an illegally produced spirit made from potato peelings. It has a reputation for being very strong and the author can testify that it tastes like paint stripper. It is now produced legally and can be purchased from shops aimed at the tourist trade, but any Irishman (or woman) will tell you it isn't as good as 'the real thing'. In every pub in Ireland you can hear stories of poteen being illicitly distilled locally, but no one ever seems to know who is doing it or where to get it.

[5]. Despite the belief of the citizens of Letterkenny, this isn't true. The spire of St Eunan's stands at 240 ft, but Salisbury Cathedral's spire is 399 ft high. Ulm Minster in Germany is the tallest church building in the world at 530 ft.

[6]. Scottish whisky, or Scotch, is spelt without an e. All other whiskies are spelt with an e.

[7]. Between 1962 and 1975, Australia sent almost 50,000 troops to fight in Vietnam. 520 died there and another 2,396 were wounded. Four Victoria crosses were awarded.

[8] Battle of Long Tan (18th August 1966). D Company of 6th Battalion, The Royal Australian Regiment, found themselves surrounded by Vietcong and North Vietnamese regular soldiers. The Australians fought against superior numbers for several hours before they were relieved by US forces. The Australians suffered 17 killed and 24 wounded, approximately one third of their strength.

[9] Kevin Barry was an 18 year medical student and IRA volunteer who was executed by the British in 1920 for his part in an attack on a British Army supply lorry. The execution of such a young man scandalised the Irish population and further hardened opposition to the British regime in Ireland. Many songs were written and sung about Kevin Barry and their popularity was revived in the early days of The Troubles as an example of a martyr for the Republican cause. He had been 15 when he joined the IRA. He was an apt example for O'Driscoll to use to illustrate his pep talk to equally young Provisional IRA volunteers from Northern Ireland. Another popular song to celebrate a young Irish martyr was Roddy McCorley, who was executed during a rebellion mounted by the United Irishmen in 1798.

[10] The Punt was the Irish name for the Pound and was used to differentiate it from the Pound Sterling before the Irish adopted the Euro.

[11] A ghillie suit is a camouflaged outfit worn by snipers and reconnaissance troops to keep themselves hidden. It was supposed to be modelled on the ones worn by 19th century Scottish gamekeepers, or ghillies, who served as scouts for deer hunting parties on Scottish estates. The ghillie suit was introduced into the British Army by the Lovat's Scouts, a Territorial Army unit raised to fight in the Second Boer War (1899 – 1902). They went on to form the first official British sniper unit during the First World War. Brigadier Simon Fraser of 4 Commando and 1st Commando Brigade was 15th Lord

Lovat and the son of Simon Fraser, 14th Lord Lovat, who raised the Scouts.

[12] Gerrymandering is a process by which constituency boundaries are manipulated to give one party a permanent electoral advantage. It is a portmanteau word believed to have originated with Elbridge Gerry who, in 1812 while governor of Massachusetts, signed a Bill that created a partisan district of Boston that had a shape similar to that of the mythical salamander, completer with feet, head and tail. This provided the other half of the word. Gerry later became Vice President of the USA. The word first appeared in print in the Boston Gazette on 26th March 1812.

[13] Tout: derogatory slang for an informant.

[14] Tullamore – a brand of Irish whiskey

[15.] Each year a "match making" festival is held in the small spa town of Lisdoonvarna, County Clare (population approx 800, so it really is small). The current matchmaker is Willie Daly, the grandson of the original matchmaker (also called Willie). Willie estimates that he has set up over 3,000 marriages during his time "in office". The festival started over 160 years ago but wasn't originally about matchmaking. It has now become an international event with up to 40,000 single people looking for love visiting the town in September each year. With the harvest over, many are bachelor farmers. While the main purpose of the festival was once matchmaking, nowadays it is more about the music and the cráic (fun).

[16] Said by Mao at an emergency meeting of the Chinese Communist Party on 7th August 1927, at the start of the Chinese Civil War (1927 – 1949).

Footnotes for Ch 3

[1]. To find out what Carter is doing on board this aircraft, see Book 8 of the Carter's Commandos series, "Operation Banyan".

[2]. First Secretary of the Communist Party of Soviet Union and defacto dictator of Russia. He succeeded Joseph Stalin on his death in1953 until he disappeared from public life in 1964 and was replaced by Leonid Brezhnev. Kruschev died of a 'heart attack' in 1971.

[3]. This actually happened in 1956 and it seems that Flamming had some advance knowledge that it might be a possibility. Sadly, the uprising was brutally suppressed by the Russians. Approximately 2,500 Hungarians died in the fighting and another 200 were later executed. Thousands more Hungarians were put on trial and 20,000 were imprisoned and another 12,000 interned without trial.

[4]. The correct name for MI6 is the Secret Intelligence Service (SIS), which is part of the Foreign Office. MI5 is properly called the Security Service and is part of the Home office. The MI names are a hangover from World War 2 and spy movies of the 1950s.

[5]. A popular euphemism for Russians during the Cold war.

[6]. Harry Houghton was a former Royal Navy Warrant Officer who was recruited by Polish Intelligence while working in the British Embassy in Warsaw. He is known to have passed at least 59 Top Secret documents to the Poles before returning to the UK in 1953. He was then passed on to the KGB for them to handle. He found new employment at the Portland naval base where he and work colleague Ethel Gee began to pass more secrets to the Russians. They were both motivated by greed rather than political ideology and were paid well for what they did. Gordon Lonsdale appeared to

be a small-time Canadian businessman but was actually a KGB agent by the name of Konon Molody. The ring was exposed when a Polish defector informed the security services that they had a spy ring working at Portland, but it took many months of investigation before Lonsdale, Houghton and Gee were identified, arrested and put on trial in 1961. MI5 had missed a chance to arrest them in 1957 when they ignored warnings that a spy ring was at work. They were sentenced to 15 years in prison. Lonsdale went back to Russia in 1964 as part of a prisoner swap for a British citizen, Greville Wynne, who was accused of spying (Wynne's story is told in his book "Wynne and Penkowsky" and in the 2020 film "The Courier"). After their release from prison in 1970, Houghton and Gee were married. Ethel Gee died in 1984, followed by Harry Houghton a year later. They were living in relative obscurity in Poole, Dorset.

Footnotes for Ch 4

[1]. Although the use of this phrase only started to become common in the late 1960s, with the rise of the modern feminist movement, according to an academic paper published by Jane Mansbridge and Katherine Flaster of Harvard University, it actually dates back all the way to 1851, when it first appeared in the new York Times. Other words revealed by the research to be older than you might think are 'sexist', 'sexual harassment' and 'feminist'.

[2]. A defensive position usually made with sandbags, with a corrugated iron roof supported by wooden posts. However, the ones constructed in Northern Ireland at permanent checkpoints were made of concrete, including a concrete roof to protect against improvised mortar bombs. From a Hindi/Pashto word meaning "stone".

[3]. A biblical prophet and author of three books of the Old Testament, known for his gloomy outlook on life.

[4] The Ulster Defence Regiment (UDR). A Territorial Army unit, part of Britain's reserve forces. they were established in 1970 to support the regular security forces in Northern Ireland. Their main tasks were to mount mobile check points, patrol the border with the Republic to prevent arms smuggling and to do the same on Northern Ireland's lengthy coastline. However, they also manned fixed checkpoints alongside regular soldiers and carried out patrols with them, using their local knowledge to aid the regular forces. They were recruited mainly from the Protestant population, so weren't trusted by the Nationalists. However, they were less partisan than the B Specials, the part time paramilitary police that they replaced. Throughout their history the regiment was prone to being infiltrated by members of paramilitary groups from both sides. The regiment grew to become the largest in the British army, with 11 battalions at their peak. They also hold the record for being the longest serving regiment in a combat zone since the Napoleonic wars. The regiment was merged with the Royal Irish Rangers in 1992 to become the Royal Irish Regiment. Since the signing of the Northern Ireland Peace Agreement, the number of part time battalions has been reduced to three. Unlike other infantry regiments at that time, the UDR also had a women's section, who were nicknamed "Greenfinches". Their original role was to permit body searches to be carried out on women. This had originally been done by female members of the Royal Military Police, but there were always too few female RMPs to meet the demand.

[5]. This is the ancestral home of the Cameron Clan. During the Second World War the family lent it to the government for wartime use and it became the training depot for the commandos. The rugged countryside surrounding the house provided ideal conditions for toughening up soldiers and preparing them for the arduous duties they were destined to perform. Approximately 25,000 trainees passed through its grounds, including members of the American equivalent of the Commandos, the Rangers. To mark its

contribution, a 15 m high memorial stands alongside the nearby A82 road between Fort William and Fort Augustus.

Footnotes for Ch 5

[1.] A long running BBC TV series that first aired in 1955 and was last shown in 1976. It starred former child actor Jack Warner (who created the character for a film) and was noted for its home spun philosophy. Each episode started with PC (later Sergeant) Dixon standing under the blue lamp outside the fictional Dock Green police station as he greeted the audience with the words "Evenin' all". He would then start to tell a story that would lead into that week's action. The episode ended with some words of wisdom about the moral of the story, before Dixon bid the audience goodnight with a tap of his fingers on the brim of his policeman's helmet and the words "Mind how you go". It would all be far too tame for modern TV audiences.

[2.] Officer Cadet Training Unit (OCTU). Several of these were established during both world wars to train junior officers. They ran short courses teaching basic military skills before the officers went on to specialist training prior to joining a regiment. Officers destined for the infantry weren't provided with any specialist training until as late as 1943, which accounted for the poor opinion that many soldiers developed regarding their fitness for command.

[3.] See Book 3 of the Carter's Commando series, 'Operation Dagger' for this story, which was loosely based on real life. The author's father completed an annual pilgrimage to Dieppe to commemorate the real life event.

[4.] British Airways was founded a few weeks after the date of this meeting, on 31st March 1974, with the merging of two existing airlines, BOAC and BEA. Prior to that date Britain's two 'flag carrier' airlines were British Overseas Airways Corporation (BOAC) for inter-continental flights and British European Airways (BEA).

Footnotes for Ch 6

[1]. Slang term for a government official, as used by the paramilitary groups in Northern Ireland. Its origins are in the USA during the 1920s and 30s where it was used by gangsters to refer to members of the FBI. Its first known written use was in the biography of Al Capone written by F D Pasley, titled "Al Capone: Biography of a Self Made Man.".

[2]. See Book 5 of the Carter's Commando series, "Operation Leonardo".

[3] Until 18th April 2005 responsibility for collecting taxes lay with the Inland Revenue service. VAT and excise duties were collected by HM Customs and Excise. Both agencies were part of the Treasury. The two agencies were merged to form Her (now His) Majesty's Revenue and Customs (HMRC).

Footnotes for Ch 7

[1]. The Black and Tans were a paramilitary police force raised between 1920 and 1922 to combat the IRA during the Irish War of Independence. Because of the terrorist risk it was difficult to also recruit proper police officers for the Royal Irish Constabulary (RIC) Special Reserve, which was their official title. Instead, they were recruited from the very worst elements of British society, including from the prisons. Their officers were no better, with many cashiered (meaning they were dismissed in disgrace) Army officers within their ranks. Over 10,000 were recruited in total. While they were used heavily in three of Irelands provinces (Connaught, Leinster and Munster) they were only lightly used in Ulster, where they raised

their own force from the majority Protestant population. Their nickname came from the mix of a dark navy police jacket and khaki army trousers they wore. They were known for the abuse of their powers and the brutality of their methods, and they were accused of several killings of unarmed civilians, including women. Comparisons have been made with behaviour of the Gestapo and SS in later decades and they were probably justified.

[2]. Eamon De Valera was the first *Taoiseach* (Prime Minister) of the newly independent Irish Free State (later the Republic of Ireland) and its third President. He left office in 1973, just as Ireland entered the Common Market (EU as it is now known) alongside the United Kingdom and Denmark. While he was credited with helping to win Ireland its independence from Britain, opinion is divided on how beneficial he was to the development of Ireland as a nation. Many Irish people share O'Driscoll's view that he was more of a handbrake than an accelerator. He was devoutly catholic and would do nothing to limit the authority of the Roman Catholic Church in Ireland. De Valera was born in New York to an Irish mother (Catherine Coll) and a Spanish American (possibly Cuban) father (Juan Vivion de Valera). However, O'Driscoll's assertion that de Valera was heavily influenced by his mother are unfounded. At the age of two, his father died and he was sent back to Ireland (Limerick) to be raised by relatives. His mother remained in America, remarried and only returned to Ireland for short visits. Eamon de Valera died of pneumonia in 1975 and was accorded a state funeral. He is buried in Glasnevin Cemetery, Dublin. The 4 mile route from St Mary's Pro-Cathedral to the cemetery was lined by over 200,000 people. (A pro-cathedral is a parish church that is filling the temporary role of a cathedral as the principal church of a diocese. While Dublin possesses two cathedrals, both belong to the minority Church of Ireland).

[3] The Griffin Brewery in Chiswick, West London, is now home to the Fullers beer brands.

[4] Checkpoint Charlie was one of the crossing points between East and West Berlin established when the Berlin Wall was erected in

1961. As it was reserved for the sole use of the military forces of the four occupying powers (United Kingdom, United States, France and the Soviet Union) it was also the best place to carry out exchanges of spies, or those arrested and accused of spying. In films, the exchange point is often portrayed as a bridge, but that was actually a civilian crossing point and wasn't used as prisoner exchange point. Checkpoint Charlie was dismantled when the Berlin Wall began to be demolished in 1989. All that now remains is a single wooden hut where tourists can have their photo taken with fake Russian or American guards. Nearby there are two small privately run museums telling the history of the wall.

[5] Glenveagh House is a restored Victorian mansion in the Glenveagh National Park. It is indeed a beautiful location. Unfortunately, it has a dark past. It's founder and builder, a land speculator by the name of John George Adair, evicted 244 families from their tenancies. While such acts had been common during the Irish Famine (1845-52), these evictions took place in 1857, after the famine had ended and the Irish economy was beginning to recover. Adair wanted to build a private deer hunting resort of the type popular amongst the gentry in Scotland. The construction of the house started in 1865 and finished in 1873 but the estate fell into decline in the 1920's when Adair's widow, an American woman, died in 1921. In 1975 the land was sold to the Irish government for the establishment of a national park and the house's last owner, an American by the name of Henry McIlhenny, gifted the house to the people of Ireland in 1983.

[6.] This model was created by Michael Collins during the Irish War of Independence (January 1919 to July 1921). It was so successful that the British themselves adopted the cell structure for organising resistance groups in the occupied countries of Europe during World War II. It is now used by almost every terrorist organisation in the world, except where they are engaged in open warfare, as ISIS were in Iraq and Syria. Michael Collins was the head of the Irish Republican Brotherhood (IRB), forerunners of the IRA, during the Irish War of Independence and was known to have masterminded a number of terrorist coups, particularly targeting Britain's intelligence services in Ireland. After Independence a civil war broke out in Ireland between those who wanted to fight on to gain the whole thirty two counties and those willing to accept the peace treaty establishing a twenty six county Free State. As Collins had been a major figure in negotiating the independence treaty, he naturally chose the Free State side. He was assassinated in an ambush on 22nd August 1922 while inspecting areas of his native Cork recently recovered from the anti-Treaty forces.

Footnotes for Ch 8

[1.] The Orange Order was founded in 1795. Although King William III had defeated the Catholic King James II at the Battle of the Boyne in 1690, tensions between Catholics and Protestants continued in Ireland, nowhere more so than in Co Armagh where fighting frequently broke out over land ownership. This resulted in the formation of the Orange Order as a Protestant defence force aimed at keeping Catholics in their place. It quickly expanded and is now an international federation. It remains fiercely anti-Catholic and the majority of Ulster Unionist politicians rely on the organisation for their support. The meeting place of the order is always known as the Orange Hall and most communities in Northern Ireland with a significant Protestant population will have one. The organisation is most visible in July of each year when a series of marches are held to commemorate centuries old victories over the Catholics, culminating in the 12th of July parade that marks the Battle of the Boyne itself. Orange Order members have a strict code of dress for parades, wearing a suit, a bowler hat and the traditional orange "sash"; their badge of membership. The significance of the colour orange is that William III was a prince of the Dutch House of Orange, but that family name has nothing to do with the colour. It is more closely related to a principality in Southern France, from which the family originated. However, the colour and the family name are now inextricably linked, which is why the Dutch national football team wears orange shirts.

2. GAA = Gaelic Athletic Association (*Cumann Lúthchleas Gael* in Irish). There are two Gaelic sports, football and hurling. The football game allows for the use of hands and is similar in some ways to Australian Rules football. Hurling is a game played with a wooden stick or *hurl*, which can propel the hard ball (or *Slioter*) a significant distance at high speed. The fact that the players wear helmets gives some indication of the dangers involved in being hit by either the stick or the ball. The two games are played on the same pitch, with football in the winter and hurling in the summer. When visiting Ireland, never suggest that hurling is similar to hockey (it isn't anyway). The GAA was founded in 1884, though the games themselves are far older, and in terms of participation Gaelic sports are far bigger in Ireland than either soccer or rugby. The sports are strictly amateur. Consequently, the GAA is immensely wealthy and ploughs a lot of its income back into the sport at grass roots level. There are national competitions at both club and county level for each sport, with the county level games being known as the "All Ireland Championships". They are knockout competitions involving county teams from both sides of the border. Participation in the North is predominantly Catholic but in the south members of both communities participate. As well as the "All Ireland" there are also leagues that cater for all abilities. Just as in Britain, where almost every village will have a football club, in Ireland every village will have a GAA club (and probably a football club too). The finals of the All Ireland competitions are played at Croke Park, Dublin. Croke Park has a special significance in Irish history, having been the scene of a massacre of civilians by British troops in what was the original Bloody Sunday (21st November 1920). The massacre took place during a Gaelic football match when a British armoured car was driven onto the pitch, stopped the game and opened fire on the spectators with a machine gun. 15 died. The attack was in retaliation for an attack by the IRA on British intelligence officers earlier in the

day in which 15 British agents died in a series of co-ordinated attacks.

[3] At this time, if you were offered a biscuit in Ireland it would almost always be a Kimberly. They are made of a thick layer of marshmallow sandwiched between two sweet biscuits. Nowadays they have been supplanted as Ireland's favourites by better known British brands, but still remain a popular choice amongst the older generations. They are available in the UK but usually have to be obtained through internet retailers.

[4]. The original Wild Geese were Catholic soldiers who left Ireland after the war between James II and William of Orange (William III) to fight in the continental wars of the 17th and 18th centuries, usually on the side of Catholic nations against those of Protestants. They found particular favour in the armies of Spain and of that of Britain's traditional enemy, France. They also served in Italy, Austria, Sweden and Poland. However, a wild goose chase has nothing to do with them. It was a form of sport, with a horseman being chased by other mounted riders. The quarry would make random changes of course to try to shake off his pursuers. The pursuers would fan out in a V formation, like a skein of wild geese, to try to pre-empt those manoeuvres. Hence the name of wild goose chase.

[5] For newcomers to the Carter's Commandos series, see Book 1, Operation Absolom.

[6] See Book 5, Operation Leonardo.

[7] Technically they were in The Netherlands. North and South Holland are the names of two areas, which we would call counties, in the southwest of the country along the North Sea coast. In the 17th and 18th centuries they gave their name to the Kingdom of Holland, but the name was officially changed in 1815, after new borders were drawn for various European countries following the defeat of Napoleon at the Battle of Waterloo.

[8] See Book 7, Operation Pegasus.

Footnotes for Ch 10

[1] In 1845 Ireland suffered an outbreak of potato blight which destroyed the staple food that fed the people of rural Ireland. Not only was it eaten as a vegetable, it was combined with flour to make bread – the origins of "potato bread" which is still eaten today. This placed a great strain on the remainder of the island's food resources, put up prices to beyond the reach of many of the population and triggered a famine that lasted until 1852. It isn't known how many people died as a result of the famine but between death and people emigrating the population fell from 8.1 million before the famine to 6.5 million afterwards. The emigration continued for many years more, further reducing the population. The current consensus estimates that around 1.1 million people died as a direct consequence of the famine or as the result of people being evicted from their homes. The irony was that there was actually plenty of food available. Throughout the famine period grain and meat were being shipped across the Irish Sea to England by the Anglo-Irish landlords, who then used the non-payment of rents by their tenants as an excuse to evict them from the land, replacing them with sheep as had been done in Scotland during the Highland Clearances (1750 – 1860). The origin of the present day Irish travellers is with the displaced people of the famine era. All this was happening on an island that Queen Victoria's government claimed was part of Great Britain and, at the time, was less than 2 days travel from London (about an hour by air today). Perhaps one of the less obvious consequences of the famine was to strengthen the support for Irish nationalism on the island.

[2] Rarely seen these days, antimacassars were cloths placed on the back of a chair to protect the upholstery against damage from hair-oil, otherwise known as macassar oil. It takes its name from Makassar in the Dutch East Indies (now Indonesia) where the recipe supposedly originated. Most likely it is a European creation using ingredients such as coconut oil from the Far East. Although the oil

itself went out of use in the early 1900s, the cloths remained in use as a protection against the products that replaced them, such as Brilliantine and Brylcreem which remained in use into the late 20th century, when they were replaced in turn by more modern products. The doilies that usually accompanied antimacassars were to protect against damage from cuff links, which are also less fashionable these days but were everyday attire in earlier times.

[3] The two main Irish political parties at the time of this story were Fine (pronounced finner) Gael, which supported the 1922 treaty between Great Britain and the Republic of Ireland, and Fianna Fáil, which opposed the treaty and wanted to hold out for a 32 county Ireland. Fine Gael weren't actually formed until 1933, when several smaller parties merged. The opposing points of view had been the cause of the Irish Civil War (1922-23). Fine Gael have now been pushed into third place by Sinn Fein who, technically, are older than both. Because of the proportional representation system of voting in use in Ireland, there is rarely a clear majority party in the *Dáil* (pronounced doyle, the lower house of the Irish parliament) which means coalition governments are common. At the time of writing the only thing preventing Sinn Fein from forming the government (they have the same number of seats as Fianna Fáil) is the lack of enough coalition partners from minor parties (Greens, Labour, Social Democrat, Solidarity and others) willing to work with them. Instead, Fianne Fáil and Fine Gael form a coalition with the help of the Green Party. The leaders of the two larger parties are taking turns to act as *Taoiseach* (Prime Minister) for 6 months each.

[4] The Republic of Ireland withdrew from the Commonwealth in 1949 and this encouraged an outbreak of IRA activity in the North during the 1950s and early 60s. However, it attracted very little support in Northern Ireland and fizzled out.

[6] Ulster Volunteer Force and Ulster Defence Association, the two principal terrorist groups on the Loyalist side.

[7] Versions of this fable vary, but the generally accepted story is that an old man collecting wood in the forest becomes weary, throws down his burden and begs for Death to take him. Death arrives to do the old man's bidding, but the old man asks him to help him shoulder his burden once more, the prospect of imminent death having changed his mind about wanting to die.

Footnotes for Ch 11

[1] OP = observation post or point.

[2] Irish slang. A yoke is a word used to describe something in vague terms. Often heard as "that old yoke" which could mean an object or a person, but it could also mean a cliché of some sort.

3. Nobody knows the identity of the person who first said "There are no atheists in foxholes". There are several candidates. It seems to have originated in the aftermath of the Battle of Battaan in the Philippines (7 – 9 January 1942).

[4] For those that do want to know, Muckish is a distinctive flat topped mountain in the Derryveigh range of Donegal, which rises to 667 m (2,189 ft). Mount Errigal, which gives its name to the hotel mentioned in this book, is the highest peak in the same range, rising to 751 m (2,464 fit).

Footnotes for Ch 13

[1] In addition to the sanctions described in this chapter, there is no official war memorial to the Irish soldiers who fell during World War II. There is a National War Memorial to the fallen of World War I, but even that wasn't finished until 1939 and no official opening was ever held because of the looming threat of World War

II. The first official function to be held there wasn't until November 1940, for Armistice Day.

[2] At this time Spain wasn't part of the European Union (known as the Common Market in 1974) and no extradition treaties existed between it and most other European countries. Consequently, the fast expanding Costas were a popular destination for British and Irish criminals wanting to evade justice. And the Spanish government of General Franco was happy to welcome the money that the criminals brought with them, no questions asked.

[3] The first form of body armour issued to troops in Northern Ireland. The flak jacket had originally been developed for issue to RAF bomber crews during World War II to protect them from the fragments of anti-aircraft shells, otherwise known as "flak". They were rushed into service in Northern Ireland as a protection against bomb fragments, but they weren't effective against bullets.

[4]. Between 1945 and 1990, when Germany became a reunified country, the Federal capital was located in the city of Bonn, on the banks of the River Rhein. In 1990 it was transferred to Berlin.

[5] See Operation Tightrope.

And Now

Both the author Robert Cubitt and Selfishgenie Publishing hope that you have enjoyed reading this story.

Please tell people about this eBook, write a review on Amazon or mention it on your favourite social networking site. Word of mouth is an author's best friend and is much appreciated. Thank you.
Find Robert Cubitt on Facebook at https://www.facebook.com/robertocubitt and 'like' his page; follow him on Twitter @Robert_Cubitt

For further titles that may be of interest to you please visit our website at selfishgenie.com where you can also sign up to receive our newsletter.

Printed in Great Britain
by Amazon